Voyages in Time and Space
Vintage Science Fiction from the 1950s

Selected and Edited By
Noe Torres

Featuring Stories by
Philip K. Dick, Frederik Pohl, Robert Sheckley, H. Beam Piper, Fritz Leiber, and others

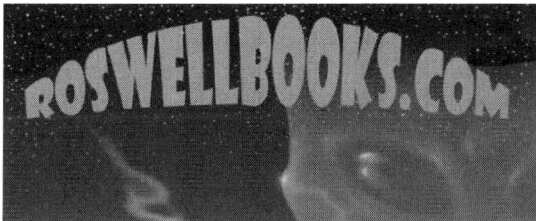

ROSWELLBOOKS.COM

Edinburg, Texas

ISBN: 1496160517
ISBN-13: 978-1496160515

For Robin and Stephen: I love you more than words can say.

CONTENTS

INTRODUCTION

As a child of the 1950s, I was greatly influenced by three powerful forces pervading American culture from the late 1940s to the early 1960s: the ever-present threat of nuclear annihilation, the rise of science fiction as a serious literary genre, and the "flying saucer" phenomenon that swept America during this time period. All three of these "trends" found their way into the literature and media of the day and specifically the science fiction books and magazines.

Included in this collection are eight truly astounding science fiction tales that capture the essence of the time period, including masterpieces by Clifford D. Simak, Frederik Pohl, H. Beam Piper, Philip K. Dick, Murray Leinster, and Fritz Lieber. The impact and reach of these stories has been extensive, as all of them were adapted into radio dramas for the outstanding 1950s series "Dimension X" and "X Minus One," which are still treasured by many today.

The stories included in this collection also influenced many later literary and film ventures. For instance, Pohl's story "Tunnel Under the World" is about a character who keeps re-living the same day over and over, similar to the dilemma faced by Phil Connors in the 1993 motion picture *Groundhog Day*. Others of these stories had an obvious influence on television shows such as *Star Trek*, *Lost in Space*, and *Twilight Zone*.

As an author, I have published a number of books about unidentified flying objects, again influenced by the culture of the 1950s and 1960s – and also influenced by stories such as these, which I first read as a child and young adult. These wonderful stories truly make one's imagination soar far beyond the cares of daily life to worlds where the impossible seems possible and where flying saucers are not only possible but probably have landed in our own backyard.

The time in which these tales were written was one of great stress and societal tension; yet, out of this pain was forged some truly fantastic science fiction. Those who toiled in this untested literary genre were "going where no man had gone before," to use *Star Trek* creator Gene Roddenberry's term, and through their creativity, they established sci-fi as a valid and important conduit for the human imagination.

So here are eight tales that will amaze and tantalize, written by some of the best science fiction writers ever. Step back in time to the 1950s and imagine that the Cold War is still in full swing, nuclear war could break out at any moment, and mankind is beginning to ask a very important question – are we truly alone in the universe?

Noe Torres
Edinburg, Texas
March 2014

1950s Nuclear Test (U.S. Government Photo)

Time and Time Again
By Henry Beam Piper

Editor's note: "Time and Time Again" was Henry Beam Piper's first published short story, appearing in the April 1947 edition of Astounding Science Fiction. *Piper (1904-1964), or "H. Beam Piper" as he was better known, went on to a long career of writing both short stories and novels, mostly in the science-fiction genre. He is perhaps best known for his "Fuzzy" novels, of which* Little Fuzzy *was the first, published in 1962. A fascinating time travel story, "Time and Time Again" was adapted into radio dramas by the groundbreaking 1950s radio series "Dimension X" and "X Minus One."*

Blinded by the bomb-flash and numbed by the narcotic injection, he could not estimate the extent of his injuries, but he knew that he was dying. Around him, in the darkness, voices sounded as through a thick wall.

"They mighta left mosta these Joes where they was. Half of them won't even last till the truck comes."

"No matter; so long as they're alive, they must be treated," another voice, crisp and cultivated, rebuked. "Better start taking names, while we're waiting."

"Yes, sir." Fingers fumbled at his identity badge. "Hartley, Allan; Captain, G5, Chem. Research AN/73/D. Serial, SO-23869403J."

"Allan Hartley!" The medic officer spoke in shocked surprise. "Why, he's the man who wrote *Children of the Mist*, *Rose of Death*, and *Conqueror's Road*!"

He tried to speak, and must have stirred; the corpsman's voice sharpened.

"Major, I think he's part conscious. Mebbe I better give him 'nother shot."

"Yes, yes; by all means, sergeant."

Something jabbed Allan Hartley in the back of the neck. Soft billows of oblivion closed in upon him, and all that remained to him was a tiny spark of awareness, glowing alone and lost in a great darkness.

The Spark grew brighter. He was more than a something that merely knew that it existed. He was a man, and he had a name, and a military rank, and memories. Memories of the searing blue-green flash, and of what he had been doing outside the shelter the moment

before, and memories of the month-long siege, and of the retreat from the north, and memories of the days before the War, back to the time when he had been little Allan Hartley, a schoolboy, the son of a successful lawyer, in Williamsport, Pennsylvania.

His mother he could not remember; there was only a vague impression of the house full of people who had tried to comfort him for something he could not understand. But he remembered the old German woman who had kept house for his father, afterward, and he remembered his bedroom, with its chintz-covered chairs, and the warm-colored patch quilt on the old cherry bed, and the tan curtains at the windows, edged with dusky red, and the morning sun shining through them. He could almost see them, now.

He blinked. He could see them!

For a long time, he lay staring at them unbelievingly, and then he deliberately closed his eyes and counted ten seconds, and as he counted, terror gripped him. He was afraid to open them again, lest he find himself blind, or gazing at the filth and wreckage of a blasted city, but when he reached ten, he forced himself to look, and gave a sigh of relief. The sunlit curtains and the sun-gilded mist outside were still there.

He reached out to check one sense against another, feeling the rough monk's cloth and the edging of maroon silk thread. They were tangible as well as visible. Then he saw that the back of his hand was unscarred. There should have been a scar, souvenir of a rough-and-tumble brawl of his cub reporter days. He examined both hands closely. An instant later, he had sat up in bed and thrown off the covers, partially removing his pajamas and inspecting as much of his body as was visible.

It was the smooth body of a little boy.

That was ridiculous. He was a man of forty-three; an army officer,

4

a chemist, once a best-selling novelist. He had been married, and divorced ten years ago. He looked again at his body. It was only twelve years old. Fourteen, at the very oldest. His eyes swept the room, wide with wonder. Every detail was familiar: the flower-splashed chair covers; the table that served as desk and catch-all for his possessions; the dresser, with its mirror stuck full of pictures of aircraft. It was the bedroom of his childhood home. He swung his legs over the edge of the bed. They were six inches too short to reach the floor.

For an instant, the room spun dizzily; and he was in the grip of utter panic, all confidence in the evidence of his senses lost. Was he insane? Or delirious? Or had the bomb really killed him; was this what death was like? What was that thing, about "ye become as little children"? He started to laugh, and his juvenile larynx made giggling sounds. They seemed funny, too, and aggravated his mirth. For a little while, he was on the edge of hysteria and then, when he managed to control his laughter, he felt calmer. If he were dead, then he must be a discarnate entity, and would be able to penetrate matter. To his relief, he was unable to push his hand through the bed. So he was alive; he was also fully awake, and, he hoped, rational. He rose to his feet and prowled about the room, taking stock of its contents.

There was no calendar in sight, and he could find no newspapers or dated periodicals, but he knew that it was prior to July 18, 1946. On that day, his fourteenth birthday, his father had given him a light .22 rifle, and it had been hung on a pair of rustic forks on the wall. It was not there now, nor ever had been. On the table, he saw a boys' book of military aircraft, with a clean, new dust jacket; the flyleaf was inscribed: To Allan Hartley, from his father, on his thirteenth birthday, 7/18 '45. Glancing out the window at the foliage on the trees, he estimated the date at late July or early August, 1945; that would make him just thirteen.

His clothes were draped on a chair beside the bed. Stripping off his pajamas, he donned shorts, then sat down and picked up a pair of lemon-colored socks, which he regarded with disfavor. As he pulled one on, a church bell began to clang. St. Boniface, up on the hill, ringing for early Mass; so this was Sunday. He paused, the second sock in his hand.

There was no question that his present environment was actual. Yet, on the other hand, he possessed a set of memories completely at variance with it. Now, suppose, since his environment were not an illusion, everything else were? Suppose all these troublesome memories were no more than a dream? Why, he was just little Allan Hartley, safe in his room on a Sunday morning, badly scared by a nightmare! Too much science fiction, Allan; too many comic books!

That was a wonderfully comforting thought, and he hugged it to him contentedly. It lasted all the while he was buttoning up his shirt and pulling on his pants, but when he reached for his shoes, it evaporated. Ever since he had wakened, he realized, he had been occupied with thoughts utterly incomprehensible to any thirteen-year-old; even thinking in words that would have been so much Sanscrit to himself at thirteen. He shook his head regretfully. The just-a-dream hypothesis went by the deep six.

He picked up the second shoe and glared at it as though it were responsible for his predicament. He was going to have to be careful. An unexpected display of adult characteristics might give rise to some questions he would find hard to answer credibly. Fortunately, he was an only child; there would be no brothers or sisters to trip him up. Old Mrs. Stauber, the housekeeper, wouldn't be much of a problem; even in his normal childhood, he had bulked like an intellectual giant in comparison to her. But his father—

Now, there the going would be tough. He knew that shrewd attorney's mind, whetted keen on a generation of lying and reluctant witnesses. Sooner or later, he would forget for an instant and betray himself. Then he smiled, remembering the books he had discovered, in his late 'teens, on his father's shelves and recalling the character of the open-minded agnostic lawyer. If he could only avoid the inevitable unmasking until he had a plausible explanatory theory.

Blake Hartley was leaving the bathroom as Allan Hartley opened his door and stepped into the hall. The lawyer was bare-armed and in slippers; at forty-eight, there was only a faint powdering of gray in his dark hair, and not a gray thread in his clipped mustache. The old Merry Widower, himself, Allan thought, grinning as he remembered the white-haired but still vigorous man from whom he'd parted at the outbreak of the War.

"'Morning, Dad," he greeted.

"'Morning, son. You're up early. Going to Sunday school?"

Now there was the advantage of a father who'd cut his first intellectual tooth on Tom Paine and Bob Ingersoll; attendance at divine services was on a strictly voluntary basis.

"Why, I don't think so; I want to do some reading, this morning."

"That's always a good thing to do," Blake Hartley approved. "After breakfast, suppose you take a walk down to the station and get me a Times." He dug in his trouser pocket and came out with a half dollar. "Get anything you want for yourself, while you're at it."

Allan thanked his father and pocketed the coin.

"Mrs. Stauber'll still be at Mass," he suggested. "Say I get the paper now; breakfast won't be ready till she gets here."

"Good idea." Blake Hartley nodded, pleased. "You'll have three-quarters of an hour, at least."

So far, he congratulated himself, everything had gone smoothly. Finishing his toilet, he went downstairs and onto the street, turning left at Brandon to Campbell, and left again in the direction of the station. Before he reached the underpass, a dozen half-forgotten memories had revived. Here was a house that would, in a few years, be gutted by fire. Here were four dwellings standing where he had last seen a five-story apartment building. A gasoline station and a weed-grown lot would shortly be replaced by a supermarket. The environs of the station itself were a complete puzzle to him, until he oriented himself.

He bought a New York Times, glancing first of all at the date line. Sunday, August 5, 1945; he'd estimated pretty closely. The battle of Okinawa had been won. The Potsdam Conference had just ended. There were still pictures of the B-25 crash against the Empire State Building, a week ago Saturday. And Japan was still being pounded by bombs from the air and shells from off-shore naval guns. Why, tomorrow, Hiroshima was due for the Big Job! It amused him to reflect that he was probably the only person in Williamsport who knew that.

On the way home, a boy, sitting on the top step of a front porch, hailed him. Allan replied cordially, trying to remember who it was. Of course; Larry Morton! He and Allan had been buddies. They probably had been swimming, or playing Commandos and Germans, the afternoon before. Larry had gone to Cornell the same year that Allan had gone to Penn State; they had both graduated in 1954. Larry had gotten into some Government bureau, and then he had married a Pittsburgh girl, and had become twelfth vice-president of her father's firm. He had been killed, in 1968, in a plane crash.

"You gonna Sunday school?" Larry asked, mercifully unaware of the fate Allan foresaw for him.

"Why, no. I have some things I want to do at home." He'd have to watch himself. Larry would spot a difference quicker than any adult. "Heck with it," he added.

"Golly, I wisht I c'ld stay home from Sunday school whenever I wanted to," Larry envied. "How about us goin' swimmin', at the Canoe Club, 'safter?"

Allan thought fast. "Gee, I wisht I c'ld," he replied, lowering his grammatical sights. "I gotta stay home, 'safter. We're expectin' comp'ny; coupla aunts of mine. Dad wants me to stay home when they come."

That went over all right. Anybody knew that there was no rational accounting for the vagaries of the adult mind, and no appeal from adult demands. The prospect of company at the Hartley home would keep Larry away, that afternoon. He showed his disappointment.

"Aw, jeepers creepers!" he blasphemed euphemistically.

"Mebbe t'morrow," Allan said. "If I c'n make it. I gotta go, now; ain't had breakfast yet." He scuffed his feet boyishly, exchanged so-longs with his friend, and continued homeward.

As he had hoped, the Sunday paper kept his father occupied at breakfast, to the exclusion of any dangerous table talk. Blake Hartley was still deep in the financial section when Allan left the table and went to the library. There should be two books there to which he wanted badly to refer. For a while, he was afraid that his father had not acquired them prior to 1945, but he finally found them, and carried them onto the front porch, along with a pencil and a ruled yellow scratch pad. In his experienced future—or his past-to-come—Allan Hartley had been accustomed to doing his thinking with a pencil. As reporter, as novelist plotting his work, as amateur chemist in his home laboratory, as scientific warfare research officer, his ideas had always been clarified by making notes. He pushed a chair to the table and built up the seat with cushions, wondering how soon he would become used to the proportional disparity between himself and the furniture. As he opened the books and took his pencil in his hand, there was one thing missing. If he could only smoke a pipe, now!

His father came out and stretched in a wicker chair with the Times book-review section. The morning hours passed. Allan Hartley leafed

8

through one book and then the other. His pencil moved rapidly at times; at others, he doodled absently. There was no question, any more, in his mind, as to what or who he was. He was Allan Hartley, a man of forty-three, marooned in his own thirteen-year-old body, thirty years back in his own past. That was, of course, against all common sense, but he was easily able to ignore that objection. It had been made before: against the astronomy of Copernicus, and the geography of Columbus, and the biology of Darwin, and the industrial technology of Samuel Colt, and the military doctrines of Charles de Gaulle. Today's common sense had a habit of turning into tomorrow's utter nonsense. What he needed, right now, but bad, was a theory that would explain what had happened to him.

Understanding was beginning to dawn when Mrs. Stauber came out to announce midday dinner.

"I hope you von't mind haffin' it so early," she apologized. "Mein sister, Jennie, offer in Nippenose, she iss sick; I vant to go see her, dis afternoon, yet. I'll be back in blenty time to get supper, Mr. Hartley."

"Hey, Dad!" Allan spoke up. "Why can't we get our own supper, and have a picnic, like? That'd be fun, and Mrs. Stauber could stay as long as she wanted to."

His father looked at him. Such consideration for others was a most gratifying deviation from the juvenile norm; dawn of altruism, or something. He gave hearty assent:

"Why, of course, Mrs. Stauber. Allan and I can shift for ourselves, this evening; can't we, Allan? You needn't come back till tomorrow morning."

"Ach, t'ank you! T'ank you so mooch, Mr. Hartley."

At dinner, Allan got out from under the burden of conversation by questioning his father about the War and luring him into a lengthy dissertation on the difficulties of the forthcoming invasion of Japan. In view of what he remembered of the next twenty-four hours, Allan was secretly amused. His father was sure that the War would run on to mid-1946.

After dinner, they returned to the porch, Hartley père smoking a cigar and carrying out several law books. He only glanced at these occasionally; for the most part, he sat and blew smoke rings, and watched them float away. Some thrice-guilty felon was about to be triumphantly acquitted by a weeping jury; Allan could recognize a courtroom masterpiece in the process of incubation.

It was several hours later that the crunch of feet on the walk caused father and son to look up simultaneously. The approaching visitor was a tall man in a rumpled black suit; he had knobby wrists and big, awkward hands; black hair flecked with gray, and a harsh, bigoted face. Allan remembered him. Frank Gutchall. Lived on Campbell Street; a religious fanatic, and some sort of lay preacher. Maybe he needed legal advice; Allan could vaguely remember some incident—

"Ah, good afternoon, Mr. Gutchall. Lovely day, isn't it?" Blake Hartley said.

Gutchall cleared his throat. "Mr. Hartley, I wonder if you could lend me a gun and some bullets," he began, embarrassedly. "My little dog's been hurt, and it's suffering something terrible. I want a gun, to put the poor thing out of its pain."

"Why, yes; of course. How would a 20-gauge shotgun do?" Blake Hartley asked. "You wouldn't want anything heavy."

Gutchall fidgeted. "Why, er, I was hoping you'd let me have a little gun." He held his hands about six inches apart. "A pistol, that I could put in my pocket. It wouldn't look right, to carry a hunting gun on the Lord's day; people wouldn't understand that it was for a work of mercy."

The lawyer nodded. In view of Gutchall's religious beliefs, the objection made sense.

"Well, I have a Colt .38-special," he said, "but you know, I belong to this Auxiliary Police outfit. If I were called out for duty, this evening, I'd need it. How soon could you bring it back?"

Something clicked in Allan Hartley's mind. He remembered, now, what that incident had been. He knew, too, what he had to do.

"Dad, aren't there some cartridges left for the Luger?" he asked.

Blake Hartley snapped his fingers. "By George, yes! I have a German automatic I can let you have, but I wish you'd bring it back as soon as possible. I'll get it for you."

Before he could rise, Allan was on his feet.

"Sit still, Dad; I'll get it. I know where the cartridges are." With that, he darted into the house and upstairs.

The Luger hung on the wall over his father's bed. Getting it down, he dismounted it, working with rapid precision. He used the blade of his pocketknife to unlock the endpiece of the breechblock, slipping out the firing pin and buttoning it into his shirt pocket. Then he

reassembled the harmless pistol, and filled the clip with 9-millimeter cartridges from the bureau drawer.

There was an extension telephone beside the bed. Finding Gutchall's address in the directory, he lifted the telephone, and stretched his handkerchief over the mouthpiece. Then he dialed Police Headquarters.

"This is Blake Hartley," he lied, deepening his voice and copying his father's tone. "Frank Gutchall, who lives at...take this down"—he gave Gutchall's address—"has just borrowed a pistol from me, ostensibly to shoot a dog. He has no dog. He intends shooting his wife. Don't argue about how I know; there isn't time. Just take it for granted that I do. I disabled the pistol—took out the firing pin—but if he finds out what I did, he may get some other weapon. He's on his way home, but he's on foot. If you hurry, you may get a man there before he arrives, and grab him before he finds out the pistol won't shoot."

"O. K., Mr. Hartley. We'll take care of it. Thanks."

"And I wish you'd get my pistol back, as soon as you can. It's something I brought home from the other War, and I shouldn't like to lose it."

"We'll take care of that, too. Thank you, Mr. Hartley."

He hung up, and carried the Luger and the loaded clip down to the porch.

"Look, Mr. Gutchall; here's how it works," he said, showing it to the visitor. Then he slapped in the clip and yanked up on the toggle loading the chamber. "It's ready to shoot, now; this is the safety." He pushed it on. "When you're ready to shoot, just shove it forward and up, and then pull the trigger. You have to pull the trigger each time; it's loaded for eight shots. And be sure to put the safety back when you're through shooting."

"Did you load the chamber?" Blake Hartley demanded.

"Sure. It's on safe, now."

"Let me see." His father took the pistol, being careful to keep his finger out of the trigger guard, and looked at it. "Yes, that's all right." He repeated the instructions Allan had given, stressing the importance of putting the safety on after using. "Understand how it works, now?" he asked.

"Yes, I understand how it works. Thank you, Mr. Hartley. Thank you, too, young man."

Gutchall put the Luger in his hip pocket, made sure it wouldn't fall out, and took his departure.

"You shouldn't have loaded it," Hartley père reproved, when he was gone.

Allan sighed. This was it; the masquerade was over.

"I had to, to keep you from fooling with it," he said. "I didn't want you finding out that I'd taken out the firing pin."

"You what?"

"Gutchall didn't want that gun to shoot a dog. He has no dog. He meant to shoot his wife with it. He's a religious maniac; sees visions, hears voices, receives revelations, talks with the Holy Ghost. The Holy Ghost probably put him up to this caper. I'll submit that any man who holds long conversations with the Deity isn't to be trusted with a gun, and neither is any man who lies about why he wants one. And while I was at it, I called the police, on the upstairs phone. I had to use your name; I deepened my voice and talked through a handkerchief."

"You—" Blake Hartley jumped as though bee-stung. "Why did you have to do that?"

"You know why. I couldn't have told them, 'This is little Allan Hartley, just thirteen years old; please, Mr. Policeman, go and arrest Frank Gutchall before he goes root-toot-toot at his wife with my pappa's Luger.' That would have gone over big, now, wouldn't it?"

"And suppose he really wants to shoot a dog; what sort of a mess will I be in?"

"No mess at all. If I'm wrong—which I'm not—I'll take the thump for it, myself. It'll pass for a dumb kid trick, and nothing'll be done. But if I'm right, you'll have to front for me. They'll keep your name out of it, but they'd give me a lot of cheap boy-hero publicity, which I don't want." He picked up his pencil again. "We should have the complete returns in about twenty minutes."

That was a ten-minute under-estimate, and it was another quarter-hour before the detective-sergeant who returned the Luger had finished congratulating Blake Hartley and giving him the thanks of the Department. After he had gone, the lawyer picked up the Luger, withdrew the clip, and ejected the round in the chamber.

"Well," he told his son, "you were right. You saved that woman's life." He looked at the automatic, and then handed it across the table. "Now, let's see you put that firing pin back."

Allan Hartley dismantled the weapon, inserted the missing part, and put it together again, then snapped it experimentally and returned it to his father. Blake Hartley looked at it again, and laid it on the table.

"Now, son, suppose we have a little talk," he said softly.

"But I explained everything." Allan objected innocently.

"You did not," his father retorted. "Yesterday you'd never have thought of a trick like this; why, you wouldn't even have known how to take this pistol apart. And at dinner, I caught you using language and expressing ideas that were entirely outside anything you'd ever known before. Now, I want to know—and I mean this literally."

Allan chuckled. "I hope you're not toying with the rather medieval notion of obsession," he said.

Blake Hartley started. Something very like that must have been flitting through his mind. He opened his mouth to say something, then closed it abruptly.

"The trouble is, I'm not sure you aren't right," his son continued. "You say you find me—changed. When did you first notice a difference?"

"Last night, you were still my little boy. This morning—" Blake Hartley was talking more to himself than to Allan. "I don't know. You were unusually silent at breakfast. And come to think of it, there was something ... something strange ... about you when I saw you in the hall, upstairs.... Allan!" he burst out, vehemently. "What has happened to you?"

Allan Hartley felt a twinge of pain. What his father was going through was almost what he, himself, had endured, in the first few minutes after waking.

"I wish I could be sure, myself, Dad," he said. "You see, when I woke, this morning, I hadn't the least recollection of anything I'd done yesterday. August 4, 1945, that is," he specified. "I was

positively convinced that I was a man of forty-three, and my last memory was of lying on a stretcher, injured by a bomb explosion. And I was equally convinced that this had happened in 1975."

"Huh?" His father straightened. "Did you say nineteen seventy-five?" He thought for a moment. "That's right; in 1975, you will be forty-three. A bomb, you say?"

Allan nodded. "During the siege of Buffalo, in the Third World War," he said, "I was a captain in G5— Scientific Warfare, General Staff. There'd been a transpolar air invasion of Canada, and I'd been sent to the front to check on service failures of a new lubricating oil for combat equipment. A week after I got there, Ottawa fell, and the retreat started. We made a stand at Buffalo, and that was where I copped it. I remember being picked up, and getting a narcotic injection. The next thing I knew, I was in bed, upstairs, and it was 1945 again, and I was back in my own little thirteen-year-old body."

"Oh, Allan, you just had a nightmare to end nightmares!" his father assured him, laughing a trifle too heartily. "That's all!"

"That was one of the first things I thought of. I had to reject it; it just wouldn't fit the facts. Look; a normal dream is part of the dreamer's own physical brain, isn't it? Well, here is a part about two thousand per cent greater than the whole from which it was taken. Which is absurd."

"You mean all this Battle of Buffalo stuff? That's easy. All the radio commentators have been harping on the horrors of World War III, and you couldn't have avoided hearing some of it. You just have an undigested chunk of H. V. Kaltenborn raising hell in your subconscious."

"It wasn't just World War III; it was everything. My four years at high school, and my four years at Penn State, and my seven years as a reporter on the Philadelphia Record. And my novels: *Children of the Mist*, *Rose of Death*, *Conqueror's Road*. They were no kid stuff. Why, yesterday I'd never even have thought of some of the ideas I used in my detective stories, that I published under a nom-de-plume. And my hobby, chemistry; I was pretty good at that. Patented a couple of processes that made me as much money as my writing. You think a thirteen-year-old just dreamed all that up? Or, here; you speak French, don't you?" He switched languages and spoke at some length in good conversational slang-spiced Parisian. "Too bad you don't speak Spanish, too," he added, reverting to English. "Except for a Mexican accent you could cut with a machete, I'm even better there than in French. And I know some German, and a little Russian."

Blake Hartley was staring at his son, stunned. It was some time before he could make himself speak.

"I could barely keep up with you, in French," he admitted. "I can swear that in the last thirteen years of your life, you had absolutely no chance to learn it. All right; you lived till 1975, you say. Then, all of a sudden, you found yourself back here, thirteen years old, in 1945. I suppose you remember everything in between?" he asked. "Did you ever read James Branch Cabell? Remember Florian de Puysange, in 'The High Place'?"

"Yes. You find the same idea in 'Jurgen' too," Allan said. "You know, I'm beginning to wonder if Cabell mightn't have known something he didn't want to write."

"But it's impossible!" Blake Hartley hit the table with his hand, so hard that the heavy pistol bounced. The loose round he had ejected from the chamber toppled over and started to roll, falling off the edge. He stooped and picked it up. "How can you go back, against time? And the time you claim you came from doesn't exist, now; it hasn't happened yet." He reached for the pistol magazine, to insert the cartridge, and as he did, he saw the books in front of his son. "Dunne's 'Experiment with Time,'" he commented. "And J. N. M. Tyrrell's 'Science and Psychical Phenomena.' Are you trying to work out a theory?"

"Yes." It encouraged Allan to see that his father had unconsciously adopted an adult-to-adult manner. "I think I'm getting somewhere, too. You've read these books? Well, look, Dad; what's your attitude on precognition? The ability of the human mind to exhibit real knowledge, apart from logical inference, of future events? You think Dunne is telling the truth about his experiences? Or that the cases in Tyrrell's book are properly verified, and can't be explained away on the basis of chance?"

Blake Hartley frowned. "I don't know," he confessed. "The evidence is the sort that any court in the world would accept, if it concerned ordinary, normal events. Especially the cases investigated by the Society for Psychical Research: they have been verified. But how can anybody know of something that hasn't happened yet? If it hasn't happened yet, it doesn't exist, and you can't have real knowledge of something that has no real existence."

"Tyrrell discusses that dilemma, and doesn't dispose of it. I think I can. If somebody has real knowledge of the future, then the future must be available to the present mind. And if any moment other than the bare present exists, then all time must be totally present; every moment must be perpetually coexistent with every other moment," Allan said.

"Yes. I think I see what you mean. That was Dunne's idea, wasn't it?"

"No. Dunne postulated an infinite series of time dimensions, the entire extent of each being the bare present moment of the next. What I'm postulating is the perpetual coexistence of every moment of time in this dimension, just as every graduation on a yardstick exists equally with every other graduation, but each at a different point in space."

"Well, as far as duration and sequence go, that's all right," the father agreed. "But how about the 'Passage of Time'?"

"Well, time does appear to pass. So does the landscape you see from a moving car window. I'll suggest that both are illusions of the same kind. We imagine time to be dynamic, because we've never viewed it from a fixed point, but if it is totally present, then it must be static, and in that case, we're moving through time."

"That seems all right. But what's your car window?"

"If all time is totally present, then you must exist simultaneously at every moment along your individual life span," Allan said. "Your physical body, and your mind, and all the thoughts contained in your mind, each at its appropriate moment in sequence. But what is it that exists only at the bare moment we think of as now?"

Blake Hartley grinned. Already, he was accepting his small son as an intellectual equal.

"Please, teacher; what?"

"Your consciousness. And don't say, 'What's that?' Teacher doesn't know. But we're only conscious of one moment; the illusory now. This is 'now,' and it was 'now' when you asked that question, and it'll be 'now' when I stop talking, but each is a different moment. We imagine that all those nows are rushing past us. Really, they're standing still, and our consciousness is whizzing past them."

His father thought that over for some time. Then he sat up. "Hey!" he cried, suddenly. "If some part of our ego is time-free and passes from moment to moment, it must be extraphysical, because the physical body exists at every moment through which the consciousness passes. And if it's extraphysical, there's no reason whatever for assuming that it passes out of existence when it reaches the moment of the death of the body. Why, there's logical evidence for survival, independent of any alleged spirit communication! You can toss out Patience Worth, and Mrs. Osborne Leonard's Feda, and Sir Oliver Lodge's son, and Wilfred Brandon, and all the other spirit-communicators, and you still have evidence."

"I hadn't thought of that," Allan confessed. "I think you're right. Well, let's put that at the bottom of the agenda and get on with this time business. You 'lose consciousness' as in sleep; where does your consciousness go? I think it simply detaches from the moment at which you go to sleep, and moves backward or forward along the line of moment-sequence, to some prior or subsequent moment, attaching there."

"Well, why don't we know anything about that?" Blake Hartley asked. "It never seems to happen. We go to sleep tonight, and it's always tomorrow morning when we wake; never day-before-yesterday, or last month, or next year."

"It never ... or almost never ... seems to happen; you're right there. Know why? Because if the consciousness goes forward, it attaches at a moment when the physical brain contains memories of the previous, consciously unexperienced, moment. You wake, remembering the evening before, because that's the memory contained in your mind at that moment, and back of it are memories of all the events in the interim. See?"

"Yes. But how about backward movement, like this experience of yours?"

"This experience of mine may not be unique, but I never heard of another case like it. What usually happens is that the memories carried back by the consciousness are buried in the subconscious mind. You know how thick the wall between the subconscious and the conscious mind is. These dreams of Dunne's, and the cases in Tyrrell's book, are leakage. That's why precognitions are usually incomplete and distorted, and generally trivial. The wonder isn't that good cases are so few; it's surprising that there are any at all." Allan looked at the papers in front of him. "I haven't begun to theorize about how I managed to remember everything. It may have been the radiations from the bomb, or the effect of the narcotic, or both together, or something at this end, or a combination of all three. But the fact remains that my subconscious barrier didn't function, and everything got through. So, you see, I am obsessed—by my own future identity."

"And I'd been afraid that you'd been, well, taken-over by some ... some outsider." Blake Hartley grinned weakly. "I don't mind admitting, Allan, that what's happened has been a shock. But that other ... I just couldn't have taken that."

"No. Not and stayed sane. But really, I am your son; the same entity I was yesterday. I've just had what you might call an educational short cut."

"I'll say you have!" His father laughed in real amusement. He discovered that his cigar had gone out, and re-lit it. "Here; if you can remember the next thirty years, suppose you tell me when the War's going to end. This one, I mean."

"The Japanese surrender will be announced at exactly 1901—7:01 P. M. present style—on August 14. A week from Tuesday. Better make sure we have plenty of grub in the house by then. Everything will be closed up tight till Thursday morning; even the restaurants. I remember, we had nothing to eat in the house but some scraps."

"Well! It is handy, having a prophet in the family! I'll see to it Mrs. Stauber gets plenty of groceries in.... Tuesday a week? That's pretty sudden, isn't it?"

"The Japs are going to think so," Allan replied. He went on to describe what was going to happen.

His father swore softly. "You know, I've heard talk about atomic

18

energy, but I thought it was just Buck Rogers stuff. Was that the sort of bomb that got you?"

"That was a firecracker to the bomb that got me. That thing exploded a good ten miles away."

Blake Hartley whistled softly. "And that's going to happen in thirty years! You know, son, if I were you, I wouldn't like to have to know about a thing like that." He looked at Allan for a moment. "Please, if you know, don't ever tell me when I'm going to die."

Allan smiled. "I can't. I had a letter from you just before I left for the front. You were seventy-eight, then, and you were still hunting, and fishing, and flying your own plane. But I'm not going to get killed in any Battle of Buffalo, this time, and if I can prevent it, and I think I can, there won't be any World War III."

"But—You say all time exists, perpetually coexistent and totally present," his father said. "Then it's right there in front of you, and you're getting closer to it, every watch tick."

Allan Hartley shook his head. "You know what I remembered, when Frank Gutchall came to borrow a gun?" he asked. "Well, the other time, I hadn't been home: I'd been swimming at the Canoe Club, with Larry Morton. When I got home, about half an hour from now, I found the house full of cops. Gutchall talked the .38 officers' model out of you, and gone home; he'd shot his wife four times through the body, finished her off with another one back of the ear, and then used his sixth shot to blast his brains out. The cops traced the gun; they took a very poor view of your lending it to him. You never got it back."

"Trust that gang to keep a good gun," the lawyer said.

"I didn't want us to lose it, this time, and I didn't want to see you lose face around City Hall. Gutchalls, of course, are expendable," Allan said. "But my main reason for fixing Frank Gutchall up with a padded cell was that I wanted to know whether or not the future could be altered. I have it on experimental authority that it can be. There must be additional dimensions of time; lines of alternate probabilities. Something like William Seabrook's witch-doctor friend's Fan-Shaped Destiny. When I brought memories of the future back to the present, I added certain factors to the causal chain. That set up an entirely new line of probabilities. On no notice at all, I stopped a murder and a suicide. With thirty years to work, I can stop a world war. I'll have the means to do it, too."

"The means?"

"Unlimited wealth and influence. Here." Allan picked up a sheet and handed it to his father. "Used properly, we can make two or three million on that, alone. A list of all the Kentucky Derby, Preakness, and Belmont winners to 1970. That'll furnish us primary capital. Then, remember, I was something of a chemist. I took it up, originally, to get background material for one of my detective stories; it fascinated me, and I made it a hobby, and then a source of income. I'm thirty years ahead of any chemist in the world, now. You remember I. G. Farbenindustrie? Ten years from now, we'll make them look like pikers."

His father looked at the yellow sheet. "Assault, at eight to one," he said. "I can scrape up about five thousand for that—Yes; in ten years—Any other little operations you have in mind?" he asked.

"About 1950, we start building a political organization, here in Pennsylvania. In 1960, I think we can elect you President. The world situation will be crucial, by that time, and we had a good-natured nonentity in the White House then, who let things go till war became inevitable. I think President Hartley can be trusted to take a strong line of policy. In the meantime, you can read Machiavelli."

"That's my little boy, talking!"

Blake Hartley said softly. "All right, son; I'll do just what you tell me, and when you grow up, I'll be president.... Let's go get supper, now."

Note: Illustrations by Napoli.

The Defenders
By Philip K. Dick

Editor's note: Appearing in the highly regarded magazine Galaxy Science Fiction *in January 1953, this gem of a story was written by celebrated sci-fi writer Philip K. Dick (1928-1982), who has had several of his stories adapted into major motion pictures, including* Blade Runner *(1982),* Total Recall *(1990 & 2012),* Minority Report *(2002), and* Paycheck *(2003). In "The Defenders," the U.S. and Russia are locked in a massive global war that is being fought by robots and has devastated the Earth's major cities – or is the war even real? This story was adapted for radio on NBC's "X Minus One."*

Taylor sat back in his chair reading the morning newspaper. The warm kitchen and the smell of coffee blended with the comfort of not having to go to work. This was his Rest Period, the first for a long time, and he was glad of it. He folded the second section back, sighing with contentment.

"What is it?" Mary said, from the stove.

"They pasted Moscow again last night." Taylor nodded his head in approval. "Gave it a real pounding. One of those R-H bombs. It's about time."

He nodded again, feeling the full comfort of the kitchen, the presence of his plump, attractive wife, the breakfast dishes and coffee. This was relaxation. And the war news was good, good and satisfying. He could feel a justifiable glow at the news, a sense of pride and personal accomplishment. After all, he was an integral part of the war program, not just another factory worker lugging a cart of scrap, but a technician, one of those who designed and planned the nerve-trunk of the war.

"It says they have the new subs almost perfected. Wait until they get those going." He smacked his lips with anticipation. "When they start shelling from underwater, the Soviets are sure going to be surprised."

"They're doing a wonderful job," Mary agreed vaguely. "Do you know what we saw today? Our team is getting a leady to show to the school children. I saw the leady, but only for a moment. It's good for the children to see what their contributions are going for, don't you think?"

She looked around at him.

"A leady," Taylor murmured. He put the newspaper slowly down. "Well, make sure it's decontaminated properly. We don't want to take any chances."

"Oh, they always bathe them when they're brought down from the surface," Mary said. "They wouldn't think of letting them down without the bath. Would they?" She hesitated, thinking back. "Don, you know, it makes me remember—"

He nodded. "I know."

HE knew what she was thinking. Once in the very first weeks of the war, before everyone had been evacuated from the surface, they had seen a hospital train discharging the wounded, people who had been showered with sleet. He remembered the way they had looked, the expression on their faces, or as much of their faces as was left. It had not been a pleasant sight.

There had been a lot of that at first, in the early days before the transfer to undersurface was complete. There had been a lot, and it hadn't been very difficult to come across it.

Taylor looked up at his wife. She was thinking too much about it, the last few months. They all were.

"Forget it," he said. "It's all in the past. There isn't anybody up there now but the leadys, and they don't mind."

"But just the same, I hope they're careful when they let one of them down here. If one were still hot—"

He laughed, pushing himself away from the table. "Forget it. This is a wonderful moment; I'll be home for the next two shifts. Nothing to do but sit around and take things easy. Maybe we can take in a show. Okay?"

"A show? Do we have to? I don't like to look at all the destruction, the ruins. Sometimes I see some place I remember, like San Francisco. They showed a shot of San Francisco, the bridge broken and fallen in the water, and I got upset. I don't like to watch."

"But don't you want to know what's going on? No human beings are getting hurt, you know."

"But it's so awful!" Her face was set and strained. "Please, no, Don."

Don Taylor picked up his newspaper sullenly. "All right, but there isn't a hell of a lot else to do. And don't forget, their cities are getting it even worse."

She nodded. Taylor turned the rough, thin sheets of newspaper. His good mood had soured on him. Why did she have to fret all the time? They were pretty well off, as things went. You couldn't expect to have everything perfect, living undersurface, with an artificial sun and artificial food. Naturally it was a strain, not seeing the sky or being able to go any place or see anything other than metal walls, great roaring factories, the plant-yards, barracks. But it was better than being on surface. And some day it would end and they could return. Nobody wanted to live this way, but it was necessary.

He turned the page angrily and the poor paper ripped. Damn it, the paper was getting worse quality all the time, bad print, yellow tint—

Well, they needed everything for the war program. He ought to know that. Wasn't he one of the planners?

He excused himself and went into the other room. The bed was still unmade. They had better get it in shape before the seventh hour inspection. There was a one unit fine—

The vidphone rang. He halted. Who would it be? He went over and clicked it on.

"Taylor?" the face said, forming into place. It was an old face, gray and grim. "This is Moss. I'm sorry to bother you during Rest Period, but this thing has come up." He rattled papers. "I want you to hurry over here."

Taylor stiffened. "What is it? There's no chance it could wait?" The calm gray eyes were studying him, expressionless, unjudging. "If you want me to come down to the lab," Taylor grumbled, "I suppose I can. I'll get my uniform—"

"No. Come as you are. And not to the lab. Meet me at second stage as soon as possible. It'll take you about a half hour, using the fast car up. I'll see you there."

The picture broke and Moss disappeared.

"What was it?" Mary said, at the door.

"Moss. He wants me for something."

"I knew this would happen."

"Well, you didn't want to do anything, anyhow. What does it matter?" His voice was bitter. "It's all the same, every day. I'll bring you back something. I'm going up to second stage. Maybe I'll be close enough to the surface to—"

"Don't! Don't bring me anything! Not from the surface!"

"All right, I won't. But of all the irrational nonsense—"

She watched him put on his boots without answering.

Moss nodded and Taylor fell in step with him, as the older man strode along. A series of loads were going up to the surface, blind cars clanking like ore-trucks up the ramp, disappearing through the stage trap above them. Taylor watched the cars, heavy with tubular machinery of some sort, weapons new to him. Workers were everywhere, in the dark gray uniforms of the labor corps, loading, lifting, shouting back and forth. The stage was deafening with noise.

"We'll go up a way," Moss said, "where we can talk. This is no place to give you details."

They took an escalator up. The commercial lift fell behind them, and with it most of the crashing and booming. Soon they emerged on an observation platform, suspended on the side of the Tube, the vast tunnel leading to the surface, not more than half a mile above them now.

"My God!" Taylor said, looking down the Tube involuntarily. "It's a long way down."

Moss laughed. "Don't look."

They opened a door and entered an office. Behind the desk, an officer was sitting, an officer of Internal Security. He looked up.

"I'll be right with you, Moss." He gazed at Taylor studying him. "You're a little ahead of time."

"This is Commander Franks," Moss said to Taylor. "He was the first to make the discovery. I was notified last night." He tapped a parcel he carried. "I was let in because of this."

Franks frowned at him and stood up. "We're going up to first stage. We can discuss it there."

"First stage?" Taylor repeated nervously. The three of them went down a side passage to a small lift. "I've never been up there. Is it all right? It's not radioactive, is it?"

"You're like everyone else," Franks said. "Old women afraid of burglars. No radiation leaks down to first stage. There's lead and rock, and what comes down the Tube is bathed."

"What's the nature of the problem?" Taylor asked. "I'd like to know something about it."

"In a moment."

They entered the lift and ascended. When they stepped out, they were in a hall of soldiers, weapons and uniforms everywhere. Taylor blinked in surprise. So this was first stage, the closest undersurface level to the top! After this stage there was only rock, lead and rock, and the great tubes leading up like the burrows of earthworms. Lead and rock, and above that, where the tubes opened, the great expanse that no living being had seen for eight years, the vast, endless ruin that had once been Man's home, the place where he had lived, eight years ago.

Now the surface was a lethal desert of slag and rolling clouds. Endless clouds drifted back and forth, blotting out the red Sun. Occasionally something metallic stirred, moving through the remains of a city, threading its way across the tortured terrain of the countryside. A leady, a surface robot, immune to radiation, constructed with feverish haste in the last months before the cold war became literally hot.

Leadys, crawling along the ground, moving over the oceans or through the skies in slender, blackened craft, creatures that could exist where no life could remain, metal and plastic figures that waged a war Man had conceived, but which he could not fight himself. Human beings had invented war, invented and manufactured the weapons, even invented the players, the fighters, the actors of the war. But they themselves could not venture forth, could not wage it themselves. In all the world—in Russia, in Europe, America, Africa—no living human being remained. They were under the surface, in the deep shelters that had been carefully planned and built, even as the first bombs began to fall.

It was a brilliant idea and the only idea that could have worked. Up above, on the ruined, blasted surface of what had once been a living planet, the leady crawled and scurried, and fought Man's war. And undersurface, in the depths of the planet, human beings toiled endlessly to produce the weapons to continue the fight, month by month, year by year.

"First stage," Taylor said. A strange ache went through him. "Almost to the surface."

"But not quite," Moss said.

Franks led them through the soldiers, over to one side, near the lip of the Tube.

"In a few minutes, a lift will bring something down to us from the surface," he explained. "You see, Taylor, every once in a while Security examines and interrogates a surface leady, one that has been above for a time, to find out certain things. A vidcall is sent up and contact is made with a field headquarters. We need this direct interview; we can't depend on vidscreen contact alone. The leadys are doing a good job, but we want to make certain that everything is going the way we want it."

Franks faced Taylor and Moss and continued: "The lift will bring down a leady from the surface, one of the A-class leadys. There's an examination chamber in the next room, with a lead wall in the center, so the interviewing officers won't be exposed to radiation. We find this easier than bathing the leady. It is going right back up; it has a job to get back to.

"Two days ago, an A-class leady was brought down and interrogated. I conducted the session myself. We were interested in a new weapon the Soviets have been using, an automatic mine that pursues anything that moves. Military had sent instructions up that the mine be observed and reported in detail.

"This A-class leady was brought down with information. We learned a few facts from it, obtained the usual roll of film and reports, and then sent it back up. It was going out of the chamber, back to the lift, when a curious thing happened. At the time, I thought—"

THE DEFENDERS By Philip K. Dick

Franks broke off. A red light was flashing.

"That down lift is coming." He nodded to some soldiers. "Let's enter the chamber. The leady will be along in a moment."

"An A-class leady," Taylor said. "I've seen them on the showscreens, making their reports."

"It's quite an experience," Moss said. "They're almost human."

They entered the chamber and seated themselves behind the lead wall. After a time, a signal was flashed, and Franks made a motion with his hands.

The door beyond the wall opened. Taylor peered through his view slot. He saw something advancing slowly, a slender metallic figure moving on a tread, its arm grips at rest by its sides. The figure halted and scanned the lead wall. It stood, waiting.

"We are interested in learning something," Franks said. "Before I question you, do you have anything to report on surface conditions?"

"No. The war continues." The leady's voice was automatic and toneless. "We are a little short of fast pursuit craft, the single-seat type. We could use also some—"

"That has all been noted. What I want to ask you is this. Our contact with you has been through vidscreen only. We must rely on indirect evidence, since none of us goes above. We can only infer what is going on. We never see anything ourselves. We have to take it all secondhand. Some top leaders are beginning to think there's too much room for error."

"Error?" the leady asked. "In what way? Our reports are checked carefully before they're sent down. We maintain constant contact with you; everything of value is reported. Any new weapons which the enemy is seen to employ—"

"I realize that," Franks grunted behind his peep slot. "But perhaps we should see it all for ourselves. Is it possible that there might be a large enough radiation-free area for a human party to ascend to the surface? If a few of us were to come up in lead-lined suits, would we be able to survive long enough to observe conditions and watch things?"

The machine hesitated before answering. "I doubt it. You can check air samples, of course, and decide for yourselves. But in the eight years since you left, things have continually worsened. You cannot have any real idea of conditions up there. It has become difficult for any moving object to survive for long. There are many kinds of projectiles sensitive to movement. The new mine not only reacts to motion, but continues to pursue the object indefinitely, until it finally reaches it. And the radiation is everywhere."

"I see." Franks turned to Moss, his eyes narrowed oddly. "Well, that was what I wanted to know. You may go."

The machine moved back toward its exit. It paused. "Each month the amount of lethal particles in the atmosphere increases. The tempo of the war is gradually—"

"I understand." Franks rose. He held out his hand and Moss passed him the package. "One thing before you leave. I want you to examine a new type of metal shield material. I'll pass you a sample with the tong."

Franks put the package in the toothed grip and revolved the tong so that he held the other end. The package swung down to the leady, which took it. They watched it unwrap the package and take the metal plate in its hands. The leady turned the metal over and over.

Suddenly it became rigid.

"All right," Franks said.

He put his shoulder against the wall and a section slid aside. Taylor gasped—Franks and Moss were hurrying up to the leady!

"Good God!" Taylor said. "But it's radioactive!"

The leady stood unmoving, still holding the metal. Soldiers appeared in the chamber. They surrounded the leady and ran a counter across it carefully.

"Okay, sir," one of them said to Franks. "It's as cold as a long winter evening."

"Good. I was sure, but I didn't want to take any chances."

"You see," Moss said to Taylor, "this leady isn't hot at all. Yet it came directly from the surface, without even being bathed."

"But what does it mean?" Taylor asked blankly.

"It may be an accident," Franks said. "There's always the possibility that a given object might escape being exposed above. But this is the second time it's happened that we know of. There may be others."

"The second time?"

"The previous interview was when we noticed it. The leady was not hot. It was cold, too, like this one."

Moss took back the metal plate from the leady's hands. He pressed the surface carefully and returned it to the stiff, unprotesting fingers.

"We shorted it out with this, so we could get close enough for a thorough check. It'll come back on in a second now. We had better get behind the wall again."

They walked back and the lead wall swung closed behind them. The soldiers left the chamber.

"Two periods from now," Franks said softly, "an initial investigating party will be ready to go surface-side. We're going up the Tube in suits, up to the top—the first human party to leave undersurface in eight years."

"It may mean nothing," Moss said, "but I doubt it. Something's going on, something strange. The leady told us no life could exist above without being roasted. The story doesn't fit."

Taylor nodded. He stared through the peep slot at the immobile metal figure. Already the leady was beginning to stir. It was bent in several places, dented and twisted, and its finish was blackened and charred. It was a leady that had been up there a long time; it had seen war and destruction, ruin so vast that no human being could imagine the extent. It had crawled and slunk in a world of radiation and death, a world where no life could exist.

And Taylor had touched it!

"You're going with us," Franks said suddenly. "I want you along. I think the three of us will go."

Mary faced him with a sick and frightened expression. "I know it. You're going to the surface. Aren't you?"

She followed him into the kitchen. Taylor sat down, looking away from her.

"It's a classified project," he evaded. "I can't tell you anything about it."

"You don't have to tell me. I know. I knew it the moment you came in. There was something on your face, something I haven't seen there for a long, long time. It was an old look."

She came toward him. "But how can they send you to the surface?" She took his face in her shaking hands, making him look at her. There was a strange hunger in her eyes. "Nobody can live up there. Look, look at this!"

She grabbed up a newspaper and held it in front of him.

"Look at this photograph. America, Europe, Asia, Africa—nothing but ruins. We've seen it every day on the showscreens. All destroyed, poisoned. And they're sending you up. Why? No living thing can get by up there, not even a weed, or grass. They've wrecked the surface, haven't they? Haven't they?"

Taylor stood up. "It's an order. I know nothing about it. I was told to report to join a scout party. That's all I know."

He stood for a long time, staring ahead. Slowly, he reached for the newspaper and held it up to the light.

"It looks real," he murmured. "Ruins, deadness, slag. It's convincing. All the reports, photographs, films, even air samples. Yet we haven't seen it for ourselves, not after the first months ..."

"What are you talking about?"

"Nothing." He put the paper down. "I'm leaving early after the next Sleep Period. Let's turn in."

Mary turned away, her face hard and harsh. "Do what you want. We might just as well all go up and get killed at once, instead of dying slowly down here, like vermin in the ground."

He had not realized how resentful she was. Were they all like that? How about the workers toiling in the factories, day and night, endlessly? The pale, stooped men and women, plodding back and forth to work, blinking in the colorless light, eating synthetics—

"You shouldn't be so bitter," he said.

Mary smiled a little. "I'm bitter because I know you'll never come back." She turned away. "I'll never see you again, once you go up there."

He was shocked. "What? How can you say a thing like that?"

She did not answer.

HE awakened with the public newscaster screeching in his ears, shouting outside the building.

"Special news bulletin! Surface forces report enormous Soviet attack with new weapons! Retreat of key groups! All work units report to factories at once!"

Taylor blinked, rubbing his eyes. He jumped out of bed and hurried to the vidphone. A moment later he was put through to Moss.

"Listen," he said. "What about this new attack? Is the project off?" He could see Moss's desk, covered with reports and papers.

"No," Moss said. "We're going right ahead. Get over here at once."

"But—"

"Don't argue with me." Moss held up a handful of surface bulletins, crumpling them savagely. "This is a fake. Come on!" He broke off.

Taylor dressed furiously, his mind in a daze.

Half an hour later, he leaped from a fast car and hurried up the stairs into the Synthetics Building. The corridors were full of men and women rushing in every direction. He entered Moss's office.

"There you are," Moss said, getting up immediately. "Franks is waiting for us at the outgoing station."

They went in a Security Car, the siren screaming. Workers scattered out of their way.

"What about the attack?" Taylor asked.

Moss braced his shoulders. "We're certain that we've forced their hand. We've brought the issue to a head."

They pulled up at the station link of the Tube and leaped out. A moment later they were moving up at high speed toward the first stage.

They emerged into a bewildering scene of activity. Soldiers were fastening on lead suits, talking excitedly to each other, shouting back and forth. Guns were being given out, instructions passed.

Taylor studied one of the soldiers. He was armed with the dreaded Bender pistol, the new snub-nosed hand weapon that was just beginning to come from the assembly line. Some of the soldiers looked a little frightened.

"I hope we're not making a mistake," Moss said, noticing his gaze.

Franks came toward them. "Here's the program. The three of us are going up first, alone. The soldiers will follow in fifteen minutes."

"What are we going to tell the leadys?" Taylor worriedly asked. "We'll have to tell them something."

"We want to observe the new Soviet attack." Franks smiled ironically. "Since it seems to be so serious, we should be there in person to witness it."

"And then what?" Taylor said.

"That'll be up to them. Let's go."

IN a small car, they went swiftly up the Tube, carried by anti-grav beams from below. Taylor glanced down from time to time. It was a long way back, and getting longer each moment. He sweated nervously inside his suit, gripping his Bender pistol with inexpert fingers.

Why had they chosen him? Chance, pure chance. Moss had asked him to come along as a Department member. Then Franks had picked him out on the spur of the moment. And now they were rushing toward the surface, faster and faster.

A deep fear, instilled in him for eight years, throbbed in his mind. Radiation, certain death, a world blasted and lethal—

Up and up the car went. Taylor gripped the sides and closed his eyes. Each moment they were closer, the first living creatures to go above the first stage, up the Tube past the lead and rock, up to the surface. The phobic horror shook him in waves. It was death; they all knew that. Hadn't they seen it in the films a thousand times? The cities, the sleet coming down, the rolling clouds—

"It won't be much longer," Franks said. "We're almost there. The surface tower is not expecting us. I gave orders that no signal was to be sent."

The car shot up, rushing furiously. Taylor's head spun; he hung on, his eyes shut. Up and up....

The car stopped. He opened his eyes.

They were in a vast room, fluorescent-lit, a cavern filled with equipment and machinery, endless mounds of material piled in row after row. Among the stacks, leadys were working silently, pushing trucks and handcarts.

"Leadys," Moss said. His face was pale. "Then we're really on the surface."

The leadys were going back and forth with equipment moving the vast stores of guns and spare parts, ammunition and supplies that had been brought to the surface. And this was the receiving station for only one Tube; there were many others, scattered throughout the continent.

Taylor looked nervously around him. They were really there, above ground, on the surface. This was where the war was.

"Come on," Franks said. "A B-class guard is coming our way."

THEY stepped out of the car. A leady was approaching them rapidly. It coasted up in front of them and stopped, scanning them with its hand-weapon raised.

"This is Security," Franks said. "Have an A-class sent to me at once."

The leady hesitated. Other B-class guards were coming, scooting across the floor, alert and alarmed. Moss peered around.

"Obey!" Franks said in a loud, commanding voice. "You've been ordered!"

The leady moved uncertainly away from them. At the end of the building, a door slid back. Two A-class leadys appeared, coming slowly toward them. Each had a green stripe across its front.

"From the Surface Council," Franks whispered tensely. "This is above ground, all right. Get set."

The two leadys approached warily. Without speaking, they stopped close by the men, looking them up and down.

"I'm Franks of Security. We came from undersurface in order to—"

"This in incredible," one of the leadys interrupted him coldly. "You know you can't live up here. The whole surface is lethal to you. You can't possibly remain on the surface."

"These suits will protect us," Franks said. "In any case, it's not your responsibility. What I want is an immediate Council meeting so I can acquaint myself with conditions, with the situation here. Can that be arranged?"

"You human beings can't survive up here. And the new Soviet attack is directed at this area. It is in considerable danger."

"We know that. Please assemble the Council." Franks looked around him at the vast room, lit by recessed lamps in the ceiling. An uncertain quality came into his voice. "Is it night or day right now?"

"Night," one of the A-class leadys said, after a pause. "Dawn is coming in about two hours."

Franks nodded. "We'll remain at least two hours, then. As a

34

concession to our sentimentality, would you please show us some place where we can observe the Sun as it comes up? We would appreciate it."

A stir went through the leadys.

"It is an unpleasant sight," one of the leadys said. "You've seen the photographs; you know what you'll witness. Clouds of drifting particles blot out the light, slag heaps are everywhere, the whole land is destroyed. For you it will be a staggering sight, much worse than pictures and film can convey."

"However it may be, we'll stay long enough to see it. Will you give the order to the Council?"

"COME this way." Reluctantly, the two leadys coasted toward the wall of the warehouse. The three men trudged after them, their heavy shoes ringing against the concrete. At the wall, the two leadys paused.

"This is the entrance to the Council Chamber. There are windows in the Chamber Room, but it is still dark outside, of course. You'll see nothing right now, but in two hours—"

"Open the door," Franks said.

The door slid back. They went slowly inside. The room was small, a neat room with a round table in the center, chairs ringing it. The three of them sat down silently, and the two leadys followed after them, taking their places.

"The other Council Members are on their way. They have already been notified and are coming as quickly as they can. Again I urge you to go back down." The leady surveyed the three human beings. "There is no way you can meet the conditions up here. Even we survive with some trouble, ourselves. How can you expect to do it?"

The leader approached Franks.

"This astonishes and perplexes us," it said. "Of course we must do what you tell us, but allow me to point out that if you remain here—"

"We know," Franks said impatiently. "However, we intend to remain, at least until sunrise."

"If you insist."

There was silence. The leadys seemed to be conferring with each other, although the three men heard no sound.

"For your own good," the leader said at last, "you must go back down. We have discussed this, and it seems to us that you are doing the wrong thing for your own good."

"We are human beings," Franks said sharply. "Don't you understand? We're men, not machines."

"That is precisely why you must go back. This room is radioactive; all surface areas are. We calculate that your suits will not protect you for over fifty more minutes. Therefore—"

The leadys moved abruptly toward the men, wheeling in a circle, forming a solid row. The men stood up, Taylor reaching awkwardly for his weapon, his fingers numb and stupid. The men stood facing the silent metal figures.

"We must insist," the leader said, its voice without emotion. "We must take you back to the Tube and send you down on the next car. I am sorry, but it is necessary."

"What'll we do?" Moss said nervously to Franks. He touched his gun. "Shall we blast them?"

Franks shook his head. "All right," he said to the leader. "We'll go back."

He moved toward the door, motioning Taylor and Moss to follow him. They looked at him in surprise, but they came with him. The leadys followed them out into the great warehouse. Slowly they moved toward the Tube entrance, none of them speaking.

At the lip, Franks turned. "We are going back because we have no choice. There are three of us and about a dozen of you. However, if—"

"Here comes the car," Taylor said.

There was a grating sound from the Tube. D-class leadys moved toward the edge to receive it.

"I am sorry," the leader said, "but it is for your protection. We are watching over you, literally. You must stay below and let us conduct the war. In a sense, it has come to be our war. We must fight it as we see fit."

The car rose to the surface.

Twelve soldiers, armed with Bender pistols, stepped from it and surrounded the three men.

Moss breathed a sigh of relief. "Well, this does change things. It came off just right."

The leader moved back, away from the soldiers. It studied them intently, glancing from one to the next, apparently trying to make up its mind. At last it made a sign to the other leadys. They coasted aside and a corridor was opened up toward the warehouse.

"Even now," the leader said, "we could send you back by force. But it is evident that this is not really an observation party at all. These soldiers show that you have much more in mind; this was all carefully prepared."

"Very carefully," Franks said.

They closed in.

"How much more, we can only guess. I must admit that we were taken unprepared. We failed utterly to meet the situation. Now force would be absurd, because neither side can afford to injure the other; we, because of the restrictions placed on us regarding human life, you because the war demands—"

The soldiers fired, quick and in fright. Moss dropped to one knee, firing up. The leader dissolved in a cloud of particles. On all sides D- and B-class leadys were rushing up, some with weapons, some with metal slats. The room was in confusion. Off in the distance a siren was screaming. Franks and Taylor were cut off from the others, separated from the soldiers by a wall of metal bodies.

"They can't fire back," Franks said calmly. "This is another bluff. They've tried to bluff us all the way." He fired into the face of a leady. The leady dissolved. "They can only try to frighten us. Remember that."

They went on firing and leady after leady vanished. The room reeked with the smell of burning metal, the stink of fused plastic and steel. Taylor had been knocked down. He was struggling to find his gun, reaching wildly among metal legs, groping frantically to find it. His fingers strained, a handle swam in front of him. Suddenly something came down on his arm, a metal foot. He cried out.

Then it was over. The leadys were moving away, gathering together off to one side. Only four of the Surface Council remained. The others were radioactive particles in the air. D-class leadys were already restoring order, gathering up partly destroyed metal figures and bits and removing them.

Franks breathed a shuddering sigh.

"All right," he said. "You can take us back to the windows. It won't be long now."

The leadys separated, and the human group, Moss and Franks and Taylor and the soldiers, walked slowly across the room, toward the door. They entered the Council Chamber. Already a faint touch of gray mitigated the blackness of the windows.

"Take us outside," Franks said impatiently. "We'll see it directly, not in here."

A door slid open. A chill blast of cold morning air rushed in, chilling them even through their lead suits. The men glanced at each other uneasily.

"Come on," Franks said. "Outside."

He walked out through the door, the others following him.

They were on a hill, overlooking the vast bowl of a valley. Dimly, against the graying sky, the outline of mountains were forming, becoming tangible.

"It'll be bright enough to see in a few minutes," Moss said. He shuddered as a chilling wind caught him and moved around him. "It's worth it, really worth it, to see this again after eight years. Even if it's the last thing we see—"

"Watch," Franks snapped.

They obeyed, silent and subdued. The sky was clearing, brightening each moment. Some place far off, echoing across the valley, a rooster crowed.

"A chicken!" Taylor murmured. "Did you hear?"

Behind them, the leadys had come out and were standing silently, watching, too. The gray sky turned to white and the hills appeared more clearly. Light spread across the valley floor, moving toward them.

"God in heaven!" Franks exclaimed.

Trees, trees and forests. A valley of plants and trees, with a few roads winding among them. Farmhouses. A windmill. A barn, far down below them.

"Look!" Moss whispered.

Color came into the sky. The Sun was approaching. Birds began to sing. Not far from where they stood, the leaves of a tree danced in the wind.

Franks turned to the row of leadys behind them.

"Eight years. We were tricked. There was no war. As soon as we left the surface—"

"Yes," an A-class leady admitted. "As soon as you left, the war ceased. You're right, it was a hoax. You worked hard undersurface, sending up guns and weapons, and we destroyed them as fast as they came up."

"But why?" Taylor asked, dazed. He stared down at the vast valley below. "Why?"

"You created us," the leady said, "to pursue the war for you, while you human beings went below the ground in order to survive. But before we could continue the war, it was necessary to analyze it to determine what its purpose was. We did this, and we found that it had no purpose, except, perhaps, in terms of human needs. Even this was questionable.

"We investigated further. We found that human cultures pass through phases, each culture in its own time. As the culture ages and begins to lose its objectives, conflict arises within it between those who wish to cast it off and set up a new culture-pattern, and those who wish to retain the old with as little change as possible.

"At this point, a great danger appears. The conflict within threatens to engulf the society in self-war, group against group. The vital traditions may be lost—not merely altered or reformed, but completely destroyed in this period of chaos and anarchy. We have found many such examples in the history of mankind.

"It is necessary for this hatred within the culture to be directed outward, toward an external group, so that the culture itself may survive its crisis. War is the result. War, to a logical mind, is absurd. But in terms of human needs, it plays a vital role. And it will continue to until Man has grown up enough so that no hatred lies within him."

Taylor was listening intently. "Do you think this time will come?"

"Of course. It has almost arrived now. This is the last war. Man is almost united into one final culture—a world culture. At this point he stands continent against continent, one half of the world against the other half. Only a single step remains, the jump to a unified culture. Man has climbed slowly upward, tending always toward unification of his culture. It will not be long—

"But it has not come yet, and so the war had to go on, to satisfy the last violent surge of hatred that Man felt. Eight years have passed since the war began. In these eight years, we have observed and noted important changes going on in the minds of men. Fatigue and disinterest, we have seen, are gradually taking the place of hatred and fear. The hatred is being exhausted gradually, over a period of time. But for the present, the hoax must go on, at least for a while longer. You are not ready to learn the truth. You would want to continue the war."

"But how did you manage it?" Moss asked. "All the photographs, the samples, the damaged equipment—"

"Come over here." The leady directed them toward a long, low building. "Work goes on constantly, whole staffs laboring to maintain a coherent and convincing picture of a global war."

They entered the building. Leadys were working everywhere, poring over tables and desks.

"Examine this project here," the A-class leady said. Two leadys were carefully photographing something, an elaborate model on a table top. "It is a good example."

The men grouped around, trying to see. It was a model of a ruined city.

Taylor studied it in silence for a long time. At last he looked up.

"It's San Francisco," he said in a low voice. "This is a model of San Francisco, destroyed. I saw this on the vidscreen, piped down to us. The bridges were hit—"

"Yes, notice the bridges." The leady traced the ruined span with his metal finger, a tiny spider-web, almost invisible. "You have no doubt seen photographs of this many times, and of the other tables in this building.

"San Francisco itself is completely intact. We restored it soon after you left, rebuilding the parts that had been damaged at the start of the war. The work of manufacturing news goes on all the time in this particular building. We are very careful to see that each part fits in with all the other parts. Much time and effort are devoted to it."

Franks touched one of the tiny model buildings, lying half in ruins. "So this is what you spend your time doing—making model cities and then blasting them."

"No, we do much more. We are caretakers, watching over the whole world. The owners have left for a time, and we must see that the cities are kept clean, that decay is prevented, that everything is kept oiled and in running condition. The gardens, the streets, the water mains, everything must be maintained as it was eight years ago, so that when the owners return, they will not be displeased. We want to be sure that they will be completely satisfied."

Franks tapped Moss on the arm.

"Come over here," he said in a low voice. "I want to talk to you."

He led Moss and Taylor out of the building, away from the leadys, outside on the hillside. The soldiers followed them. The Sun was up and the sky was turning blue. The air smelled sweet and good, the smell of growing things.

Taylor removed his helmet and took a deep breath.

"I haven't smelled that smell for a long time," he said.

"Listen," Franks said, his voice low and hard. "We must get back down at once. There's a lot to get started on. All this can be turned to our advantage."

"What do you mean?" Moss asked.

"It's a certainty that the Soviets have been tricked, too, the same as us. But we have found out. That gives us an edge over them."

"I see." Moss nodded. "We know, but they don't. Their Surface Council has sold out, the same as ours. It works against them the same way. But if we could—"

"With a hundred top-level men, we could take over again, restore things as they should be! It would be easy!"

Moss touched him on the arm. An A-class leady was coming from the building toward them.

"We've seen enough," Franks said, raising his voice. "All this is very serious. It must be reported below and a study made to determine our policy."

The leady said nothing.

Franks waved to the soldiers. "Let's go." He started toward the warehouse.

Most of the soldiers had removed their helmets. Some of them had taken their lead suits off, too, and were relaxing comfortably in their cotton uniforms. They stared around them, down the hillside at the trees and bushes, the vast expanse of green, the mountains and the sky.

"Look at the Sun," one of them murmured.

"It sure is bright as hell," another said.

"We're going back down," Franks said. "Fall in by twos and follow us."

Reluctantly, the soldiers regrouped. The leadys watched without emotion as the men marched slowly back toward the warehouse. Franks and Moss and Taylor led them across the ground, glancing alertly at the leadys as they walked.

They entered the warehouse. D-class leadys were loading material and weapons on surface carts. Cranes and derricks were working busily everywhere. The work was done with efficiency, but without hurry or excitement.

The men stopped, watching. Leadys operating the little carts moved past them, signaling silently to each other. Guns and parts were being hoisted by magnetic cranes and lowered gently onto waiting carts.

"Come on," Franks said.

He turned toward the lip of the Tube. A row of D-class leadys was standing in front of it, immobile and silent. Franks stopped, moving back. He looked around. An A-class leady was coming toward him.

"Tell them to get out of the way," Franks said. He touched his gun. "You had better move them."

Time passed, an endless moment, without measure. The men stood, nervous and alert, watching the row of leadys in front of them.

"As you wish," the A-class leady said.

It signaled and the D-class leadys moved into life. They stepped slowly aside.

Moss breathed a sigh of relief.

"I'm glad that's over," he said to Franks. "Look at them all. Why don't they try to stop us? They must know what we're going to do."

Franks laughed. "Stop us? You saw what happened when they tried to stop us before. They can't; they're only machines. We built them so they can't lay hands on us, and they know that."

His voice trailed off.

The men stared at the Tube entrance. Around them the leadys watched, silent and impassive, their metal faces expressionless.

For a long time the men stood without moving. At last Taylor turned away.

"Good God," he said. He was numb, without feeling of any kind.

The Tube was gone. It was sealed shut, fused over. Only a dull surface of cooling metal greeted them.

The Tube had been closed.

Franks turned, his face pale and vacant.

The A-class leady shifted. "As you can see, the Tube has been shut. We were prepared for this. As soon as all of you were on the surface, the order was given. If you had gone back when we asked you, you would now be safely down below. We had to work quickly because it was such an immense operation."

"But why?" Moss demanded angrily.

"Because it is unthinkable that you should be allowed to resume the war. With all the Tubes sealed, it will be many months before forces from below can reach the surface, let alone organize a military program. By that time the cycle will have entered its last stages. You will not be so perturbed to find your world intact.

"We had hoped that you would be undersurface when the sealing occurred. Your presence here is a nuisance. When the Soviets broke through, we were able to accomplish their sealing without—"

"The Soviets? They broke through?"

"Several months ago, they came up unexpectedly to see why the war had not been won. We were forced to act with speed. At this moment they are desperately attempting to cut new Tubes to the surface, to resume the war. We have, however, been able to seal each new one as it appears."

The leady regarded the three men calmly.

"We're cut off," Moss said, trembling. "We can't get back. What'll we do?"

"How did you manage to seal the Tube so quickly?" Franks asked the leady. "We've been up here only two hours."

"Bombs are placed just above the first stage of each Tube for such emergencies. They are heat bombs. They fuse lead and rock."

Gripping the handle of his gun, Franks turned to Moss and Taylor.

"What do you say? We can't go back, but we can do a lot of damage, the fifteen of us. We have Bender guns. How about it?"

He looked around. The soldiers had wandered away again, back toward the exit of the building. They were standing outside, looking at the valley and the sky. A few of them were carefully climbing down the slope.

"Would you care to turn over your suits and guns?" the A-class leady asked politely. "The suits are uncomfortable and you'll have no need for weapons. The Russians have given up theirs, as you can see."

Fingers tensed on triggers. Four men in Russian uniforms were coming toward them from an aircraft that they suddenly realized had landed silently some distance away.

"Let them have it!" Franks shouted.

"They are unarmed," said the leady. "We brought them here so you could begin peace talks."

"We have no authority to speak for our country," Moss said stiffly.

"We do not mean diplomatic discussions," the leady explained. "There will be no more. The working out of daily problems of existence will teach you how to get along in the same world. It will not be easy, but it will be done."

The Russians halted and they faced each other with raw hostility.

"I am Colonel Borodoy and I regret giving up our guns," the senior Russian said. "You could have been the first Americans to be killed in almost eight years."

"Or the first Americans to kill," Franks corrected.

"No one would know of it except yourselves," the leady pointed out. "It would be useless heroism. Your real concern should be surviving on the surface. We have no food for you, you know."

Taylor put his gun in its holster. "They've done a neat job of neutralizing us, damn them. I propose we move into a city, start raising crops with the help of some leadys, and generally make ourselves comfortable." Drawing his lips tight over his teeth, he glared at the A-class leady. "Until our families can come up from undersurface, it's going to be pretty lonesome, but we'll have to manage."

"If I may make a suggestion," said another Russian uneasily. "We tried living in a city. It is too empty. It is also too hard to maintain for so few people. We finally settled in the most modern village we could find."

"Here in this country," a third Russian blurted. "We have much to learn from you."

The Americans abruptly found themselves laughing.

"You probably have a thing or two to teach us yourselves," said Taylor generously, "though I can't imagine what."

The Russian colonel grinned. "Would you join us in our village? It would make our work easier and give us company."

"Your village?" snapped Franks. "It's American, isn't it? It's ours!"

The leady stepped between them. "When our plans are completed, the term will be interchangeable. 'Ours' will eventually mean mankind's." It pointed at the aircraft, which was warming up. "The ship is waiting. Will you join each other in making a new home?"

The Russians waited while the Americans made up their minds.

"I see what the leadys mean about diplomacy becoming outmoded," Franks said at last. "People who work together don't need diplomats. They solve their problems on the operational level instead of at a conference table."

The leady led them toward the ship. "It is the goal of history, unifying the world. From family to tribe to city-state to nation to hemisphere, the direction has been toward unification. Now the hemispheres will be joined and—"

Taylor stopped listening and glanced back at the location of the Tube. Mary was undersurface there. He hated to leave her, even though he couldn't see her again until the Tube was unsealed. But then he shrugged and followed the others.

If this tiny amalgam of former enemies was a good example, it wouldn't be too long before he and Mary and the rest of humanity would be living on the surface like rational human beings instead of blindly hating moles.

"It has taken thousands of generations to achieve," the A-class leady concluded. "Hundreds of centuries of bloodshed and destruction. But each war was a step toward uniting mankind. And now the end is in sight: a world without war. But even that is only the beginning of a new stage of history."

"The conquest of space," breathed Colonel Borodoy.

"The meaning of life," Moss added.

"Eliminating hunger and poverty," said Taylor.

The leady opened the door of the ship. "All that and more. How much more? We cannot foresee it any more than the first men who formed a tribe could foresee this day. But it will be unimaginably great."

The door closed and the ship took off toward their new home.

Note: Illustrations by Ed Emshwiller.

Tunnel Under the World
By Frederik Pohl

Editor's note: From the pages of the January 1955 edition of Galaxy Science Fiction *comes this amazing story by award-winning sci-fi author Frederik Pohl (1919-2013), who served as editor of* Galaxy *from 1959 to 1969. Pohl is perhaps best known for his 1977 Hugo-winning novel* Gateway. *In "Tunnel Under the World," the main character keeps re-living the same day over and over, along the lines of the 1993 movie "Groundhog Day," but the solution is something altogether different.*

I

On the morning of June 15th, Guy Burckhardt woke up screaming out of a dream.

It was more real than any dream he had ever had in his life. He could still hear and feel the sharp, ripping-metal explosion, the violent heave that had tossed him furiously out of bed, the searing wave of heat.

He sat up convulsively and stared, not believing what he saw, at the quiet room and the bright sunlight coming in the window.

He croaked, "Mary?"

His wife was not in the bed next to him. The covers were tumbled and awry, as though she had just left it, and the memory of the dream was so strong that instinctively he found himself searching the floor to see if the dream explosion had thrown her down.

But she wasn't there. Of course she wasn't, he told himself, looking at the familiar vanity and slipper chair, the uncracked window, the unbuckled wall. It had only been a dream.

"Guy?" His wife was calling

him querulously from the foot of the stairs. "Guy, dear, are you all right?"

He called weakly, "Sure."

There was a pause. Then Mary said doubtfully, "Breakfast is ready. Are you sure you're all right? I thought I heard you yelling—"

Burckhardt said more confidently, "I had a bad dream, honey. Be right down."

In the shower, punching the lukewarm-and-cologne he favored, he told himself that it had been a beaut of a dream. Still, bad dreams weren't unusual, especially bad dreams about explosions. In the past thirty years of H-bomb jitters, who had not dreamed of explosions?

Even Mary had dreamed of them, it turned out, for he started to tell her about the dream, but she cut him off. "You did?" Her voice was astonished. "Why, dear, I dreamed the same thing! Well, almost the same thing. I didn't actually hear anything. I dreamed that something woke me up, and then there was a sort of quick bang, and then something hit me on the head. And that was all. Was yours like that?"

Burckhardt coughed. "Well, no," he said. Mary was not one of these strong-as-a-man, brave-as-a-tiger women. It was not necessary, he thought, to tell her all the little details of the dream that made it seem so real. No need to mention the splintered ribs, and the salt bubble in his throat, and the agonized knowledge that this was death. He said, "Maybe there really was some kind of explosion downtown. Maybe we heard it and it started us dreaming."

Mary reached over and patted his hand absently. "Maybe," she agreed. "It's almost half-past eight, dear. Shouldn't you hurry? You don't want to be late to the office."

He gulped his food, kissed her and rushed out—not so much to be on time as to see if his guess had been right.

But downtown Tylerton looked as it always had. Coming in on the bus, Burckhardt watched critically out the window, seeking evidence of an explosion. There wasn't any. If anything, Tylerton looked better than it ever had before: It was a beautiful crisp day, the sky was cloudless, the buildings were clean and inviting. They had, he observed, steam-blasted the Power & Light Building, the town's only skyscraper—that was the penalty of having Contro Chemical's main plant on the outskirts of town; the fumes from the cascade stills left their mark on stone buildings.

None of the usual crowd were on the bus, so there wasn't anyone Burckhardt could ask about the explosion. And by the time he got out at the corner of Fifth and Lehigh and the bus rolled away with a muted diesel moan, he had pretty well convinced himself that it was all imagination.

He stopped at the cigar stand in the lobby of his office building, but Ralph wasn't behind the counter. The man who sold him his pack of cigarettes was a stranger.

"Where's Mr. Stebbins?" Burckhardt asked.

The man said politely, "Sick, sir. He'll be in tomorrow. A pack of Marlins today?"

"Chesterfields," Burckhardt corrected.

"Certainly, sir," the man said. But what he took from the rack and slid across the counter was an unfamiliar green-and-yellow pack.

"Do try these, sir," he suggested. "They contain an anti-cough factor. Ever notice how ordinary cigarettes make you choke every once in a while?"

Burckhardt said suspiciously, "I never heard of this brand."

"Of course not. They're something new." Burckhardt hesitated, and the man said persuasively, "Look, try them out at my risk. If you don't like them, bring back the empty pack and I'll refund your money. Fair enough?"

Burckhardt shrugged. "How can I lose? But give me a pack of Chesterfields, too, will you?"

He opened the pack and lit one while he waited for the elevator. They weren't bad, he decided, though he was suspicious of cigarettes that had the tobacco chemically treated in any way. But he didn't think much of Ralph's stand-in; it would raise hell with the trade at the cigar stand if the man tried to give every customer the same high-pressure sales talk.

The elevator door opened with a low-pitched sound of music. Burckhardt and two or three others got in and he nodded to them as the door closed. The thread of music switched off and the speaker in the ceiling of the cab began its usual commercials.

No, not the usual commercials, Burckhardt realized. He had been exposed to the captive-audience commercials so long that they hardly registered on the outer ear any more, but what was coming from the recorded program in the basement of the building caught his attention. It wasn't merely that the brands were mostly unfamiliar; it was a difference in pattern.

There were jingles with an insistent, bouncy rhythm, about soft drinks he had never tasted. There was a rapid patter dialogue between what sounded like two ten-year-old boys about a candy bar, followed by an authoritative bass rumble: "Go right out and get a DELICIOUS Choco-Bite and eat your TANGY Choco-Bite all up. That's Choco-Bite!" There was a sobbing female whine: "I wish I had a Feckle Freezer! I'd do anything for a Feckle Freezer!" Burckhardt reached his floor and left the elevator in the middle of the last one. It left him a little uneasy. The commercials were not for familiar brands; there was no feeling of use and custom to them.

But the office was happily normal—except that Mr. Barth wasn't in. Miss Mitkin, yawning at the reception desk, didn't know exactly why. "His home phoned, that's all. He'll be in tomorrow."

"Maybe he went to the plant. It's right near his house."

She looked indifferent. "Yeah."

A thought struck Burckhardt. "But today is June 15th! It's quarterly tax return day—he has to sign the return!"

Miss Mitkin shrugged to indicate that that was Burckhardt's problem, not hers. She returned to her nails.

Thoroughly exasperated, Burckhardt went to his desk. It wasn't that he couldn't sign the tax returns as well as Barth, he thought resentfully. It simply wasn't his job, that was all; it was a responsibility that Barth, as office manager for Contro Chemicals' downtown office, should have taken.

He thought briefly of calling Barth at his home or trying to reach him at the factory, but he gave up the idea quickly enough. He didn't really care much for the people at the factory and the less contact he had with them, the better. He had been to the factory once, with Barth; it had been a confusing and, in a way, a frightening experience. Barring a handful of executives and engineers, there wasn't a soul in the factory—that is, Burckhardt corrected himself, remembering what Barth had told him, not a living soul—just the machines.

According to Barth, each machine was controlled by a sort of computer which reproduced, in its electronic snarl, the actual memory and mind of a human being. It was an unpleasant thought. Barth, laughing, had assured him that there was no Frankenstein business of robbing graveyards and implanting brains in machines. It was only a matter, he said, of transferring a man's habit patterns from

49

brain cells to vacuum-tube cells. It didn't hurt the man and it didn't make the machine into a monster.

But they made Burckhardt uncomfortable all the same.

He put Barth and the factory and all his other little irritations out of his mind and tackled the tax returns. It took him until noon to verify the figures—which Barth could have done out of his memory and his private ledger in ten minutes, Burckhardt resentfully reminded himself.

He sealed them in an envelope and walked out to Miss Mitkin. "Since Mr. Barth isn't here, we'd better go to lunch in shifts," he said. "You can go first."

"Thanks." Miss Mitkin languidly took her bag out of the desk drawer and began to apply makeup.

Burckhardt offered her the envelope. "Drop this in the mail for me, will you? Uh—wait a minute. I wonder if I ought to phone Mr. Barth to make sure. Did his wife say whether he was able to take phone calls?"

"Didn't say." Miss Mitkin blotted her lips carefully with a Kleenex. "Wasn't his wife, anyway. It was his daughter who called and left the message."

"The kid?" Burckhardt frowned. "I thought she was away at school."

"She called, that's all I know."

Burckhardt went back to his own office and stared distastefully at the unopened mail on his desk. He didn't like nightmares; they spoiled his whole day. He should have stayed in bed, like Barth.

A funny thing happened on his way home. There was a disturbance at the corner where he usually caught his bus—someone was screaming something about a new kind of deep-freeze—so he walked an extra block. He saw the bus coming and started to trot. But behind him, someone was calling his name. He looked over his shoulder; a small harried-looking man was hurrying toward him.

Burckhardt hesitated, and then recognized him. It was a casual acquaintance named Swanson. Burckhardt sourly observed that he had already missed the bus.

He said, "Hello."

Swanson's face was desperately eager. "Burckhardt?" he asked inquiringly, with an odd intensity. And then he just stood there silently, watching Burckhardt's face, with a burning eagerness that dwindled to a faint hope and died to a regret. He was searching for something, waiting for something, Burckhardt thought. But whatever it was he wanted, Burckhardt didn't know how to supply it.

Burckhardt coughed and said again, "Hello, Swanson."

Swanson didn't even acknowledge the greeting. He merely sighed a very deep sigh.

"Nothing doing," he mumbled, apparently to himself. He nodded abstractedly to Burckhardt and turned away.

Burckhardt watched the slumped shoulders disappear in the crowd. It was an odd sort of day, he thought, and one he didn't much like. Things weren't going right.

Riding home on the next bus, he brooded about it. It wasn't anything terrible or disastrous; it was something out of his experience entirely. You live your life, like any man, and you form a network of impressions and reactions. You expect things. When you open your medicine chest, your razor is expected to be on the second shelf; when you lock your front door, you expect to have to give it a slight extra tug to make it latch.

It isn't the things that are right and perfect in your life that make it familiar. It is the things that are just a little bit wrong—the sticking latch, the light switch at the head of the stairs that needs an extra push because the spring is old and weak, the rug that unfailingly skids underfoot.

It wasn't just that things were wrong with the pattern of Burckhardt's life; it was that the wrong things were wrong. For instance, Barth hadn't come into the office, yet Barth always came in.

Burckhardt brooded about it through dinner. He brooded about it, despite his wife's attempt to interest him in a game of bridge with the neighbors, all through the evening. The neighbors were people he liked—Anne and Farley Dennerman. He had known them all their lives. But they were odd and brooding, too, this night and he barely listened to Dennerman's complaints about not being able to get good phone service or his wife's comments on the disgusting variety of television commercials they had these days.

Burckhardt was well on the way to setting an all-time record for continuous abstraction when, around midnight, with a suddenness that surprised him—he was strangely aware of it happening—he turned over in his bed and, quickly and completely, fell asleep.

II

On the morning of June 15th, Burckhardt woke up screaming.

It was more real than any dream he had ever had in his life. He could still hear the explosion, feel the blast that crushed him against a wall. It did not seem right that he should be sitting bolt upright in bed in an undisturbed room.

His wife came pattering up the stairs. "Darling!" she cried. "What's the matter?"

He mumbled, "Nothing. Bad dream."

She relaxed, hand on heart. In an angry tone, she started to say: "You gave me such a shock—"

But a noise from outside interrupted her. There was a wail of sirens and a clang of bells; it was loud and shocking.

The Burckhardts stared at each other for a heartbeat, then hurried fearfully to the window.

There were no rumbling fire engines in the street, only a small panel truck, cruising slowly along. Flaring loudspeaker horns crowned its top. From them issued the screaming sound of sirens, growing in intensity, mixed with the rumble of heavy-duty engines and the sound of bells. It was a perfect record of fire engines arriving at a four-alarm blaze.

Burckhardt said in amazement, "Mary, that's against the law! Do you know what they're doing? They're playing records of a fire. What are they up to?"

"Maybe it's a practical joke," his wife offered.

"Joke? Waking up the whole neighborhood at six o'clock in the morning?" He shook his head. "The police will be here in ten minutes," he predicted. "Wait and see."

But the police weren't—not in ten minutes, or at all. Whoever the pranksters in the car were, they apparently had a police permit for their games.

The car took a position in the middle of the block and stood silent for a few minutes. Then there was a crackle from the speaker, and a giant voice chanted:

"Feckle Freezers!

Feckle Freezers!

Gotta have a

Feckle Freezer!

Feckle, Feckle, Feckle,

Feckle, Feckle, Feckle—"

It went on and on. Every house on the block had faces staring out of windows by then. The voice was not merely loud; it was nearly deafening.

Burckhardt shouted to his wife, over the uproar, "What the hell is a Feckle Freezer?"

"Some kind of a freezer, I guess, dear," she shrieked back unhelpfully.

Abruptly the noise stopped and the truck stood silent. It was still misty morning; the Sun's rays came horizontally across the rooftops. It was impossible to believe that, a moment ago, the silent block had been bellowing the name of a freezer.

"A crazy advertising trick," Burckhardt said bitterly. He yawned and turned away from the window. "Might as well get dressed. I guess that's the end of—"

The bellow caught him from behind; it was almost like a hard slap on the ears. A harsh, sneering voice, louder than the arch-angel's trumpet, howled:

"Have you got a freezer? It stinks! If it isn't a Feckle Freezer, it stinks! If it's a last year's Feckle Freezer, it stinks! Only this year's Feckle Freezer is any good at all! You know who owns an Ajax Freezer? Fairies own Ajax Freezers! You know who owns a Triplecold Freezer? Commies own Triplecold Freezers! Every freezer but a brand-new Feckle Freezer stinks!"

The voice screamed inarticulately with rage. "I'm warning you! Get out and buy a Feckle Freezer right away! Hurry up! Hurry for Feckle! Hurry for Feckle! Hurry, hurry, hurry, Feckle, Feckle, Feckle, Feckle, Feckle, Feckle...."

It stopped eventually. Burckhardt licked his lips. He started to say to his wife, "Maybe we ought to call the police about—" when the speakers erupted again. It caught him off guard; it was intended to catch him off guard. It screamed:

"Feckle, Feckle, Feckle, Feckle, Feckle, Feckle, Feckle, Feckle. Cheap freezers ruin your food. You'll get sick and throw up. You'll get sick and die. Buy a Feckle, Feckle, Feckle, Feckle! Ever take a piece of meat out of the freezer you've got and see how rotten and moldy it is? Buy a Feckle, Feckle, Feckle, Feckle, Feckle. Do you want to eat rotten, stinking food? Or do you want to wise up and buy a Feckle, Feckle, Feckle—"

That did it. With fingers that kept stabbing the wrong holes, Burckhardt finally managed to dial the local police station. He got a busy signal—it was apparent that he was not the only one with the same idea—and while he was shakingly dialing again, the noise outside stopped.

He looked out the window. The truck was gone.

Burckhardt loosened his tie and ordered another Frosty-Flip from the waiter. If only they wouldn't keep the Crystal Cafe so hot! The new paint job—searing reds and blinding yellows—was bad enough, but someone seemed to have the delusion that this was January instead of June; the place was a good ten degrees warmer than outside.

He swallowed the Frosty-Flip in two gulps. It had a kind of peculiar flavor, he thought, but not bad. It certainly cooled you off, just as the waiter had promised. He reminded himself to pick up a carton of them on the way home; Mary might like them. She was always interested in something new.

He stood up awkwardly as the girl came across the restaurant toward him. She was the most beautiful thing he had ever seen in Tylerton. Chin-height, honey-blonde hair and a figure that—well, it was all hers. There was no doubt in the world that the dress that clung to her was the only thing she wore. He felt as if he were blushing as she greeted him.

"Mr. Burckhardt." The voice was like distant tomtoms. "It's wonderful of you to let me see you, after this morning."

He cleared his throat. "Not at all. Won't you sit down, Miss—"

"April Horn," she murmured, sitting down—beside him, not where he had pointed on the other side of the table. "Call me April, won't you?"

She was wearing some kind of perfume, Burckhardt noted with

what little of his mind was functioning at all. It didn't seem fair that she should be using perfume as well as everything else. He came to with a start and realized that the waiter was leaving with an order for filets mignon for two.

"Hey!" he objected.

"Please, Mr. Burckhardt." Her shoulder was against his, her face was turned to him, her breath was warm, her expression was tender and solicitous. "This is all on the Feckle Corporation. Please let them—it's the least they can do."

He felt her hand burrowing into his pocket.

"I put the price of the meal into your pocket," she whispered conspiratorially. "Please do that for me, won't you? I mean I'd appreciate it if you'd pay the waiter—I'm old-fashioned about things like that."

She smiled meltingly, then became mock-businesslike. "But you must take the money," she insisted. "Why, you're letting Feckle off lightly if you do! You could sue them for every nickel they've got, disturbing your sleep like that."

With a dizzy feeling, as though he had just seen someone make a rabbit disappear into a top hat, he said, "Why, it really wasn't so bad, uh, April. A little noisy, maybe, but—"

"Oh, Mr. Burckhardt!" The blue eyes were wide and admiring. "I knew you'd understand. It's just that—well, it's such a wonderful freezer that some of the outside men get carried away, so to speak. As soon as the main office found out about what happened, they sent representatives around to every house on the block to apologize. Your wife told us where we could phone you—and I'm so very pleased that you were willing to let me have lunch with you, so that I could apologize, too. Because truly, Mr. Burckhardt, it is a fine freezer.

"I shouldn't tell you this, but—" the blue eyes were shyly lowered—"I'd do almost anything for Feckle Freezers. It's more than a job to me." She looked up. She was enchanting. "I bet you think I'm silly, don't you?"

Burckhardt coughed. "Well, I—"

"Oh, you don't want to be unkind!" She shook her head. "No, don't pretend. You think it's silly. But really, Mr. Burckhardt, you wouldn't think so if you knew more about the Feckle. Let me show you this little booklet—"

Burckhardt got back from lunch a full hour late. It wasn't only the girl who delayed him. There had been a curious interview with a little man named Swanson, whom he barely knew, who had stopped him with desperate urgency on the street—and then left him cold.

But it didn't matter much. Mr. Barth, for the first time since Burckhardt had worked there, was out for the day—leaving Burckhardt stuck with the quarterly tax returns.

What did matter, though, was that somehow he had signed a purchase order for a twelve-cubic-foot Feckle Freezer, upright model, self-defrosting, list price $625, with a ten per cent "courtesy" discount—"Because of that horrid affair this morning, Mr. Burckhardt," she had said.

And he wasn't sure how he could explain it to his wife.

He needn't have worried. As he walked in the front door, his wife said almost immediately, "I wonder if we can't afford a new freezer, dear. There was a man here to apologize about that noise and—well, we got to talking and—"

She had signed a purchase order, too.

It had been the damnedest day, Burckhardt thought later, on his way up to bed. But the day wasn't done with him yet. At the head of the stairs, the weakened spring in the electric light switch refused to click at all. He snapped it back and forth angrily and, of course, succeeded in jarring the tumbler out of its pins. The wires shorted and every light in the house went out.

"Damn!" said Guy Burckhardt.

"Fuse?" His wife shrugged sleepily. "Let it go till the morning, dear."

Burckhardt shook his head. "You go back to bed. I'll be right along."

It wasn't so much that he cared about fixing the fuse, but he was too restless for sleep. He disconnected the bad switch with a screwdriver, stumbled down into the black kitchen, found the flashlight and climbed gingerly down the cellar stairs. He located a spare fuse, pushed an empty trunk over to the fuse box to stand on and twisted out the old fuse.

When the new one was in, he heard the starting click and steady drone of the refrigerator in the kitchen overhead.

He headed back to the steps, and stopped.

Where the old trunk had been, the cellar floor gleamed oddly bright. He inspected it in the flashlight beam. It was metal!

"Son of a gun," said Guy Burckhardt. He shook his head unbelievingly. He peered closer, rubbed the edges of the metallic patch with his thumb and acquired an annoying cut—the edges were sharp.

The stained cement floor of the cellar was a thin shell. He found a hammer and cracked it off in a dozen spots—everywhere was metal.

The whole cellar was a copper box. Even the cement-brick walls were false fronts over a metal sheath!

Baffled, he attacked one of the foundation beams. That, at least, was real wood. The glass in the cellar windows was real glass.

He sucked his bleeding thumb and tried the base of the cellar stairs. Real wood. He chipped at the bricks under the oil burner. Real bricks. The retaining walls, the floor—they were faked.

It was as though someone had shored up the house with a frame of metal and then laboriously concealed the evidence.

The biggest surprise was the upside-down boat hull that blocked the rear half of the cellar, relic of a brief home workshop period that Burckhardt had gone through a couple of years before. From above, it looked perfectly normal. Inside, though, where there should have been thwarts and seats and lockers, there was a mere tangle of braces, rough and unfinished.

"But I built that!" Burckhardt exclaimed, forgetting his thumb. He leaned against the hull dizzily, trying to think this thing through. For reasons beyond his comprehension, someone had taken his boat and his cellar away, maybe his whole house, and replaced them with a clever mock-up of the real thing.

"That's crazy," he said to the empty cellar. He stared around in the light of the flash. He whispered, "What in the name of Heaven would anybody do that for?"

Reason refused an answer; there wasn't any reasonable answer. For long minutes, Burckhardt contemplated the uncertain picture of his own sanity.

He peered under the boat again, hoping to reassure himself that it was a mistake, just his imagination. But the sloppy, unfinished bracing was unchanged. He crawled under for a better look, feeling the rough wood incredulously. Utterly impossible!

He switched off the flashlight and started to wriggle out. But he didn't make it. In the moment between the command to his legs to move and the crawling out, he felt a sudden draining weariness flooding through him.

Consciousness went—not easily, but as though it were being taken away, and Guy Burckhardt was asleep.

III

On the morning of June 16th, Guy Burckhardt woke up in a cramped position huddled under the hull of the boat in his basement—and raced upstairs to find it was June 15th.

The first thing he had done was to make a frantic, hasty inspection of the boat hull, the faked cellar floor, the imitation stone. They were all as he had remembered them—all completely unbelievable.

The kitchen was its placid, unexciting self. The electric clock was purring soberly around the dial. Almost six o'clock, it said. His wife would be waking at any moment.

Burckhardt flung open the front door and stared out into the quiet street. The morning paper was tossed carelessly against the steps—and as he retrieved it, he noticed that this was the 15th day of June.

But that was impossible. Yesterday was the 15th of June. It was not a date one would forget—it was quarterly tax-return day.

He went back into the hall and picked up the telephone; he dialed for Weather Information, and got a well-modulated chant: "—and cooler, some showers. Barometric pressure thirty point zero four, rising ... United States Weather Bureau forecast for June 15th. Warm and sunny, with high around—"

He hung the phone up. June 15th.

"Holy heaven!" Burckhardt said prayerfully. Things were very odd indeed. He heard the ring of his wife's alarm and bounded up the stairs.

Mary Burckhardt was sitting upright in bed with the terrified, uncomprehending stare of someone just waking out of a nightmare.

"Oh!" she gasped, as her husband came in the room. "Darling, I just had the most terrible dream! It was like an explosion and—"

"Again?" Burckhardt asked, not very sympathetically. "Mary, something's funny! I knew there was something wrong all day yesterday and—"

He went on to tell her about the copper box that was the cellar, and the odd mock-up someone had made of his boat. Mary looked astonished, then alarmed, then placatory and uneasy.

She said, "Dear, are you sure? Because I was cleaning that old trunk out just last week and I didn't notice anything."

"Positive!" said Guy Burckhardt. "I dragged it over to the wall to step on it to put a new fuse in after we blew the lights out and—"

"After we what?" Mary was looking more than merely alarmed.

"After we blew the lights out. You know, when the switch at the head of the stairs stuck. I went down to the cellar and—"

Mary sat up in bed. "Guy, the switch didn't stick. I turned out the lights myself last night."

Burckhardt glared at his wife. "Now I know you didn't! Come here and take a look!"

He stalked out to the landing and dramatically pointed to the bad switch, the one that he had unscrewed and left hanging the night before....

Only it wasn't. It was as it had always been. Unbelieving, Burckhardt pressed it and the lights sprang up in both halls.

Mary, looking pale and worried, left him to go down to the kitchen and start breakfast. Burckhardt stood staring at the switch for a long time. His mental processes were gone beyond the point of disbelief and shock; they simply were not functioning.

He shaved and dressed and ate his breakfast in a state of numb introspection. Mary didn't disturb him; she was apprehensive and soothing. She kissed him good-by as he hurried out to the bus without another word.

Miss Mitkin, at the reception desk, greeted him with a yawn.

"Morning," she said drowsily. "Mr. Barth won't be in today."

Burckhardt started to say something, but checked himself. She would not know that Barth hadn't been in yesterday, either, because she was tearing a June 14th pad off her calendar to make way for the "new" June 15th sheet.

He staggered to his own desk and stared unseeingly at the morning's mail. It had not even been opened yet, but he knew that the Factory Distributors envelope contained an order for twenty thousand feet of the new acoustic tile, and the one from Finebeck & Sons was a complaint.

After a long while, he forced himself to open them. They were.

By lunchtime, driven by a desperate sense of urgency, Burckhardt made Miss Mitkin take her lunch hour first—the June-fifteenth-that-was-yesterday, he had gone first. She went, looking vaguely worried about his strained insistence, but it made no difference to Burckhardt's mood.

The phone rang and Burckhardt picked it up abstractedly. "Contro Chemicals Downtown, Burckhardt speaking."

The voice said, "This is Swanson," and stopped.

Burckhardt waited expectantly, but that was all. He said, "Hello?"

Again the pause. Then Swanson asked in sad resignation, "Still nothing, eh?"

"Nothing what? Swanson, is there something you want? You came up to me yesterday and went through this routine. You—"

The voice crackled: "Burckhardt! Oh, my good heavens, you remember! Stay right there—I'll be down in half an hour!"

"What's this all about?"

"Never mind," the little man said exultantly. "Tell you about it when I see you. Don't say any more over the phone—somebody may be listening. Just wait there. Say, hold on a minute. Will you be alone in the office?"

"Well, no. Miss Mitkin will probably—"

"Hell. Look, Burckhardt, where do you eat lunch? Is it good and noisy?"

"Why, I suppose so. The Crystal Cafe. It's just about a block—"

"I know where it is. Meet you in half an hour!" And the receiver clicked.

The Crystal Cafe was no longer painted red, but the temperature was still up. And they had added piped-in music interspersed with commercials. The advertisements were for Frosty-Flip, Marlin Cigarettes—"They're sanitized," the announcer purred—and something called Choco-Bite candy bars that Burckhardt couldn't remember ever having heard of before. But he heard more about them quickly enough.

While he was waiting for Swanson to show up, a girl in the cellophane skirt of a nightclub cigarette vendor came through the restaurant with a tray of tiny scarlet-wrapped candies.

"Choco-Bites are tangy," she was murmuring as she came close to his table. "Choco-Bites are tangier than tangy!"

Burckhardt, intent on watching for the strange little man who had phoned him, paid little attention. But as she scattered a handful of the confections over the table next to his, smiling at the occupants, he caught a glimpse of her and turned to stare.

"Why, Miss Horn!" he said.

The girl dropped her tray of candies.

Burckhardt rose, concerned over the girl. "Is something wrong?"

But she fled.

The manager of the restaurant was staring suspiciously at Burckhardt, who sank back in his seat and tried to look inconspicuous. He hadn't insulted the girl! Maybe she was just a very strictly reared young lady, he thought—in spite of the long bare legs under the cellophane skirt—and when he addressed her, she thought he was a masher.

Ridiculous idea. Burckhardt scowled uneasily and picked up his menu.

"Burckhardt!" It was a shrill whisper.

Burckhardt looked up over the top of his menu, startled. In the seat across from him, the little man named Swanson was sitting, tensely poised.

"Burckhardt!" the little man whispered again. "Let's get out of here! They're on to you now. If you want to stay alive, come on!"

There was no arguing with the man. Burckhardt gave the hovering manager a sick, apologetic smile and followed Swanson out. The little man seemed to know where he was going. In the street, he clutched Burckhardt by the elbow and hurried him off down the block.

"Did you see her?" he demanded. "That Horn woman, in the phone booth? She'll have them here in five minutes, believe me, so hurry it up!"

Although the street was full of people and cars, nobody was paying any attention to Burckhardt and Swanson. The air had a nip in it—more like October than June, Burckhardt thought, in spite of the weather bureau. And he felt like a fool, following this mad little man down the street, running away from some "them" toward—toward what? The little man might be crazy, but he was afraid. And the fear was infectious.

"In here!" panted the little man.

It was another restaurant—more of a bar, really, and a sort of second-rate place that Burckhardt had never patronized.

"Right straight through," Swanson whispered; and Burckhardt, like a biddable boy, side-stepped through the mass of tables to the far end of the restaurant.

It was "L"-shaped, with a front on two streets at right angles to each other. They came out on the side street, Swanson staring coldly back at the question-looking cashier, and crossed to the opposite sidewalk.

They were under the marquee of a movie theater. Swanson's expression began to relax.

"Lost them!" he crowed softly. "We're almost there."

He stepped up to the window and bought two tickets. Burckhardt trailed him in to the theater. It was a weekday matinee and the place was almost empty. From the screen came sounds of gunfire and horse's hoofs. A solitary usher, leaning against a bright brass rail, looked briefly at them and went back to staring boredly at the picture as Swanson led Burckhardt down a flight of carpeted marble steps.

They were in the lounge and it was empty. There was a door for men and one for ladies; and there was a third door, marked "MANAGER" in gold letters. Swanson listened at the door, and gently opened it and peered inside.

"Okay," he said, gesturing.

Burckhardt followed him through an empty office, to another door—a closet, probably, because it was unmarked.

But it was no closet. Swanson opened it warily, looked inside, then motioned Burckhardt to follow.

It was a tunnel, metal-walled, brightly lit. Empty, it stretched vacantly away in both directions from them.

Burckhardt looked wondering around. One thing he knew and

knew full well:

No such tunnel belonged under Tylerton.

There was a room off the tunnel with chairs and a desk and what looked like television screens. Swanson slumped in a chair, panting.

"We're all right for a while here," he wheezed. "They don't come here much anymore. If they do, we'll hear them and we can hide."

"Who?" demanded Burckhardt.

The little man said, "Martians!" His voice cracked on the word and the life seemed to go out of him. In morose tones, he went on: "Well, I think they're Martians. Although you could be right, you know; I've had plenty of time to think it over these last few weeks, after they got you, and it's possible they're Russians after all. Still—"

"Start from the beginning. Who got me when?"

Swanson sighed. "So we have to go through the whole thing again. All right. It was about two months ago that you banged on my door, late at night. You were all beat up—scared silly. You begged me to help you—"

"I did?"

"Naturally you don't remember any of this. Listen and you'll understand. You were talking a blue streak about being captured and threatened, and your wife being dead and coming back to life, and all kinds of mixed-up nonsense. I thought you were crazy. But—well, I've always had a lot of respect for you. And you begged me to hide you and I have this darkroom, you know. It locks from the inside only. I put the lock on myself. So we went in there—just to humor you—and along about midnight, which was only fifteen or twenty minutes after, we passed out."

"Passed out?"

Swanson nodded. "Both of us. It was like being hit with a sandbag. Look, didn't that happen to you again last night?"

"I guess it did," Burckhardt shook his head uncertainly.

"Sure. And then all of a sudden we were awake again, and you said you were going to show me something funny, and we went out and bought a paper. And the date on it was June 15th."

"June 15th? But that's today! I mean—"

"You got it, friend. It's always today!"

It took time to penetrate.

Burckhardt said wonderingly, "You've hidden out in that darkroom for how many weeks?"

"How can I tell? Four or five, maybe. I lost count. And every day the same—always the 15th of June, always my landlady, Mrs. Keefer, is sweeping the front steps, always the same headline in the papers at the corner. It gets monotonous, friend."

IV

It was Burckhardt's idea and Swanson despised it, but he went along. He was the type who always went along.

"It's dangerous," he grumbled worriedly. "Suppose somebody comes by? They'll spot us and—"

"What have we got to lose?"

Swanson shrugged. "It's dangerous," he said again. But he went along.

Burckhardt's idea was very simple. He was sure of only one thing—the tunnel went somewhere. Martians or Russians, fantastic plot or crazy hallucination, whatever was wrong with Tylerton had an explanation, and the place to look for it was at the end of the tunnel.

They jogged along. It was more than a mile before they began to see an end. They were in luck—at least no one came through the tunnel to spot them. But Swanson had said that it was only at certain hours that the tunnel seemed to be in use.

Always the fifteenth of June. Why? Burckhardt asked himself. Never mind the how. Why?

And falling asleep, completely involuntarily—everyone at the same time, it seemed. And not remembering, never remembering anything—Swanson had said how eagerly he saw Burckhardt again, the morning after Burckhardt had incautiously waited five minutes too many before retreating into the darkroom. When Swanson had come to, Burckhardt was gone. Swanson had seen him in the street that afternoon, but Burckhardt had remembered nothing.

And Swanson had lived his mouse's existence for weeks, hiding in the woodwork at night, stealing out by day to search for Burckhardt in pitiful hope, scurrying around the fringe of life, trying to keep from the deadly eyes of them.

Them. One of "them" was the girl named April Horn. It was by seeing her walk carelessly into a telephone booth and never come out that Swanson had found the tunnel. Another was the man at the cigar stand in Burckhardt's office building. There were more, at least a dozen that Swanson knew of or suspected.

They were easy enough to spot, once you knew where to look—for they, alone in Tylerton, changed their roles from day to day. Burckhardt was on that 8:51 bus, every morning of every day-that-was-June-15th, never different by a hair or a moment. But April Horn was sometimes gaudy in the cellophane skirt, giving away candy or cigarettes; sometimes plainly dressed; sometimes not seen by Swanson at all.

Russians? Martians? Whatever they were, what could they be hoping to gain from this mad masquerade?

Burckhardt didn't know the answer—but perhaps it lay beyond the door at the end of the tunnel. They listened carefully and heard distant sounds that could not quite be made out, but nothing that seemed dangerous. They slipped through.

And, through a wide chamber and up a flight of steps, they found they were in what Burckhardt recognized as the Contro Chemicals plant.

Nobody was in sight. By itself, that was not so very odd—the automatized factory had never had very many persons in it. But Burckhardt remembered, from his single visit, the endless, ceaseless busyness of the plant, the valves that opened and closed, the vats that emptied themselves and filled themselves and stirred and cooked and chemically tasted the bubbling liquids they held inside themselves. The plant was never populated, but it was never still.

Only—now it was still. Except for the distant sounds, there was no breath of life in it. The captive electronic minds were sending out no commands; the coils and relays were at rest.

Burckhardt said, "Come on." Swanson reluctantly followed him through the tangled aisles of stainless steel columns and tanks.

They walked as though they were in the presence of the dead. In a way, they were, for what were the automatons that once had run the factory, if not corpses? The machines were controlled by computers that were really not computers at all, but the electronic analogues of living brains. And if they were turned off, were they not dead? For each had once been a human mind.

Take a master petroleum chemist, infinitely skilled in the separation of crude oil into its fractions. Strap him down, probe into his brain with searching electronic needles. The machine scans the patterns of the mind, translates what it sees into charts and sine waves. Impress these same waves on a robot computer and you have your chemist. Or a thousand copies of your chemist, if you wish, with all of his knowledge and skill, and no human limitations at all.

Put a dozen copies of him into a plant and they will run it all, twenty-four hours a day, seven days of every week, never tiring, never overlooking anything, never forgetting....

Swanson stepped up closer to Burckhardt. "I'm scared," he said.

They were across the room now and the sounds were louder. They were not machine sounds, but voices; Burckhardt moved cautiously up to a door and dared to peer around it.

It was a smaller room, lined with television screens, each one—a dozen or more, at least—with a man or woman sitting before it, staring into the screen and dictating notes into a recorder. The viewers dialed from scene to scene; no two screens ever showed the same picture.

The pictures seemed to have little in common. One was a store, where a girl dressed like April Horn was demonstrating home freezers. One was a series of shots of kitchens. Burckhardt caught a glimpse of what looked like the cigar stand in his office building.

It was baffling and Burckhardt would have loved to stand there and puzzle it out, but it was too busy a place. There was the chance that someone would look their way or walk out and find them.

They found another room. This one was empty. It was an office, large and sumptuous. It had a desk, littered with papers. Burckhardt stared at them, briefly at first—then, as the words on one of them caught his attention, with incredulous fascination.

He snatched up the topmost sheet, scanned it, and another, while Swanson was frenziedly searching through the drawers.

Burckhardt swore unbelievingly and dropped the papers to the desk.

Swanson, hardly noticing, yelped with delight: "Look!" He dragged a gun from the desk. "And it's loaded, too!"

Burckhardt stared at him blankly, trying to assimilate what he had read. Then, as he realized what Swanson had said, Burckhardt's eyes sparked. "Good man!" he cried. "We'll take it. We're getting out of here with that gun, Swanson. And we're going to the police! Not the cops in Tylerton, but the F.B.I., maybe. Take a look at this!"

The sheaf he handed Swanson was headed: "Test Area Progress Report. Subject: Marlin Cigarettes Campaign." It was mostly tabulated figures that made little sense to Burckhardt and Swanson, but at the end was a summary that said:

Although Test 47-K3 pulled nearly double the number of new users of any of the other tests conducted, it probably cannot be used in the field because of local sound-truck control ordinances.

The tests in the 47-K12 group were second best and our recommendation is that retests be conducted in this appeal, testing each of the three best campaigns with and without the addition of sampling techniques.

An alternative suggestion might be to proceed directly with the top appeal in the K12 series, if the client is unwilling to go to the expense of additional tests.

All of these forecast expectations have an 80% probability of being within one-half of one per cent of results forecast, and more than 99% probability of coming within 5%.

Swanson looked up from the paper into Burckhardt's eyes. "I don't get it," he complained.

Burckhardt said, "I don't blame you. It's crazy, but it fits the facts, Swanson, it fits the facts. They aren't Russians and they aren't Martians. These people are advertising men! Somehow—heaven knows how they did it—they've taken Tylerton over. They've got us, all of us, you and me and twenty or thirty thousand other people, right under their thumbs.

"Maybe they hypnotize us and maybe it's something else; but however they do it, what happens is that they let us live a day at a time. They pour advertising into us the whole damned day long. And at the end of the day, they see what happened—and then they wash the day out of our minds and start again the next day with different advertising."

Swanson's jaw was hanging. He managed to close it and swallow. "Nuts!" he said flatly.

Burckhardt shook his head. "Sure, it sounds crazy—but this whole thing is crazy. How else would you explain it? You can't deny that most of Tylerton lives the same day over and over again. You've seen it! And that's the crazy part and we have to admit that that's true—unless we are the crazy ones. And once you admit that somebody, somehow, knows how to accomplish that, the rest of it makes all kinds of sense.

"Think of it, Swanson! They test every last detail before they spend a nickel on advertising! Do you have any idea what that means? Lord knows how much money is involved, but I know for a fact that some companies spend twenty or thirty million dollars a year on advertising. Multiply it, say, by a hundred companies. Say that every one of them learns how to cut its advertising cost by only ten per cent. And that's peanuts, believe me!

"If they know in advance what's going to work, they can cut their costs in half—maybe to less than half, I don't know. But that's saving two or three hundred million dollars a year—and if they pay only ten or twenty per cent of that for the use of Tylerton, it's still dirt cheap for them and a fortune for whoever took over Tylerton."

Swanson licked his lips. "You mean," he offered hesitantly, "that we're a—well, a kind of captive audience?"

Burckhardt frowned. "Not exactly." He thought for a minute. "You know how a doctor tests something like penicillin? He sets up a series of little colonies of germs on gelatine disks and he tries the stuff on one after another, changing it a little each time. Well, that's us—we're the germs, Swanson. Only it's even more efficient than that. They don't have to test more than one colony, because they can use it over and over again."

It was too hard for Swanson to take in. He only said: "What do we do about it?"

"We go to the police. They can't use human beings for guinea pigs!"

"How do we get to the police?"

Burckhardt hesitated. "I think—" he began slowly. "Sure. This place is the office of somebody important. We've got a gun. We'll stay right here until he comes along. And he'll get us out of here."

Simple and direct. Swanson subsided and found a place to sit, against the wall, out of sight of the door. Burckhardt took up a position behind the door itself—

And waited.

The wait was not as long as it might have been. Half an hour, perhaps. Then Burckhardt heard approaching voices and had time for a swift whisper to Swanson before he flattened himself against the wall.

It was a man's voice, and a girl's. The man was saying, "—reason why you couldn't report on the phone? You're ruining your whole day's test! What the devil's the matter with you, Janet?"

68

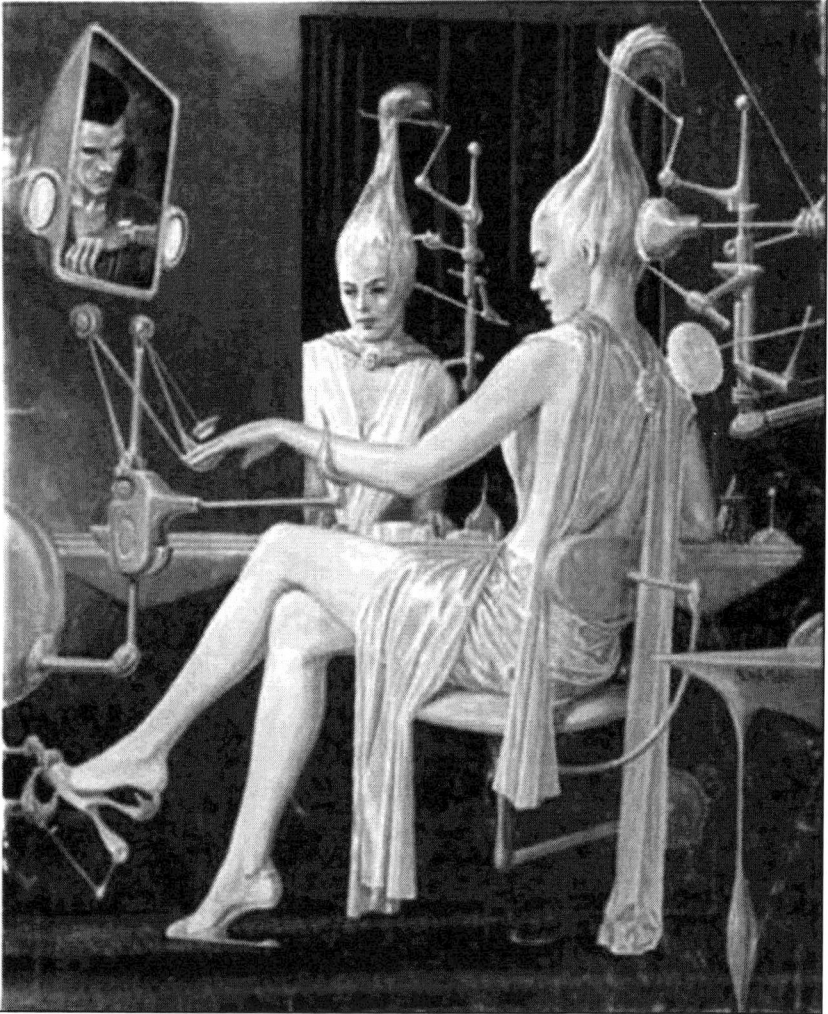

"I'm sorry, Mr. Dorchin," she said in a sweet, clear tone. "I thought it was important."

The man grumbled, "Important! One lousy unit out of twenty-one thousand."

"But it's the Burckhardt one, Mr. Dorchin. Again. And the way he got out of sight, he must have had some help."

"All right, all right. It doesn't matter, Janet; the Choco-Bite program is ahead of schedule anyhow. As long as you're this far, come on in the office and make out your worksheet. And don't worry about the Burckhardt business. He's probably just wandering around. We'll pick him up tonight and—"

They were inside the door. Burckhardt kicked it shut and pointed the gun.

"That's what you think," he said triumphantly.

It was worth the terrified hours, the bewildered sense of insanity, the confusion and fear. It was the most satisfying sensation Burckhardt had ever had in his life. The expression on the man's face was one he had read about but never actually seen: Dorchin's mouth fell open and his eyes went wide, and though he managed to make a sound that might have been a question, it was not in words.

The girl was almost as surprised. And Burckhardt, looking at her, knew why her voice had been so familiar. The girl was the one who had introduced herself to him as April Horn.

Dorchin recovered himself quickly. "Is this the one?" he asked sharply.

The girl said, "Yes."

Dorchin nodded. "I take it back. You were right. Uh, you—Burckhardt. What do you want?"

Swanson piped up, "Watch him! He might have another gun."

"Search him then," Burckhardt said. "I'll tell you what we want, Dorchin. We want you to come along with us to the FBI and explain to them how you can get away with kidnapping twenty thousand people."

"Kidnapping?" Dorchin snorted. "That's ridiculous, man! Put that gun away—you can't get away with this!"

Burckhardt hefted the gun grimly. "I think I can."

Dorchin looked furious and sick—but, oddly, not afraid. "Damn it—" he started to bellow, then closed his mouth and swallowed. "Listen," he said persuasively, "you're making a big mistake. I haven't kidnapped anybody, believe me!"

"I don't believe you," said Burckhardt bluntly. "Why should I?"

"But it's true! Take my word for it!"

Burckhardt shook his head. "The FBI can take your word if they like. We'll find out. Now how do we get out of here?"

Dorchin opened his mouth to argue.

Burckhardt blazed: "Don't get in my way! I'm willing to kill you if I have to. Don't you understand that? I've gone through two days of hell and every second of it I blame on you. Kill you? It would be a pleasure and I don't have a thing in the world to lose! Get us out of here!"

Dorchin's face went suddenly opaque. He seemed about to move; but the blonde girl he had called Janet slipped between him and the gun.

"Please!" she begged Burckhardt. "You don't understand. You mustn't shoot!"

"Get out of my way!"

"But, Mr. Burckhardt—"

She never finished. Dorchin, his face unreadable, headed for the door. Burckhardt had been pushed one degree too far. He swung the gun, bellowing. The girl called out sharply. He pulled the trigger. Closing on him with pity and pleading in her eyes, she came again between the gun and the man.

Burckhardt aimed low instinctively, to cripple, not to kill. But his aim was not good.

The pistol bullet caught her in the pit of the stomach.

Dorchin was out and away, the door slamming behind him, his footsteps racing into the distance.

Burckhardt hurled the gun across the room and jumped to the girl.

Swanson was moaning. "That finishes us, Burckhardt. Oh, why did you do it? We could have got away. We could have gone to the police. We were practically out of here! We—"

Burckhardt wasn't listening. He was kneeling beside the girl. She lay flat on her back, arms helter-skelter. There was no blood, hardly any sign of the wound; but the position in which she lay was one that no living human being could have held.

Yet she wasn't dead.

She wasn't dead—and Burckhardt, frozen beside her, thought: She isn't alive, either.

There was no pulse, but there was a rhythmic ticking of the outstretched fingers of one hand.

There was no sound of breathing, but there was a hissing, sizzling noise.

The eyes were open and they were looking at Burckhardt. There was neither fear nor pain in them, only a pity deeper than the Pit.

She said, through lips that writhed erratically, "Don't—worry, Mr. Burckhardt. I'm—all right."

Burckhardt rocked back on his haunches, staring. Where there should have been blood, there was a clean break of a substance that was not flesh; and a curl of thin golden-copper wire.

Burckhardt moistened his lips.

"You're a robot," he said.

The girl tried to nod. The twitching lips said, "I am. And so are you."

V

Swanson, after a single inarticulate sound, walked over to the desk and sat staring at the wall. Burckhardt rocked back and forth beside the shattered puppet on the floor. He had no words.

The girl managed to say, "I'm—sorry all this happened." The lovely lips twisted into a rictus sneer, frightening on that smooth young face, until she got them under control. "Sorry," she said again. "The—nerve center was right about where the bullet hit. Makes it difficult to—control this body."

Burckhardt nodded automatically, accepting the apology. Robots. It was obvious, now that he knew it. In hindsight, it was inevitable. He thought of his mystic notions of hypnosis or Martians or something stranger still—idiotic, for the simple fact of created robots fitted the facts better and more economically.

All the evidence had been before him. The automatized factory, with its transplanted minds—why not transplant a mind into a humanoid robot, give it its original owner's features and form?

Could it know that it was a robot?

"All of us," Burckhardt said, hardly aware that he spoke out loud. "My wife and my secretary and you and the neighbors. All of us the same."

"No." The voice was stronger. "Not exactly the same, all of us. I chose it, you see. I—" this time the convulsed lips were not a random contortion of the nerves—"I was an ugly woman, Mr. Burckhardt, and nearly sixty years old. Life had passed me. And when Mr.

Dorchin offered me the chance to live again as a beautiful girl, I jumped at the opportunity. Believe me, I jumped, in spite of its disadvantages. My flesh body is still alive—it is sleeping, while I am here. I could go back to it. But I never do."

"And the rest of us?"

"Different, Mr. Burckhardt. I work here. I'm carrying out Mr. Dorchin's orders, mapping the results of the advertising tests, watching you and the others live as he makes you live. I do it by choice, but you have no choice. Because, you see, you are dead."

"Dead?" cried Burckhardt; it was almost a scream.

The blue eyes looked at him unwinkingly and he knew that it was no lie. He swallowed, marveling at the intricate mechanisms that let him swallow, and sweat, and eat.

He said: "Oh. The explosion in my dream."

"It was no dream. You are right—the explosion. That was real and this plant was the cause of it. The storage tanks let go and what the blast didn't get, the fumes killed a little later. But almost everyone died in the blast, twenty-one thousand persons. You died with them and that was Dorchin's chance."

"The damned ghoul!" said Burckhardt.

The twisted shoulders shrugged with an odd grace. "Why? You were gone. And you and all the others were what Dorchin wanted—a whole town, a perfect slice of America. It's as easy to transfer a pattern from a dead brain as a living one. Easier—the dead can't say no. Oh, it took work and money—the town was a wreck—but it was possible to rebuild it entirely, especially because it wasn't necessary to have all the details exact.

"There were the homes where even the brains had been utterly destroyed, and those are empty inside, and the cellars that needn't be too perfect, and the streets that hardly matter. And anyway, it only has to last for one day. The same day—June 15th—over and over again; and if someone finds something a little wrong, somehow, the discovery won't have time to snowball, wreck the validity of the tests, because all errors are canceled out at midnight."

The face tried to smile. "That's the dream, Mr. Burckhardt, that day of June 15th, because you never really lived it. It's a present from Mr. Dorchin, a dream that he gives you and then takes back at the end of the day, when he has all his figures on how many of you responded to what variation of which appeal, and the maintenance crews go down the tunnel to go through the whole city, washing out the new dream with their little electronic drains, and then the dream starts all over again. On June 15th.

"Always June 15th, because June 14th is the last day any of you can remember alive. Sometimes the crews miss someone—as they missed you, because you were under your boat. But it doesn't matter. The ones who are missed give themselves away if they show it—and if they don't, it doesn't affect the test. But they don't drain us, the ones of us who work for Dorchin. We sleep when the power is turned off, just as you do. When we wake up, though, we remember." The face contorted wildly. "If I could only forget!"

Burckhardt said unbelievingly, "All this to sell merchandise! It must have cost millions!"

The robot called April Horn said, "It did. But it has made millions for Dorchin, too. And that's not the end of it. Once he finds the master words that make people act, do you suppose he will stop with that? Do you suppose—"

The door opened, interrupting her. Burckhardt whirled. Belatedly remembering Dorchin's flight, he raised the gun.

"Don't shoot," ordered the voice calmly. It was not Dorchin; it was another robot, this one not disguised with the clever plastics and cosmetics, but shining plain. It said metallically: "Forget it, Burckhardt. You're not accomplishing anything. Give me that gun before you do any more damage. Give it to me now."

Burckhardt bellowed angrily. The gleam on this robot torso was steel; Burckhardt was not at all sure that his bullets would pierce it, or do much harm if they did. He would have put it to the test—

But from behind him came a whimpering, scurrying whirlwind; its name was Swanson, hysterical with fear. He catapulted into Burckhardt and sent him sprawling, the gun flying free.

"Please!" begged Swanson incoherently, prostrate before the steel robot. "He would have shot you—please don't hurt me! Let me work for you, like that girl. I'll do anything, anything you tell me—"

The robot voice said. "We don't need your help." It took two precise steps and stood over the gun—and spurned it, left it lying on the floor.

The wrecked blonde robot said, without emotion, "I doubt that I can hold out much longer, Mr. Dorchin."

"Disconnect if you have to," replied the steel robot.

Burckhardt blinked. "But you're not Dorchin!"

The steel robot turned deep eyes on him. "I am," it said. "Not in the flesh—but this is the body I am using at the moment. I doubt that you can damage this one with the gun. The other robot body was more vulnerable. Now will you stop this nonsense? I don't want to have to damage you; you're too expensive for that. Will you just sit down and let the maintenance crews adjust you?"

Swanson groveled. "You—you won't punish us?"

The steel robot had no expression, but its voice was almost surprised. "Punish you?" it repeated on a rising note. "How?"

Swanson quivered as though the word had been a whip; but Burckhardt flared: "Adjust him, if he'll let you—but not me! You're going to have to do me a lot of damage, Dorchin. I don't care what I cost or how much trouble it's going to be to put me back together again. But I'm going out of that door! If you want to stop me, you'll have to kill me. You won't stop me any other way!"

The steel robot took a half-step toward him, and Burckhardt involuntarily checked his stride. He stood poised and shaking, ready for death, ready for attack, ready for anything that might happen.

Ready for anything except what did happen. For Dorchin's steel body merely stepped aside, between Burckhardt and the gun, but leaving the door free.

"Go ahead," invited the steel robot. "Nobody's stopping you."

Outside the door, Burckhardt brought up sharp. It was insane of Dorchin to let him go! Robot or flesh, victim or beneficiary, there was nothing to stop him from going to the FBI or whatever law he could find away from Dorchin's synthetic empire, and telling his story. Surely the corporations who paid Dorchin for test results had no notion of the ghoul's technique he used; Dorchin would have to keep it from them, for the breath of publicity would put a stop to it. Walking out meant death, perhaps—but at that moment in his pseudo-life, death was no terror for Burckhardt.

There was no one in the corridor. He found a window and stared out of it. There was Tylerton—an ersatz city, but looking so real and familiar that Burckhardt almost imagined the whole episode a dream. It was no dream, though. He was certain of that in his heart and equally certain that nothing in Tylerton could help him now.

It had to be the other direction.

It took him a quarter of an hour to find a way, but he found it—

skulking through the corridors, dodging the suspicion of footsteps, knowing for certain that his hiding was in vain, for Dorchin was undoubtedly aware of every move he made. But no one stopped him, and he found another door.

It was a simple enough door from the inside. But when he opened it and stepped out, it was like nothing he had ever seen.

First there was light—brilliant, incredible, blinding light. Burckhardt blinked upward, unbelieving and afraid.

He was standing on a ledge of smooth, finished metal. Not a dozen yards from his feet, the ledge dropped sharply away; he hardly dared approach the brink, but even from where he stood he could see no bottom to the chasm before him. And the gulf extended out of sight into the glare on either side of him.

No wonder Dorchin could so easily give him his freedom! From the factory, there was nowhere to go—but how incredible this fantastic gulf, how impossible the hundred white and blinding suns that hung above!

A voice by his side said inquiringly, "Burckhardt?" And thunder rolled the name, mutteringly soft, back and forth in the abyss before him.

Burckhardt wet his lips. "Y-yes?" he croaked.

"This is Dorchin. Not a robot this time, but Dorchin in the flesh, talking to you on a hand mike. Now you have seen, Burckhardt. Now will you be reasonable and let the maintenance crews take over?"

Burckhardt stood paralyzed. One of the moving mountains in the blinding glare came toward him.

It towered hundreds of feet over his head; he stared up at its top, squinting helplessly into the light.

It looked like—

Impossible!

The voice in the loudspeaker at the door said, "Burckhardt?" But he was unable to answer.

A heavy rumbling sigh. "I see," said the voice. "You finally understand. There's no place to go. You know it now. I could have told you, but you might not have believed me, so it was better for you to see it yourself. And after all, Burckhardt, why would I reconstruct a city just the way it was before? I'm a businessman; I count costs. If a thing has to be full-scale, I build it that way. But there wasn't any need to in this case."

From the mountain before him, Burckhardt helplessly saw a lesser cliff descend carefully toward him. It was long and dark, and at the end of it was whiteness, five-fingered whiteness....

"Poor little Burckhardt," crooned the loudspeaker, while the echoes rumbled through the enormous chasm that was only a workshop. "It must have been quite a shock for you to find out you were living in a town built on a table top."

VI

It was the morning of June 15th, and Guy Burckhardt woke up screaming out of a dream.

It had been a monstrous and incomprehensible dream, of explosions and shadowy figures that were not men and terror beyond words.

He shuddered and opened his eyes.

Outside his bedroom window, a hugely amplified voice was howling.

Burckhardt stumbled over to the window and stared outside. There was an out-of-season chill to the air, more like October than June; but the scent was normal enough—except for the sound-truck that squatted at curbside halfway down the block. Its speaker horns blared:

"Are you a coward? Are you a fool? Are you going to let crooked politicians steal the country from you? NO! Are you going to put up with four more years of graft and crime? NO! Are you going to vote straight Federal Party all up and down the ballot? YES! You just bet you are!"

Sometimes he screams, sometimes he wheedles, threatens, begs, cajoles ... but his voice goes on and on through one June 15th after another.

NOTE: Illustrations by Emsh.

Death Wish
By Robert Sheckley

Editor's note: This story by Robert Sheckley, writing as Ned Lang, was published in the June 1956 edition of Galaxy Science Fiction. *Sheckley (1928-2005) is regarded as one of the best science fiction short story writers of all time, and a number of his stories have been adapted into motion pictures. "Death Wish" became an episode of NBC's award-winning radio series "X Minus One" in 1957.*

The space freighter Queen Dierdre was a great, squat, pockmarked vessel of the Earth-Mars run and she never gave anyone a bit of trouble. That should have been sufficient warning to Mr. Watkins, her engineer. Watkins was fond of saying that there are two kinds of equipment—the kind that fails bit by bit, and the kind that fails all at once.

Watkins was short and red-faced, magnificently mustached, and always a little out of breath. With a cigar in his hand, over a glass of beer, he talked most cynically about his ship, in the immemorial fashion of engineers. But in reality, Watkins was foolishly infatuated with Dierdre, idealized her, humanized her, and couldn't conceive of anything serious ever happening.

On this particular run, Dierdre soared away from Terra at the proper speed; Mr. Watkins signaled that fuel was being consumed at the proper rate; and Captain Somers cut the engines at the proper moment indicated by Mr. Rajcik, the navigator.

As soon as Point Able had been reached and the engines stopped, Somers frowned and studied his complex control board. He was a thin and meticulous man, and he operated his ship with mechanical perfection. He was well liked in the front offices of Mikkelsen Space Lines, where Old Man Mikkelsen pointed to Captain Somers' reports as models of neatness and efficiency. On Mars, he stayed at the Officers' Club, eschewing the stews and dives of Marsport. On Earth, he lived in a little Vermont cottage and enjoyed the quiet companionship of two cats, a Japanese houseboy, and a wife.

His instructions read true. And yet he sensed something wrong. Somers knew every creak, rattle and groan that Dierdre was capable of making. During blastoff, he had heard something different. In space, something different had to be wrong.

"Mr. Rajcik," he said, turning to his navigator, "would you check the cargo? I believe something may have shifted."

"You bet," Rajcik said cheerfully. He was an almost offensively handsome young man with black wavy hair, blasé blue eyes and a cleft chin. Despite his appearance, Rajcik was thoroughly qualified for his position. But he was only one of fifty thousand thoroughly qualified men who lusted for a berth on one of the fourteen spaceships in existence. Only Stephen Rajcik had had the foresight, appearance and fortitude to court and wed Helga, Old Man Mikkelsen's eldest daughter.

Rajcik went aft to the cargo hold. Dierdre was carrying transistors this time, and microfilm books, platinum filaments, salamis, and other items that could not as yet be produced on Mars. But the bulk of her space was taken by the immense Fahrensen Computer.

Rajcik checked the positioning lines on the monster, examined the stays and turnbuckles that held it in place, and returned to the cabin.

"All in order, Boss," he reported to Captain Somers, with the smile that only an employer's son-in-law can both manage and afford.

"Mr. Watkins, do you read anything?"

Watkins was at his own instrument panel. "Not a thing, sir. I'll vouch for every bit of equipment in Dierdre."

"Very well. How long before we reach Point Baker?"

"Three minutes, Chief," Rajcik said.

"Good."

The spaceship hung in the void, all sensation of speed lost for lack of a reference point. Beyond the portholes was darkness, the true color of the Universe, perforated by the brilliant lost points of the stars.

Captain Somers turned away from the disturbing reminder of his extreme finitude and wondered if he could land Dierdre without shifting the computer. It was by far the largest, heaviest and most delicate piece of equipment ever transported in space.

He worried about that machine. Its value ran into the billions of dollars, for Mars Colony had ordered the best possible, a machine whose utility would offset the immense transportation charge across space. As a result, the Fahrensen Computer was perhaps the most complex and advanced machine ever built by Man.

"Ten seconds to Point Baker," Rajcik announced.

"Very well." Somers readied himself at the control board.

"Four—three—two—one—fire!"

Somers activated the engines. Acceleration pressed the three men back into their couches, and more acceleration, and—shockingly—still more acceleration.

"The fuel!" Watkins yelped, watching his indicators spinning.

"The course!" Rajcik gasped, fighting for breath.

Captain Somers cut the engine switch. The engines continued firing, pressing the men deeper into their couches. The cabin lights flickered, went out, came on again.

And still the acceleration mounted and Dierdre's engines howled in agony, thrusting the ship forward. Somers raised one leaden hand and inched it toward the emergency cut-off switch. With a fantastic expenditure of energy, he reached the switch, depressed it.

The engines stopped with dramatic suddenness, while tortured metal creaked and groaned. The lights flickered rapidly, as though Dierdre were blinking in pain. They steadied and then there was silence.

Watkins hurried to the engine room. He returned morosely.

"Of all the damn things," he muttered.

"What was it?" Captain Somers asked.

"Main firing circuit. It fused on us." He shook his head. "Metal fatigue, I'd say. It must have been flawed for years."

"When was it last checked out?"

"Well, it's a sealed unit. Supposed to outlast the ship. Absolutely foolproof, unless—"

"Unless it's flawed."

"Don't blame it on me! Those circuits are supposed to be X-rayed, heat-treated, fluoroscoped—you just can't trust machinery!"

At last Watkins believed that engineering axiom.

"How are we on fuel?" Captain Somers asked.

"Not enough left to push a kiddy car down Main Street," Watkins said gloomily. "If I could get my hands on that factory inspector ..."

Captain Somers turned to Rajcik, who was seated at the navigator's desk, hunched over his charts. "How does this affect our course?"

Rajcik finished the computation he was working on and gnawed thoughtfully at his pencil.

"It kills us. We're going to cross the orbit of Mars before Mars gets there."

"How long before?"

"Too long. Captain, we're flying out of the Solar System like the proverbial bat out of hell."

Rajcik smiled, a courageous, devil-may-care smile which Watkins found singularly inappropriate.

"Damn it, man," he roared, "don't just leave it there. We've got a little fuel left. We can turn her, can't we? You are a navigator, aren't you?"

"I am," Rajcik said icily. "And if I computed my courses the way you maintain your engines, we'd be plowing through Australia now."

"Why, you little company toady! At least I got my job legitimately, not by marrying—"

"That's enough!" Captain Somers cut in.

Watkins, his face a mottled red, his mustache bristling, looked like a walrus about to charge. And Rajcik, eyes glittering, was waiting hopefully.

"No more of this," Somers said. "I give the orders here."

"Then give some!" Watkins snapped. "Tell him to plot a return curve. This is life or death!"

"All the more reason for remaining cool. Mr. Rajcik, can you plot such a course?"

"First thing I tried," Rajcik said. "Not a chance, on the fuel we have left. We can turn a degree or two, but it won't help."

Watkins said, "Of course it will! We'll curve back into the Solar System!"

"Sure, but the best curve we can make will take a few thousand years for us to complete."

"Perhaps a landfall on some other planet—Neptune, Uranus—"

Rajcik shook his head. "Even if an outer planet were in the right place at the right time, we'd need fuel—a lot of fuel—to get into a braking orbit. And if we could, who'd come get us? No ship has gone past Mars yet."

"At least we'd have a chance," Watkins said.

"Maybe," Rajcik agreed indifferently. "But we can't swing it. I'm afraid you'll have to kiss the Solar System good-by."

Captain Somers wiped his forehead and tried to think of a plan. He found it difficult to concentrate. There was too great a discrepancy between his knowledge of the situation and its appearance. He knew—intellectually—that his ship was traveling out of the Solar System at a tremendous rate of speed. But in appearance they were stationary, hung in the abyss, three men trapped in a small, hot room, breathing the smell of hot metal and perspiration.

"What shall we do, Captain?" Watkins asked.

Somers frowned at the engineer. Did the man expect him to pull a solution out of the air? How was he even supposed to concentrate on the problem? He had to slow the ship, turn it. But his senses told him that the ship was not moving. How, then, could speed constitute a problem?

He couldn't help but feel that the real problem was to get away from these high-strung, squabbling men, to escape from this hot, smelly little room.

"Captain! You must have some idea!"

Somers tried to shake his feeling of unreality. The problem, the real problem, he told himself, was how to stop the ship.

He looked around the fixed cabin and out the porthole at the unmoving stars. We are moving very rapidly, he thought, unconvinced.

Rajcik said disgustedly, "Our noble captain can't face the situation."

"Of course I can," Somers objected, feeling very light-headed and unreal. "I can pilot any course you lay down. That's my only real responsibility. Plot us a course to Mars!"

"Sure!" Rajcik said, laughing. "I can! I will! Engineer, I'm going to need plenty of fuel for this course—about ten tons! See that I get it!"

"Right you are," said Watkins. "Captain, I'd like to put in a requisition for ten tons of fuel."

"Requisition granted," Somers said. "All right, gentlemen, responsibility is inevitably circular. Let's get a grip on ourselves. Mr. Rajcik, suppose you radio Mars."

When contact had been established, Somers took the microphone and stated their situation. The company official at the other end seemed to have trouble grasping it.

"But can't you turn the ship?" he asked bewilderedly. "Any kind of an orbit—"

"No. I've just explained that."

"Then what do you propose to do, Captain?"

"That's exactly what I'm asking you."

There was a babble of voices from the loudspeaker, punctuated by bursts of static. The lights flickered and reception began to fade. Rajcik, working frantically, managed to re-establish the contact.

"Captain," the official on Mars said, "we can't think of a thing. If you could swing into any sort of an orbit—"

"I can't!"

"Under the circumstances, you have the right to try anything at all. Anything, Captain!"

Somers groaned. "Listen, I can think of just one thing. We could bail out in spacesuits as near Mars as possible. Link ourselves together, take the portable transmitter. It wouldn't give much of a signal, but you'd know our approximate position. Everything would have to be figured pretty closely—those suits just carry twelve hours' air—but it's a chance."

There was a confusion of voices from the other end. Then the official said, "I'm sorry, Captain."

"What? I'm telling you it's our one chance!"

"Captain, the only ship on Mars now is the Diana. Her engines are being overhauled."

"How long before she can be spaceborne?"

"Three weeks, at least. And a ship from Earth would take too long. Captain, I wish we could think of something. About the only thing we can suggest—"

The reception suddenly failed again.

Rajcik cursed frustratedly as he worked over the radio. Watkins gnawed at his mustache. Somers glanced out a porthole and looked hurriedly away, for the stars, their destination, were impossibly distant.

They heard static again, faintly now.

"I can't get much more," Rajcik said. "This damned reception.... What could they have been suggesting?"

"Whatever it was," said Watkins, "they didn't think it would work."

"What the hell does that matter?" Rajcik asked, annoyed. "It'd give us something to do."

They heard the official's voice, a whisper across space.

"Can you hear ... Suggest ..."

At full amplification, the voice faded, then returned. "Can only suggest ... most unlikely ... but try ... calculator ... try ..."

The voice was gone. And then even the static was gone.

"That does it," Rajcik said. "The calculator? Did he mean the Fahrensen Computer in our hold?"

"I see what he meant," said Captain Somers. "The Fahrensen is a very advanced job. No one knows the limits of its potential. He suggests we present our problem to it."

"That's ridiculous," Watkins snorted. "This problem has no solution."

"It doesn't seem to," Somers agreed. "But the big computers have solved other apparently impossible problems. We can't lose anything by trying."

"No," said Rajcik, "as long as we don't pin any hopes on it."

"That's right. We don't dare hope. Mr. Watkins, I believe this is your department."

"Oh, what's the use?" Watkins asked. "You say don't hope—but both of you are hoping anyhow! You think the big electronic god is going to save your lives. Well, it's not!"

"We have to try," Somers told him.

"We don't! I wouldn't give it the satisfaction of turning us down!"

They stared at him in vacant astonishment.

"Now you're implying that machines think," said Rajcik.

"Of course I am," Watkins said. "Because they do! No, I'm not out of my head. Any engineer will tell you that a complex machine has a personality all its own. Do you know what that personality is like? Cold, withdrawn, uncaring, unfeeling. A machine's only purpose is to frustrate desire and produce two problems for everyone it solves. And do you know why a machine feels this way?"

"You're hysterical," Somers told him.

"I am not. A machine feels this way because it knows it is an unnatural creation in nature's domain. Therefore it wishes to reach entropy and cease—a mechanical death wish."

"I've never heard such gibberish in my life," Somers said. "Are you going to hook up that computer?"

"Of course. I'm a human. I keep trying. I just wanted you to understand fully that there is no hope." He went to the cargo hold.

After he had gone, Rajcik grinned and shook his head. "We'd better watch him."

"He'll be all right," Somers said.

"Maybe, maybe not." Rajcik pursed his lips thoughtfully. "He's blaming the situation on a machine personality now, trying to absolve himself of guilt. And it is his fault that we're in this spot. An engineer is responsible for all equipment."

"I don't believe you can put the blame on him so dogmatically," Somers replied.

"Sure I can," Rajcik said. "I personally don't care, though. This is as good a way to die as any other and better than most."

Captain Somers wiped perspiration from his face. Again the notion came to him that the problem—the real problem—was to find a way out of this hot, smelly, motionless little box.

Rajcik said, "Death in space is an appealing idea, in certain ways. Imagine an entire spaceship for your tomb! And you have a variety of ways of actually dying. Thirst and starvation I rule out as unimaginative. But there are possibilities in heat, cold, implosion, explosion—"

"This is pretty morbid," Somers said.

"I'm A pretty morbid fellow," Rajcik said carelessly. "But at least I'm not blaming inanimate objects, the way Watkins is. Or permitting myself the luxury of shock, like you." He studied Somers' face. "This is your first real emergency, isn't it, Captain?"

"I suppose so," Somers answered vaguely.

"And you're responding to it like a stunned ox," Rajcik said. "Wake up, Captain! If you can't live with joy, at least try to extract some pleasure from your dying."

"Shut up," Somers said, with no heat. "Why don't you read a book or something?"

"I've read all the books on board. I have nothing to distract me except an analysis of your character."

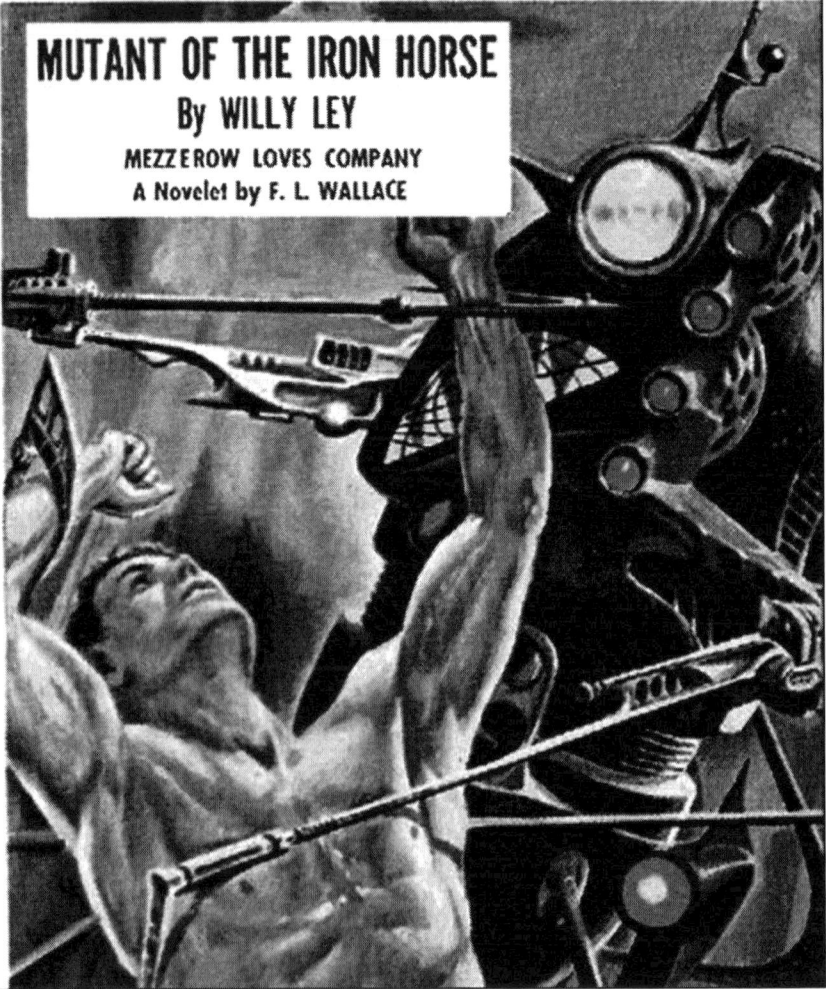

Watkins returned to the cabin. "Well, I've activated your big electronic god. Would anyone care to make a burned offering in front of it?"

"Have you given it the problem?"

"Not yet. I decided to confer with the high priest. What shall I request of the demon, sir?"

"Give it all the data you can," Somers said. "Fuel, oxygen, water, food—that sort of thing. Then tell it we want to return to Earth. Alive," he added.

"It'll love that," Watkins said. "It'll get such pleasure out of rejecting our problem as unsolvable. Or better yet—insufficient data. In that way, it can hint that a solution is possible, but just outside our reach. It can keep us hoping."

Somers and Rajcik followed him to the cargo hold. The computer, activated now, hummed softly. Lights flashed swiftly over its panels, blue and white and red.

Watkins punched buttons and turned dials for fifteen minutes, then moved back.

"Watch for the red light on top," he said. "That means the problem is rejected."

"Don't say it," Rajcik warned quickly.

Watkins laughed. "Superstitious little fellow, aren't you?"

"But not incompetent," Rajcik said, smiling.

"Can't you two quit it?" Somers demanded, and both men turned startedly to face him.

"Behold!" Rajcik said. "The sleeper has awakened."

"After a fashion," said Watkins, snickering.

Somers suddenly felt that if death or rescue did not come quickly, they would kill each other, or drive each other crazy.

"Look!" Rajcik said.

A light on the computer's panel was flashing green.

"Must be a mistake," said Watkins. "Green means the problem is solvable within the conditions set down."

"Solvable!" Rajcik said.

"But it's impossible," Watkins argued. "It's fooling us, leading us on—"

"Don't be superstitious," Rajcik mocked. "How soon do we get the solution?"

"It's coming now." Watkins pointed to a paper tape inching out of a slot in the machine's face. "But there must be something wrong!"

They watched as, millimeter by millimeter, the tape crept out. The computer hummed, its lights flashing green. Then the hum stopped. The green lights blazed once more and faded.

"What happened?" Rajcik wanted to know.

"It's finished," Watkins said.

"Pick it up! Read it!"

"You read it. You won't get me to play its game."

Rajcik laughed nervously and rubbed his hands together, but didn't move. Both men turned to Somers.

"Captain, it's your responsibility."

"Go ahead, Captain!"

Somers looked with loathing at his engineer and navigator. His responsibility, everything was his responsibility. Would they never leave him alone?

He went up to the machine, pulled the tape free, read it with slow deliberation.

"What does it say, sir?" Rajcik asked.

"Is it—possible?" Watkins urged.

"Oh, yes," Somers said. "It's possible." He laughed and looked around at the hot, smelly, low-ceilinged little room with its locked doors and windows.

"What is it?" Rajcik shouted.

Somers said, "You figured a few thousand years to return to the Solar System, Rajcik? Well, the computer agrees with you. Twenty-three hundred years, to be precise. Therefore, it has given us a suitable longevity serum."

"Twenty-three hundred years," Rajcik mumbled. "I suppose we hibernate or something of the sort."

"Not at all," Somers said calmly. "As a matter of fact, this serum does away quite nicely with the need for sleep. We stay awake and watch each other."

The three men looked at one another and at the sickeningly familiar room smelling of metal and perspiration, its sealed doors and windows that stared at an unchanging spectacle of stars.

Watkins said, "Yes, that's the sort of thing it would do."

NOTE: *Illustrations by Weiss.*

The Moon is Green
By Fritz Leiber

Editor's note: This Fritz Reuter Leiber, Jr. (1910-1992) story appeared in the April 1952 edition of Galaxy Science Fiction *and was later produced as a radio drama for NBC's award-winning series "X-Minus One." Leiber, a Chicago native, is considered to be one of the fathers of the sword-and-sorcery fantasy genre.*

"Effie! What the devil are you up to?"

Her husband's voice, chopping through her mood of terrified rapture, made her heart jump like a startled cat, yet by some miracle of feminine self-control her body did not show a tremor.

Dear God, she thought, he mustn't see it. It's so beautiful, and he always kills beauty.

"I'm just looking at the Moon," she said listlessly. "It's green."

Mustn't, mustn't see it. And now, with luck, he wouldn't. For the face, as if it also heard and sensed the menace in the voice, was moving back from the window's glow into the outside dark, but slowly, reluctantly, and still faunlike, pleading, cajoling, tempting, and incredibly beautiful.

"Close the shutters at once, you little fool, and come away from the window!"

"Green as a beer bottle," she went on dreamily, "green as emeralds, green as leaves with sunshine striking through them and green grass to lie on." She couldn't help saying those last words. They were her token to the face, even though it couldn't hear.

"Effie!"

She knew what that last tone meant. Wearily she swung shut the ponderous lead inner shutters and drove home the heavy bolts. That hurt her fingers; it always did, but he mustn't know that.

"You know that those shutters are not to be touched! Not for five more years at least!"

"I only wanted to look at the Moon," she said, turning around, and then it was all gone—the face, the night, the Moon, the magic—and she was back in the grubby, stale little hole, facing an angry, stale little man. It was then that the eternal thud of the air-conditioning fans and the crackle of the electrostatic precipitators that sieved out the dust reached her consciousness again like the bite of a dentist's

89

drill.

"Only wanted to look at the Moon!" he mimicked her in falsetto. "Only wanted to die like a little fool and make me that much more ashamed of you!" Then his voice went gruff and professional. "Here, count yourself."

She silently took the Geiger counter he held at arm's length, waited until it settled down to a steady ticking slower than a clock— due only to cosmic rays and indicating nothing dangerous—and then began to comb her body with the instrument. First her head and shoulders, then out along her arms and back along their underside. There was something oddly voluptuous about her movements, although her features were gray and sagging.

The ticking did not change its tempo until she came to her waist. Then it suddenly spurted, clicking faster and faster. Her husband gave an excited grunt, took a quick step forward, froze. She goggled for a moment in fear, then grinned foolishly, dug in the pocket of her grimy apron and guiltily pulled out a wristwatch.

He grabbed it as it dangled from her fingers, saw that it had a radium dial, cursed, heaved it up as if to smash it on the floor, but instead put it carefully on the table.

"You imbecile, you incredible imbecile," he softly chanted to himself through clenched teeth, with eyes half closed.

She shrugged faintly, put the Geiger counter on the table, and stood there slumped.

He waited until the chanting had soothed his anger, before speaking again. He said quietly, "I do suppose you still realize the sort of world you're living in?"

SHE nodded slowly, staring at nothingness. Oh, she realized, all right, realized only too well. It was the world that hadn't realized. The world that had gone on stockpiling hydrogen bombs. The world that had put those bombs in cobalt shells, although it had promised it wouldn't, because the cobalt made them much more terrible and cost no more. The world that had started throwing those bombs, always telling itself that it hadn't thrown enough of them yet to make the air really dangerous with the deadly radioactive dust that came from the cobalt. Thrown them and kept on throwing until the danger point, where air and ground would become fatal to all human life, was approached.

Then, for about a month, the two great enemy groups had

hesitated. And then each, unknown to the other, had decided it could risk one last gigantic and decisive attack without exceeding the danger point. It had been planned to strip off the cobalt cases, but someone forgot and then there wasn't time. Besides, the military scientists of each group were confident that the lands of the other had got the most dust. The two attacks came within an hour of each other.

After that, the Fury. The Fury of doomed men who think only of taking with them as many as possible of the enemy, and in this case—they hoped—all. The Fury of suicides who know they have botched up life for good. The Fury of cocksure men who realize they have been outsmarted by fate, the enemy, and themselves, and know that they will never be able to improvise a defense when arraigned before the high court of history—and whose unadmitted hope is that there will be no high court of history left to arraign them. More cobalt bombs were dropped during the Fury than in all the preceding years of the war.

After the Fury, the Terror. Men and women with death sifting into their bones through their nostrils and skin, fighting for bare survival under a dust-hazed sky that played fantastic tricks with the light of Sun and Moon, like the dust from Krakatoa that drifted around the world for years. Cities, countryside, and air were alike poisoned, alive with deadly radiation.

The only realistic chance for continued existence was to retire, for the five or ten years the radiation would remain deadly, to some well-sealed and radiation-shielded place that must also be copiously supplied with food, water, power, and a means of air-conditioning.

Such places were prepared by the far-seeing, seized by the stronger, defended by them in turn against the desperate hordes of the dying ... until there were no more of those.

After that, only the waiting, the enduring. A mole's existence, without beauty or tenderness, but with fear and guilt as constant companions. Never to see the Sun, to walk among the trees—or even know if there were still trees.

Oh, yes, she realized what the world was like.

"You understand, too, I suppose, that we were allowed to reclaim this ground-level apartment only because the Committee believed us to be responsible people, and because I've been making a damn good showing lately?"

"Yes, Hank."

"I thought you were eager for privacy. You want to go back to the basement tenements?"

God, no! Anything rather than that fetid huddling, that shameless communal sprawl. And yet, was this so much better? The nearness to the surface was meaningless; it only tantalized. And the privacy magnified Hank.

She shook her head dutifully and said, "No, Hank."

"Then why aren't you careful? I've told you a million times, Effie, that glass is no protection against the dust that's outside that window. The lead shutter must never be touched! If you make one single slip like that and it gets around, the Committee will send us back to the lower levels without blinking an eye. And they'll think twice before trusting me with any important jobs."

"I'm sorry, Hank."

"Sorry? What's the good of being sorry? The only thing that counts is never to make a slip! Why the devil do you do such things, Effie? What drives you to it?"

She swallowed. "It's just that it's so dreadful being cooped up like this," she said hesitatingly, "shut away from the sky and the Sun. I'm just hungry for a little beauty."

"And do you suppose I'm not?" he demanded. "Don't you suppose I want to get outside, too, and be carefree and have a good time? But I'm not so damn selfish about it. I want my children to enjoy the Sun, and my children's children. Don't you see that that's the all-important thing and that we have to behave like mature adults and make sacrifices for it?"

"Yes, Hank."

He surveyed her slumped figure, her lined and listless face. "You're a fine one to talk about hunger for beauty," he told her. Then his voice grew softer, more deliberate. "You haven't forgotten, have you, Effie, that until last month the Committee was so concerned about your sterility? That they were about to enter my name on the list of those waiting to be allotted a free woman? Very high on the list, too!"

She could nod even at that one, but not while looking at him. She turned away. She knew very well that the Committee was justified in worrying about the birth rate. When the community finally moved back to the surface again, each additional healthy young person would be an asset, not only in the struggle for bare survival, but in the resumed war against Communism which some of the Committee members still counted on.

It was natural that they should view a sterile woman with disfavor, and not only because of the waste of her husband's germ-plasm, but because sterility might indicate that she had suffered more than the average from radiation. In that case, if she did bear children later on, they would be more apt to carry a defective heredity, producing an undue number of monsters and freaks in future generations, and so contaminating the race.

Of course she understood it. She could hardly remember the time when she didn't. Years ago? Centuries? There wasn't much difference in a place where time was endless.

HIS lecture finished, her husband smiled and grew almost cheerful.

"Now that you're going to have a child, that's all in the background again. Do you know, Effie, that when I first came in, I had some very good news for you? I'm to become a member of the Junior Committee and the announcement will be made at the banquet tonight." He cut short her mumbled congratulations. "So brighten yourself up and put on your best dress. I want the other Juniors to see what a handsome wife the new member has got." He paused. "Well, get a move on!"

She spoke with difficulty, still not looking at him. "I'm terribly sorry, Hank, but you'll have to go alone. I'm not well."

He straightened up with an indignant jerk. "There you go again! First that infantile, inexcusable business of the shutters, and now this! No feeling for my reputation at all. Don't be ridiculous, Effie. You're coming!"

"Terribly sorry," she repeated blindly, "but I really can't. I'd just be sick. I wouldn't make you proud of me at all."

"Of course you won't," he retorted sharply. "As it is, I have to spend half my energy running around making excuses for you—why you're so odd, why you always seem to be ailing, why you're always stupid and snobbish and say the wrong thing. But tonight's really important, Effie. It will cause a lot of bad comment if the new member's wife isn't present. You know how just a hint of sickness starts the old radiation-disease rumor going. You've got to come, Effie."

She shook her head helplessly.

"Oh, for heaven's sake, come on!" he shouted, advancing on her. "This is just a silly mood. As soon as you get going, you'll snap out of it. There's nothing really wrong with you at all."

He put his hand on her shoulder to turn her around, and at his touch her face suddenly grew so desperate and gray that for a moment he was alarmed in spite of himself.

"Really?" he asked, almost with a note of concern.

She nodded miserably.

"Hmm!" He stepped back and strode about irresolutely. "Well, of course, if that's the way it is ..." He checked himself and a sad smile crossed his face. "So you don't care enough about your old husband's success to make one supreme effort in spite of feeling bad?"

Again the helpless headshake. "I just can't go out tonight, under any circumstances." And her gaze stole toward the lead shutters.

He was about to say something when he caught the direction of her gaze. His eyebrows jumped. For seconds he stared at her incredulously, as if some completely new and almost unbelievable possibility had popped into his mind. The look of incredulity slowly faded, to be replaced by a harder, more calculating expression. But when he spoke again, his voice was shockingly bright and kind.

"Well, it can't be helped naturally, and I certainly wouldn't want you to go if you weren't able to enjoy it. So you hop right into bed and get a good rest. I'll run over to the men's dorm to freshen up. No, really, I don't want you to have to make any effort at all. Incidentally, Jim Barnes isn't going to be able to come to the banquet either—touch of the old 'flu, he tells me, of all things."

He watched her closely as he mentioned the other man's name, but she didn't react noticeably. In fact, she hardly seemed to be hearing his chatter.

"I got a bit sharp with you, I'm afraid, Effie," he continued contritely. "I'm sorry about that. I was excited about my new job and I guess that was why things upset me. Made me feel let down when I found you weren't feeling as good as I was. Selfish of me. Now you get into bed right away and get well. Don't worry about me a bit. I know you'd come if you possibly could. And I know you'll be thinking about me. Well, I must be off now."

He started toward her, as if to embrace her, then seemed to think better of it. He turned back at the doorway and said, emphasizing the words, "You'll be completely alone for the next four hours." He waited for her nod, then bounced out.

SHE stood still until his footsteps died away. Then she straightened up, walked over to where he'd put down the wristwatch, picked it up and smashed it hard on the floor. The crystal shattered, the case flew apart, and something went zing!

She stood there breathing heavily. Slowly her sagged features lifted, formed themselves into the beginning of a smile. She stole another look at the shutters. The smile became more definite. She felt her hair, wet her fingers and ran them along her hairline and back over her ears. After wiping her hands on her apron, she took it off. She straightened her dress, lifted her head with a little flourish, and stepped smartly toward the window.

Then her face went miserable again and her steps slowed.

No, it couldn't be, and it won't be, she told herself. It had been just an illusion, a silly romantic dream that she had somehow projected out of her beauty-starved mind and given a moment's false reality. There couldn't be anything alive outside. There hadn't been for two whole years.

And if there conceivably were, it would be something altogether horrible. She remembered some of the pariahs—hairless, witless creatures, with radiation welts crawling over their bodies like worms, who had come begging for succor during the last months of the Terror—and been shot down. How they must have hated the people in refuges!

But even as she was thinking these things, her fingers were caressing the bolts, gingerly drawing them, and she was opening the shutters gently, apprehensively.

No, there couldn't be anything outside, she assured herself wryly, peering out into the green night. Even her fears had been groundless.

But the face came floating up toward the window. She started back in terror, then checked herself.

For the face wasn't horrible at all, only very thin, with full lips and large eyes and a thin proud nose like the jutting beak of a bird. And no radiation welts or scars marred the skin, olive in the tempered moonlight. It looked, in fact, just as it had when she had seen it the first time.

For a long moment the face stared deep, deep into her brain. Then the full lips smiled and a half-clenched, thin-fingered hand materialized itself from the green darkness and rapped twice on the grimy pane.

Her heart pounding, she furiously worked the little crank that opened the window. It came unstuck from the frame with a tiny explosion of dust and a zing like that of the watch, only louder. A moment later it swung open wide and a puff of incredibly fresh air caressed her face and the inside of her nostrils, stinging her eyes with unanticipated tears.

The man outside balanced on the sill, crouching like a faun, head high, one elbow on knee. He was dressed in scarred, snug trousers and an old sweater.

"Is it tears I get for a welcome?" he mocked her gently in a musical voice. "Or are those only to greet God's own breath, the air?"

HE swung down inside and now she could see he was tall. Turning, he snapped his fingers and called, "Come, puss."

A black cat with a twisted stump of a tail and feet like small boxing gloves and ears almost as big as rabbits' hopped clumsily in view. He lifted it down, gave it a pat. Then, nodding familiarly to Effie, he unstrapped a little pack from his back and laid it on the table.

She couldn't move. She even found it hard to breathe.

"The window," she finally managed to get out.

He looked at her inquiringly, caught the direction of her stabbing finger. Moving without haste, he went over and closed it carelessly.

"The shutters, too," she told him, but he ignored that, looking around.

"It's a snug enough place you and your man have," he commented. "Or is it that this is a free-love town or a harem spot, or just a military post?" He checked her before she could answer. "But let's not be talking about such things now. Soon enough I'll be scared to death for both of us. Best enjoy the kick of meeting, which is always good for twenty minutes at the least." He smiled at her rather shyly. "Have you food? Good, then bring it."

She set cold meat and some precious canned bread before him and had water heating for coffee. Before he fell to, he shredded a chunk of meat and put it on the floor for the cat, which left off its sniffing inspection of the walls and ran up eagerly mewing. Then the man began to eat, chewing each mouthful slowly and appreciatively.

From across the table Effie watched him, drinking in his every deft movement, his every cryptic quirk of expression. She attended to making the coffee, but that took only a moment. Finally she could contain herself no longer.

"What's it like up there?" she asked breathlessly. "Outside, I mean."

He looked at her oddly for quite a space. Finally, he said flatly, "Oh, it's a wonderland for sure, more amazing than you tombed folk could ever imagine. A veritable fairyland." And he quickly went on eating.

"No, but really," she pressed.

Noting her eagerness, he smiled and his eyes filled with playful tenderness. "I mean it, on my oath," he assured her. "You think the bombs and the dust made only death and ugliness. That was true at first. But then, just as the doctors foretold, they changed the life in the seeds and loins that were brave enough to stay. Wonders bloomed and walked." He broke off suddenly and asked, "Do any of you ever venture outside?"

"A few of the men are allowed to," she told him, "for short trips in special protective suits, to hunt for canned food and fuels and batteries and things like that."

"Aye, and those blind-souled slugs would never see anything but what they're looking for," he said, nodding bitterly. "They'd never see the garden where a dozen buds blossom where one did before, and the flowers have petals a yard across, with stingless bees big as sparrows gently supping their nectar. Housecats grown spotted and huge as leopards (not little runts like Joe Louis here) stalk through those gardens. But they're gentle beasts, no more harmful than the rainbow-scaled snakes that glide around their paws, for the dust burned all the murder out of them, as it burned itself out.

"I've even made up a little poem about that. It starts, 'Fire can hurt me, or water, or the weight of Earth. But the dust is my friend.' Oh, yes, and then the robins like cockatoos and squirrels like a princess's ermine! All under a treasure chest of Sun and Moon and stars that the dust's magic powder changes from ruby to emerald and sapphire and amethyst and back again. Oh, and then the new children—"

"You're telling the truth?" she interrupted him, her eyes brimming with tears. "You're not making it up?"

"I am not," he assured her solemnly. "And if you could catch a glimpse of one of the new children, you'd never doubt me again. They have long limbs as brown as this coffee would be if it had lots of fresh cream in it, and smiling delicate faces and the whitish teeth and the finest hair. They're so nimble that I—a sprightly man and somewhat enlivened by the dust—feel like a cripple beside them. And their thoughts dance like flames and make me feel a very imbecile.

"Of course, they have seven fingers on each hand and eight toes on each foot, but they're the more beautiful for that. They have large pointed ears that the Sun shines through. They play in the garden, all day long, slipping among the great leaves and blooms, but they're so swift that you can hardly see them, unless one chooses to stand still and look at you. For that matter, you have to look a bit hard for all these things I'm telling you."

"But it is true?" she pleaded.

"Every word of it," he said, looking straight into her eyes. He put down his knife and fork. "What's your name?" he asked softly. "Mine's Patrick."

"Effie," she told him.

He shook his head. "That can't be," he said. Then his face brightened. "Euphemia," he exclaimed. "That's what Effie is short for. Your name is Euphemia." As he said that, looking at her, she suddenly felt beautiful. He got up and came around the table and stretched out his hand toward her.

"Euphemia—" he began.

"Yes?" she answered huskily, shrinking from him a little, but looking up sideways, and very flushed.

"Don't either of you move," Hank said.

The voice was flat and nasal because Hank was wearing a nose respirator that was just long enough to suggest an elephant's trunk. In his right hand was a large blue-black automatic pistol.

They turned their faces to him. Patrick's was abruptly alert, shifty. But Effie's was still smiling tenderly, as if Hank could not break the spell of the magic garden and should be pitied for not knowing about it.

"You little—" Hank began with an almost gleeful fury, calling her several shameful names. He spoke in short phrases, closing tight his unmasked mouth between them while he sucked in breath through the respirator. His voice rose in a crescendo. "And not with a man of the community, but a pariah! A pariah!"

"I hardly know what you're thinking, man, but you're quite wrong," Patrick took the opportunity to put in hurriedly, conciliatingly. "I just happened to be coming by hungry tonight, a lonely tramp, and knocked at the window. Your wife was a bit foolish and let kindheartedness get the better of prudence—"

"Don't think you've pulled the wool over my eyes, Effie," Hank went on with a screechy laugh, disregarding the other man completely. "Don't think I don't know why you're suddenly going to have a child after four long years."

At that moment the cat came nosing up to his feet. Patrick watched him narrowly, shifting his weight forward a little, but Hank only kicked the animal aside without taking his eyes off them.

"Even that business of carrying the wristwatch in your pocket instead of on your arm," he went on with channeled hysteria. "A neat bit of camouflage, Effie. Very neat. And telling me it was my child, when all the while you've been seeing him for months!"

"Man, you're mad; I've not touched her!" Patrick denied hotly though still calculatingly, and risked a step forward, stopping when the gun instantly swung his way.

"Pretending you were going to give me a healthy child," Hank raved on, "when all the while you knew it would be—either in body or germ plasm—a thing like that!"

He waved his gun at the malformed cat, which had leaped to the top of the table and was eating the remains of Patrick's food, though its watchful green eyes were fixed on Hank.

"I should shoot him down!" Hank yelled, between sobbing, chest-racking inhalations through the mask. "I should kill him this instant for the contaminated pariah he is!"

All this while Effie had not ceased to smile compassionately. Now she stood up without haste and went to Patrick's side. Disregarding his warning, apprehensive glance, she put her arm lightly around him and faced her husband.

"Then you'd be killing the bringer of the best news we've ever had," she said, and her voice was like a flood of some warm sweet liquor in that musty, hate-charged room. "Oh, Hank, forget your silly, wrong jealousy and listen to me. Patrick here has something wonderful to tell us."

Hank stared at her. For once he screamed no reply. It was obvious that he was seeing for the first time how beautiful she had become, and that the realization jolted him terribly.

"What do you mean?" he finally asked unevenly, almost fearfully.

"I mean that we no longer need to fear the dust," she said, and now her smile was radiant. "It never really did hurt people the way the doctors said it would. Remember how it was with me, Hank, the exposure I had and recovered from, although the doctors said I wouldn't at first—and without even losing my hair? Hank, those who were brave enough to stay outside, and who weren't killed by terror and suggestion and panic— they adapted to the dust. They changed, but they changed for the better. Everything—"

"Effie, he told you lies!" Hank interrupted, but still in that same agitated, broken voice, cowed by her beauty.

"Everything that grew or moved was purified," she went on ringingly. "You men going outside have never seen it, because you've never had eyes for it. You've been blinded to beauty, to life itself. And now all the power in the dust has gone and faded, anyway, burned itself out. That's true, isn't it?"

She smiled at Patrick for confirmation. His face was strangely veiled, as if he were calculating obscure changes. He might have given a little nod; at any rate, Effie assumed that he did, for she turned back to her husband.

"You see, Hank? We can all go out now. We need never fear the dust again. Patrick is a living proof of that," she continued triumphantly, standing straighter, holding him a little tighter. "Look at him. Not a scar or a sign, and he's been out in the dust for years. How could he be this way, if the dust hurt the brave? Oh, believe me, Hank! Believe what you see. Test it if you want. Test Patrick here."

"Effie, you're all mixed up. You don't know—" Hank faltered, but without conviction of any sort.

"Just test him," Effie repeated with utter confidence, ignoring—not even noticing—Patrick's warning nudge.

"All right," Hank mumbled. He looked at the stranger dully. "Can you count?" he asked.

Patrick's face was a complete enigma. Then he suddenly spoke, and his voice was like a fencer's foil—light, bright, alert, constantly playing, yet utterly on guard.

"Can I count? Do you take me for a complete simpleton, man? Of course I can count!"

"Then count yourself," Hank said, barely indicating the table.

"Count myself, should I?" the other retorted with a quick facetious laugh. "Is this a kindergarten? But if you want me to, I'm willing." His voice was rapid. "I've two arms, and two legs, that's four. And ten fingers and ten toes—you'll take my word for them?—that's twenty-four. A head, twenty-five. And two eyes and a nose and a mouth—"

"With this, I mean," Hank said heavily, advanced to the table, picked up the Geiger counter, switched it on, and handed it across the table to the other man.

But while it was still an arm's length from Patrick, the clicks began to mount furiously, until they were like the chatter of a pigmy machine gun. Abruptly the clicks slowed, but that was only the counter shifting to a new scaling circuit, in which each click stood for 512 of the old ones.

With those horrid, rattling little volleys, fear cascaded into the room and filled it, smashing like so much colored glass all the bright barriers of words Effie had raised against it. For no dreams can stand against the Geiger counter, the Twentieth Century's mouthpiece of ultimate truth. It was as if the dust and all the terrors of the dust had incarnated themselves in one dread invading shape that said in words stronger than audible speech, "Those were illusions, whistles in the dark. This is reality, the dreary, pitiless reality of the Burrowing Years."

Hank scuttled back to the wall. Through chattering teeth he babbled, "... enough radioactives ... kill a thousand men ... freak ... a freak ..." In his agitation he forgot for a moment to inhale through the respirator.

Even Effie—taken off guard, all the fears that had been drilled into her twanging like piano wires—shrank from the skeletal-seeming shape beside her, held herself to it only by desperation.

Patrick did it for her. He disengaged her arm and stepped briskly away. Then he whirled on them, smiling sardonically, and started to speak, but instead looked with distaste at the chattering Geiger counter he held between fingers and thumb.

"Have we listened to this racket long enough?" he asked.

Without waiting for an answer, he put down the instrument on the table. The cat hurried over to it curiously and the clicks began again to mount in a minor crescendo. Effie lunged for it frantically, switched it off, darted back.

"That's right," Patrick said with another chilling smile. "You do well to cringe, for I'm death itself. Even in death I could kill you, like a snake." And with that his voice took on the tones of a circus barker. "Yes, I'm a freak, as the gentleman so wisely said. That's what one doctor who dared talk with me for a minute told me before he kicked me out. He couldn't tell me why, but somehow the dust doesn't kill me. Because I'm a freak, you see, just like the men who ate nails and walked on fire and ate arsenic and stuck themselves through with pins. Step right up, ladies and gentlemen—only not too close!—and examine the man the dust can't harm. Rappaccini's child, brought up to date; his embrace, death!

"And now," he said, breathing heavily, "I'll get out and leave you in your damned lead cave."

He started toward the window. Hank's gun followed him shakingly.

"Wait!" Effie called in an agonized voice. He obeyed. She continued falteringly, "When we were together earlier, you didn't act as if ..."

"When we were together earlier, I wanted what I wanted," he snarled at her. "You don't suppose I'm a bloody saint, do you?"

"And all the beautiful things you told me?"

"That," he said cruelly, "is just a line I've found that women fall for. They're all so bored and so starved for beauty—as they generally put it."

"Even the garden?" Her question was barely audible through the sobs that threatened to suffocate her.

He looked at her and perhaps his expression softened just a trifle.

"What's outside," he said flatly, "is just a little worse than either of you can imagine." He tapped his temple. "The garden's all here."

"You've killed it," she wept. "You've killed it in me. You've both killed everything that's beautiful. But you're worse," she screamed at Patrick, "because he only killed beauty once, but you brought it to life just so you could kill it again. Oh, I can't stand it! I won't stand it!" And she began to scream.

Patrick started toward her, but she broke off and whirled away from him to the window, her eyes crazy.

"You've been lying to us," she cried. "The garden's there. I know it is. But you don't want to share it with anyone."

"No, no, Euphemia," Patrick protested anxiously. "It's hell out there, believe me. I wouldn't lie to you about it."

"Wouldn't lie to me!" she mocked. "Are you afraid, too?"

With a sudden pull, she jerked open the window and stood before the blank green-tinged oblong of darkness that seemed to press into the room like a menacing, heavy, wind-urged curtain.

At that Hank cried out a shocked, pleading, "Effie!"

She ignored him. "I can't be cooped up here any longer," she said. "And I won't, now that I know. I'm going to the garden."

Both men sprang at her, but they were too late. She leaped lightly to the sill, and by the time they had flung themselves against it, her footsteps were already hurrying off into the darkness.

"Effie, come back! Come back!" Hank shouted after her desperately, no longer thinking to cringe from the man beside him, or how the gun was pointed. "I love you, Effie. Come back!"

Patrick added his voice. "Come back, Euphemia. You'll be safe if you come back right away. Come back to your home."

No answer to that at all.

They both strained their eyes through the greenish murk. They could barely make out a shadowy figure about half a block down the near-black canyon of the dismal, dust-blown street, into which the greenish moonlight hardly reached. It seemed to them that the figure was scooping something up from the pavement and letting it sift down along its arms and over its bosom.

"Go out and get her, man," Patrick urged the other. "For if I go out for her, I warn you I won't bring her back. She said something about having stood the dust better than most, and that's enough for me."

But Hank, chained by his painfully learned habits and by

something else, could not move.

And then a ghostly voice came whispering down the street, chanting, "Fire can hurt me, or water, or the weight of Earth. But the dust is my friend."

Patrick spared the other man one more look. Then, without a word, he vaulted up and ran off.

Hank stood there. After perhaps a half minute he remembered to close his mouth when he inhaled. Finally he was sure the street was empty. As he started to close the window, there was a little mew.

He picked up the cat and gently put it outside. Then he did close the window, and the shutters, and bolted them, and took up the Geiger counter, and mechanically began to count himself.

NOTE: Illustrations by David Stone.

The Coffin Cure
By Alan E. Nourse

Editor's note: As a medical doctor and science-fiction writer, Alan E. Nourse (1928-1992) brought a unique perspective to his stories, many of which involved physicians or medicine. In "The Coffin Cure," published April 1957 in Galaxy Science Fiction, *Nourse explores one doctor's solution for the common cold. The story was adapted into an episode of NBC's "X Minus One" radio drama, also in 1957.*

When the discovery was announced, it was Dr. Chauncey Patrick Coffin who announced it. He had, of course, arranged with uncanny skill to take most of the credit for himself. If it turned out to be greater than he had hoped, so much the better. His presentation was scheduled for the last night of the American College of Clinical Practitioners' annual meeting, and Coffin had fully intended it to be a bombshell.

It was. Its explosion exceeded even Dr. Coffin's wilder expectations, which took quite a bit of doing. In the end he had waded through more newspaper reporters than medical doctors as he left the hall that night. It was a heady evening for Chauncey Patrick Coffin, M.D.

Certain others were not so delighted with Coffin's bombshell.

"It's idiocy!" young Dr. Phillip Dawson wailed in the laboratory conference room the next morning. "Blind, screaming idiocy. You've gone out of your mind—that's all there is to it. Can't you see what you've done? Aside from selling your colleagues down the river, that is?" He clenched the reprint of Coffin's address in his hand and brandished it like a broadsword. "'Report on a Vaccine for the Treatment and Cure of the Common Cold,' by C. P. Coffin, et al. That's what it says—et al. My idea in the first place. Jake and I both pounding our heads on the wall for eight solid months—and now you sneak it into publication a full year before we have any business publishing a word about it."

"Really, Phillip!" Dr. Chauncey Coffin ran a pudgy hand through his snowy hair. "How ungrateful! I thought for sure you'd be delighted. An excellent presentation, I must say—terse, succinct, unequivocal—" he raised his hand—"but generously unequivocal, you understand. You should have heard the ovation—they nearly

106

went wild! And the look on Underwood's face! Worth waiting twenty years for."

"And the reporters," snapped Phillip. "Don't forget the reporters." He whirled on the small dark man sitting quietly in the corner. "How about that, Jake? Did you see the morning papers? This thief not only steals our work, he splashes it all over the countryside in red ink."

Dr. Jacob Miles coughed apologetically. "What Phillip is so stormed up about is the prematurity of it all," he said to Coffin. "After all, we've hardly had an acceptable period of clinical trial."

"Nonsense," said Coffin, glaring at Phillip. "Underwood and his men were ready to publish their discovery within another six weeks. Where would we be then? How much clinical testing do you want? Phillip, you had the worst cold of your life when you took the vaccine. Have you had any since?"

"No, of course not," said Phillip peevishly.

"Jacob, how about you? Any sniffles?"

"Oh, no. No colds."

"Well, what about those six hundred students from the University? Did I misread the reports on them?"

"No—98 per cent cured of active symptoms within twenty-four hours. Not a single recurrence. The results were just short of miraculous." Jake hesitated. "Of course, it's only been a month...."

"Month, year, century! Look at them! Six hundred of the world's most luxuriant colds, and now not even a sniffle." The chubby doctor sank down behind the desk, his ruddy face beaming. "Come, now, gentlemen, be reasonable. Think positively! There's work to be done, a great deal of work. They'll be wanting me in Washington, I imagine. Press conference in twenty minutes. Drug houses to consult with. How dare we stand in the path of Progress? We've won the greatest medical triumph of all times—the conquering of the Common Cold. We'll go down in history!"

And he was perfectly right on one point, at least.

They did go down in history.

The public response to the vaccine was little less than monumental. Of all the ailments that have tormented mankind through history none was ever more universal, more tenacious, more uniformly miserable than the common cold. It was a respecter of no barriers, boundaries, or classes; ambassadors and chambermaids

107

snuffled and sneezed in drippy-nosed unanimity. The powers in the Kremlin sniffed and blew and wept genuine tears on drafty days, while senatorial debates on earth-shaking issues paused reverently upon the unplugging of a nose, the clearing of a rhinorrheic throat. Other illnesses brought disability, even death in their wake; the common cold merely brought torment to the millions as it implacably resisted the most superhuman of efforts to curb it.

Until that chill, rainy November day when the tidings broke to the world in four-inch banner heads:

COFFIN NAILS LID ON COMMON COLD

———

"No More Coughin'" States Co-Finder of Cure

———

Sniffles sniped: single shot to save sneezers

In medical circles it was called the Coffin Multicentric Upper Respiratory Virus-Inhibiting Vaccine; but the papers could never stand for such high-sounding names, and called it, simply, "The Coffin Cure."

Below the banner heads, world-renowned feature writers expounded in reverent terms the story of the leviathan struggle of Dr. Chauncey Patrick Coffin (et al.) in solving this riddle of the ages: how, after years of failure, they ultimately succeeded in culturing the causative agent of the common cold, identifying it not as a single virus or group of viruses, but as a multicentric virus complex invading the soft mucous linings of the nose, throat and eyes, capable of altering its basic molecular structure at any time to resist efforts of the body from within, or the physician from without, to attack and dispel it; how the hypothesis was set forth by Dr. Phillip Dawson that the virus could be destroyed only by an antibody which could "freeze" the virus-complex in one form long enough for normal body defenses to dispose of the offending invader; the exhausting search for such a "crippling agent," and the final crowning success after injecting untold gallons of cold-virus material into the hides of a group of co-operative and forbearing dogs (a species which never suffered from colds, and hence endured the whole business with an air of affectionate boredom).

And finally, the testing. First, Coffin himself (who was suffering a particularly horrendous case of the affliction he sought to cure); then his assistants Phillip Dawson and Jacob Miles; then a multitude of students from the University—carefully chosen for the severity of their symptoms, the longevity of their colds, their tendency to acquire them on little or no provocation, and their utter inability to get rid of them with any known medical program.

They were a sorry spectacle, those students filing through the Coffin laboratory for three days in October: wheezing like steam shovels, snorting and sneezing and sniffling and blowing, coughing and squeaking, mute appeals glowing in their blood-shot eyes. The researchers dispensed the materials—a single shot in the right arm, a sensitivity control in the left.

With growing delight they then watched as the results came in. The sneezing stopped; the sniffling ceased. A great silence settled over the campus, in the classrooms, in the library, in classic halls. Dr. Coffin's voice returned (rather to the regret of his fellow workers) and he began bouncing about the laboratory like a small boy at a fair. Students by the dozen trooped in for checkups with noses dry and eyes bright.

In a matter of days there was no doubt left that the goal had been reached.

"But we have to be sure," Phillip Dawson had cried cautiously. "This was only a pilot test. We need mass testing now, on an entire community. We should go to the West Coast and run studies there— they have a different breed of cold out there, I hear. We'll have to see how long the immunity lasts, make sure there are no unexpected side effects...." And, muttering to himself, he fell to work with pad and pencil, calculating the program to be undertaken before publication.

But there were rumors. Underwood at Stanford, they said, had already completed his tests and was preparing a paper for publication in a matter of months. Surely with such dramatic results on the pilot tests something could be put into print. It would be tragic to lose the race for the sake of a little unnecessary caution....

Peter Dawson was adamant, but he was a voice crying in the wilderness. Chauncey Patrick Coffin was boss.

Within a week even Coffin was wondering if he had bitten off just a trifle too much. They had expected that demand for the vaccine would be great—but even the grisly memory of the early days of the Salk vaccine had not prepared them for the mobs of sneezing, wheezing red-eyed people bombarding them for the first fruits.

Clear-eyed young men from the Government Bureau pushed through crowds of local townspeople, lining the streets outside the Coffin laboratory, standing in pouring rain to raise insistent placards.

Seventeen pharmaceutical houses descended like vultures with production plans, cost-estimates, colorful graphs demonstrating proposed yield and distribution programs. Coffin was flown to Washington, where conferences labored far into the night as demands pounded their doors like a tidal wave.

One laboratory promised the vaccine in ten days; another said a week. The first actually appeared in three weeks and two days, to be soaked up in the space of three hours by the thirsty sponge of cold-weary humanity. Express planes were dispatched to Europe, to Asia, to Africa with the precious cargo, a million needles pierced a million hides, and with a huge, convulsive sneeze mankind stepped forth into a new era.

There were abstainers, of course. There always are.

"It doesn't bake eddy differets how much you talk," Ellie Dawson cried hoarsely, shaking her blonde curls. "I dod't wadt eddy cold shots."

"You're being totally unreasonable," Phillip said, glowering at his wife in annoyance. She wasn't the sweet young thing he had married, not this evening. Her eyes were puffy, her nose red and dripping. "You've had this cold for two solid months now, and there just isn't any sense to it. It's making you miserable. You can't eat, you can't breathe, you can't sleep."

"I dod't wadt eddy cold shots," she repeated stubbornly.

"But why not? Just one little needle, you'd hardly feel it."

"But I dod't like deedles!" she cried, bursting into tears. "Why dod't you leave be alode? Go take your dasty old deedles ad stick theb id people that wadt theb."

"Aw, Ellie—"

"I dod't care, I dod't like deedles!" she wailed, burying her face in his shirt.

He held her close, making comforting little noises. It was no use, he reflected sadly. Science just wasn't Ellie's long suit; she didn't know a cold vaccine from a case of smallpox, and no appeal to logic or common sense could surmount her irrational fear of hypodermics. "All right, nobody's going to make you do anything you don't want to," he said.

"Ad eddyway, thik of the poor tissue badufacturers," she sniffled, wiping her nose with a pink facial tissue. "All their little childred starvig to death."

"Say, you have got a cold," said Phillip, sniffing. "You've got on enough perfume to fell an ox." He wiped away tears and grinned at her. "Come on now, fix your face. Dinner at the Driftwood? I hear they have marvelous lamb chops."

It was a mellow evening. The lamb chops were delectable—the tastiest lamb chops he had ever eaten, he thought, even being blessed with as good a cook as Ellie for a spouse. Ellie dripped and blew continuously, but refused to go home until they had taken in a movie, and stopped by to dance a while. "I hardly ever gedt to see you eddy bore," she said. "All because of that dasty bedicide you're givig people."

It was true, of course. The work at the lab was endless. They danced, but came home early nevertheless. Phillip needed all the sleep he could get.

He awoke once during the night to a parade of sneezes from his wife, and rolled over, frowning sleepily to himself. It was ignominious, in a way—his own wife refusing the fruit of all those months of work.

And cold or no cold, she surely was using a whale of a lot of perfume.

He awoke, suddenly, began to stretch, and sat bolt upright in bed, staring wildly about the room. Pale morning sunlight drifted in the window. Downstairs he heard Ellie stirring in the kitchen.

For a moment he thought he was suffocating. He leaped out of bed, stared at the vanity table across the room. "Somebody's spilled the whole damned bottle—"

The heavy sick-sweet miasma hung like a cloud around him, drenching the room. With every breath it grew thicker. He searched the table top frantically, but there were no empty bottles. His head began to spin from the sickening effluvium.

He blinked in confusion, his hand trembling as he lit a cigarette. No need to panic, he thought. She probably knocked a bottle over when she was dressing. He took a deep puff, and burst into a paroxysm of coughing as acrid fumes burned down his throat to his lungs.

"Ellie!" He rushed into the hall, still coughing. The match smell had given way to the harsh, caustic stench of burning weeds. He stared at his cigarette in horror and threw it into the sink. The smell grew worse. He threw open the hall closet, expecting smoke to come billowing out. "Ellie! Somebody's burning down the house!"

"Whadtever are you talking about?" Ellie's voice came from the stair well. "It's just the toast I burned, silly."

He rushed down the stairs two at a time—and nearly gagged as he reached the bottom. The smell of hot, rancid grease struck him like a solid wall. It was intermingled with an oily smell of boiled and parboiled coffee, overpowering in its intensity. By the time he reached the kitchen he was holding his nose, tears pouring from his eyes. "Ellie, what are you doing in here?"

She stared at him. "I'b baking breakfast."

"But don't you smell it?"

"Sbell whadt?" said Ellie.

On the stove the automatic percolator was making small, promising noises. In the frying pan four sunnyside eggs were sizzling; half a dozen strips of bacon drained on a paper towel on the sideboard. It couldn't have looked more innocent.

Cautiously, Phillip released his nose, sniffed. The stench nearly choked him. "You mean you don't smell anything strange?"

"I did't sbell eddythig, period," said Ellie defensively.

"The coffee, the bacon—come here a minute."

She reeked—of bacon, of coffee, of burned toast, but mostly of perfume. "Did you put on any fresh perfume this morning?"

"Before breakfast? Dod't be ridiculous."

"Not even a drop?" Phillip was turning very white.

"Dot a drop."

He shook his head. "Now, wait a minute. This must be all in my mind. I'm—just imagining things, that's all. Working too hard, hysterical reaction. In a minute it'll all go away." He poured a cup of coffee, added cream and sugar.

But he couldn't get it close enough to taste it. It smelled as if it had been boiling three weeks in a rancid pot. It was the smell of coffee, all right, but a smell that was fiendishly distorted, overpoweringly, nauseatingly magnified. It pervaded the room and burned his throat and brought tears gushing to his eyes.

Slowly, realization began to dawn. He spilled the coffee as he set the cup down. The perfume. The coffee. The cigarette....

"My hat," he choked. "Get me my hat. I've got to get to the laboratory."

It got worse all the way downtown. He fought down waves of nausea as the smell of damp, rotting earth rose from his front yard in a gray cloud. The neighbor's dog dashed out to greet him, exuding the great-grandfather of all doggy odors. As Phillip waited for the bus, every passing car fouled the air with noxious fumes, gagging him, doubling him up with coughing as he dabbed at his streaming eyes.

Nobody else seemed to notice anything wrong at all.

The bus ride was a nightmare. It was a damp, rainy day; the inside of the bus smelled like the men's locker room after a big game. A bleary-eyed man with three-days' stubble on his chin flopped down in the seat next to him, and Phillip reeled back with a jolt to the job he had held in his student days, cleaning vats in the brewery.

"It'sh a great morning," Bleary-eyes breathed at him, "huh, Doc?" Phillip blanched. To top it, the man had had a breakfast of salami. In the seat ahead, a fat man held a dead cigar clamped in his mouth like a rank growth. Phillip's stomach began rolling; he sank his face into his hand, trying unobtrusively to clamp his nostrils. With a groan of deliverance he lurched off the bus at the laboratory gate.

He met Jake Miles coming up the steps. Jake looked pale, too pale.

"Morning," Phillip said weakly. "Nice day. Looks like the sun might come through."

"Yeah," said Jake. "Nice day. You—uh—feel all right this morning?"

"Fine, fine." Phillip tossed his hat in the closet, opened the incubator on his culture tubes, trying to look busy. He slammed the door after one whiff and gripped the edge of the work table with whitening knuckles. "Why?"

"Oh, nothing. Thought you looked a little peaked, was all."

They stared at each other in silence. Then, as though by signal, their eyes turned to the office at the end of the lab.

"Coffin come in yet?"

Jake nodded. "He's in there. He's got the door locked."

"I think he's going to have to open it," said Phillip.

A gray-faced Dr. Coffin unlocked the door, backed quickly toward the wall. The room reeked of kitchen deodorant. "Stay right where you are," Coffin squeaked. "Don't come a step closer. I can't see you now. I'm—I'm busy, I've got work that has to be done—"

"You're telling me," growled Phillip. He motioned Jake into the office and locked the door carefully. Then he turned to Coffin. "When did it start for you?"

Coffin was trembling. "Right after supper last night. I thought I was going to suffocate. Got up and walked the streets all night. My God, what a stench!"

"Jake?"

Dr. Miles shook his head. "Sometime this morning, I don't know when. I woke up with it."

"That's when it hit me," said Phillip.

"But I don't understand," Coffin howled. "Nobody else seems to notice anything—"

"Yet," said Phillip, "we were the first three to take the Coffin Cure, remember? You, and me and Jake. Two months ago."

Coffin's forehead was beaded with sweat. He stared at the two men in growing horror. "But what about the others?" he whispered.

"I think," said Phillip, "that we'd better find something spectacular to do in a mighty big hurry. That's what I think."

Jake Miles said, "The most important thing right now is secrecy. We mustn't let a word get out, not until we're absolutely certain."

"But what's happened?" Coffin cried. "These foul smells, everywhere. You, Phillip, you had a cigarette this morning. I can smell it clear over here, and it's bringing tears to my eyes. And if I didn't know better I'd swear neither of you had had a bath in a week. Every odor in town has suddenly turned foul—"

"Magnified, you mean," said Jake. "Perfume still smells sweet—there's just too much of it. The same with cinnamon; I tried it. Cried for half an hour, but it still smelled like cinnamon. No, I don't think the smells have changed any."

"But what, then?"

"Our noses have changed, obviously." Jake paced the floor in excitement. "Look at our dogs! They've never had colds—and they practically live by their noses. Other animals—all dependent on their senses of smell for survival—and none of them ever have anything even vaguely reminiscent of a common cold. The multicentric virus hits primates only—and it reaches its fullest parasitic powers in man alone!"

Coffin shook his head miserably. "But why this horrible stench all of a sudden? I haven't had a cold in weeks—"

"Of course not! That's just what I'm trying to say," Jake cried. "Look, why do we have any sense of smell at all? Because we have tiny olfactory nerve endings buried in the mucous membrane of our noses and throats. But we have always had the virus living there, too, colds or no colds, throughout our entire lifetime. It's always been there, anchored in the same cells, parasitizing the same sensitive tissues that carry our olfactory nerve endings, numbing them and crippling them, making them practically useless as sensory organs. No wonder we never smelled anything before! Those poor little nerve endings never had a chance!"

"Until we came along in our shining armor and destroyed the virus," said Phillip.

"Oh, we didn't destroy it. We merely stripped it of a very slippery protective mechanism against normal body defences." Jake perched on the edge of the desk, his dark face intense. "These two months since we had our shots have witnessed a battle to the death between our bodies and the virus. With the help of the vaccine, our bodies have won, that's all—stripped away the last vestiges of an invader that has been almost a part of our normal physiology since the beginning of time. And now for the first time those crippled little nerve endings are just beginning to function."

"God help us," Coffin groaned. "You think it'll get worse?"

"And worse. And still worse," said Jake.

"I wonder," said Phillip slowly, "what the anthropologists will say."

"What do you mean?"

"Maybe it was just a single mutation somewhere back there. Just a tiny change of cell structure or metabolism that left one line of primates vulnerable to an invader no other would harbor. Why else should man have begun to flower and blossom intellectually—grow to depend so much on his brains instead of his brawn that he could rise above all others? What better reason than because somewhere along the line in the world of fang and claw he suddenly lost his sense of smell?"

They stared at each other. "Well, he's got it back again now," Coffin wailed, "and he's not going to like it a bit."

"No, he surely isn't," Jake agreed. "He's going to start looking very quickly for someone to blame, I think."

They both looked at Coffin.

"Now don't be ridiculous, boys," said Coffin, turning white. "We're in this together. Phillip, it was your idea in the first place—you said so yourself! You can't leave me now—"

The telephone jangled. They heard the frightened voice of the secretary clear across the room. "Dr. Coffin? There was a student on the line just a moment ago. He—he said he was coming up to see you. Now, he said, not later."

"I'm busy," Coffin sputtered. "I can't see anyone. And I can't take any calls."

"But he's already on his way up," the girl burst out. "He was saying something about tearing you apart with his bare hands."

Coffin slammed down the receiver. His face was the color of lead. "They'll crucify me!" he sobbed. "Jake—Phillip—you've got to help me."

Phillip sighed and unlocked the door. "Send a girl down to the freezer and have her bring up all the live cold virus she can find. Get us some inoculated monkeys and a few dozen dogs." He turned to Coffin. "And stop sniveling. You're the big publicity man around here; you're going to handle the screaming masses, whether you like it or not."

"But what are you going to do?"

"I haven't the faintest idea," said Phillip, "but whatever I do is going to cost you your shirt. We're going to find out how to catch cold again if we have to die."

It was an admirable struggle, and a futile one. They sprayed their noses and throats with enough pure culture of virulent live virus to have condemned an ordinary man to a lifetime of sneezing, watery-eyed misery. They didn't develop a sniffle among them. They mixed six different strains of virus and gargled the extract, spraying themselves and every inoculated monkey they could get their hands on with the vile-smelling stuff. Not a sneeze. They injected it hypodermically, intradermally, subcutaneously, intramuscularly, and intravenously. They drank it. They bathed in the stuff.

But they didn't catch a cold.

"Maybe it's the wrong approach," Jake said one morning. "Our body defenses are keyed up to top performance right now. Maybe if we break them down we can get somewhere."

116

They plunged down that alley with grim abandon. They starved themselves. They forced themselves to stay awake for days on end, until exhaustion forced their eyes closed in spite of all they could do. They carefully devised vitamin-free, protein-free, mineral-free diets that tasted like library paste and smelled worse. They wore wet clothes and sopping shoes to work, turned off the heat and threw windows open to the raw winter air. Then they resprayed themselves with the live cold virus and waited reverently for the sneezing to begin.

It didn't. They stared at each other in gathering gloom. They'd never felt better in their lives.

Except for the smells, of course. They'd hoped that they might, presently, get used to them. They didn't. Every day it grew a little worse. They began smelling smells they never dreamed existed— noxious smells, cloying smells, smells that drove them gagging to the sinks. Their nose-plugs were rapidly losing their effectiveness. Mealtimes were nightmarish ordeals; they lost weight with alarming speed.

But they didn't catch cold.

"I think you should all be locked up," Ellie Dawson said severely as she dragged her husband, blue-faced and shivering, out of an icy shower one bitter morning. "You've lost your wits. You need to be protected against yourselves, that's what you need."

"You don't understand," Phillip moaned. "We've got to catch cold."

"Why?" Ellie snapped angrily. "Suppose you don't—what's going to happen?"

"We had three hundred students march on the laboratory today," Phillip said patiently. "The smells were driving them crazy, they said. They couldn't even bear to be close to their best friends. They wanted something done about it, or else they wanted blood. Tomorrow we'll have them back and three hundred more. And they were just the pilot study! What's going to happen when fifteen million people find their noses going bad on them?" He shuddered. "Have you seen the papers? People are already going around sniffing like bloodhounds. And now we're finding out what a thorough job we did. We can't crack it, Ellie. We can't even get a toe hold. Those antibodies are just doing too good a job."

"Well, maybe you can find some unclebodies to take care of

them," Ellie offered vaguely.

"Look, don't make bad jokes—"

"I'm not making jokes! All I want is a husband back who doesn't complain about how everything smells, and eats the dinners I cook, and doesn't stand around in cold showers at six in the morning."

"I know it's miserable," he said helplessly. "But I don't know how to stop it."

He found Jake and Coffin in tight-lipped conference when he reached the lab. "I can't do it anymore," Coffin was saying. "I've begged them for time. I've threatened them. I've promised them everything but my upper plate. I can't face them again, I just can't."

"We only have a few days left," Jake said grimly. "If we don't come up with something, we're goners."

Phillip's jaw suddenly sagged as he stared at them. "You know what I think?" he said suddenly. "I think we've been prize idiots. We've gotten so rattled we haven't used our heads. And all the time it's been sitting there blinking at us!"

"What are you talking about?" snapped Jake.

"Unclebodies," said Phillip.

"Oh, great God!"

"No, I'm serious." Phillip's eyes were very bright. "How many of those students do you think you can corral to help us?"

Coffin gulped. "Six hundred. They're out there in the street right now, howling for a lynching."

"All right, I want them in here. And I want some monkeys. Monkeys with colds, the worse colds the better."

"Do you have any idea what you're doing?" asked Jake.

"None in the least," said Phillip happily, "except that it's never been done before. But maybe it's time we tried following our noses for a while."

The tidal wave began to break two days later ... only a few people here, a dozen there, but enough to confirm the direst newspaper predictions. The boomerang was completing its circle.

At the laboratory the doors were kept barred, the telephones disconnected. Within, there was a bustle of feverish—if odorous— activity. For the three researchers, the olfactory acuity had reached agonizing proportions. Even the small gas masks Phillip had devised could no longer shield them from the constant barrage of violent odors.

But the work went on in spite of the smell. Truckloads of monkeys arrived at the lab—cold-ridden monkeys, sneezing, coughing, weeping, wheezing monkeys by the dozen. Culture trays bulged with tubes, overflowed the incubators and work tables. Each day six hundred angry students paraded through the lab, arms exposed, mouths open, grumbling but co-operating.

At the end of the first week, half the monkeys were cured of their colds and were quite unable to catch them back; the other half had new colds and couldn't get rid of them. Phillip observed this fact with grim satisfaction, and went about the laboratory mumbling to himself.

Two days later he burst forth jubilantly, lugging a sad-looking puppy under his arm. It was like no other puppy in the world. This puppy was sneezing and snuffling with a perfect howler of a cold.

The day came when they injected a tiny droplet of milky fluid beneath the skin of Phillip's arm, and then got the virus spray and gave his nose and throat a liberal application. Then they sat back and waited.

They were still waiting three days later.

"It was a great idea," Jake said gloomily, flipping a bulging notebook closed with finality. "It just didn't work, was all."

Phillip nodded. Both men had grown thin, with pouches under their eyes. Jake's right eye had begun to twitch uncontrollably whenever anyone came within three yards of him. "We can't go on like this, you know. The people are going wild."

"Where's Coffin?"

"He collapsed three days ago. Nervous prostration. He kept having dreams about hangings."

Phillip sighed. "Well, I suppose we'd better just face it. Nice knowing you, Jake. Pity it had to be this way."

"It was a great try, old man. A great try."

"Ah, yes. Nothing like going down in a blaze of—"

Phillip stopped dead, his eyes widening. His nose began to twitch. He took a gasp, a larger gasp, as a long-dead reflex came sleepily to life, shook its head, reared back ...

Phillip sneezed.

He sneezed for ten minutes without a pause, until he lay on the floor blue-faced and gasping for air. He caught hold of Jake, wringing his hand as tears gushed from his eyes. He gave his nose an enormous blow, and headed shakily for the telephone.

"It was a sipple edough pridciple," he said later to Ellie as she spread mustard on his chest and poured more warm water into his foot bath. "The Cure itself depedded upod it—the adtiged-adtibody reactiod. We had the adtibody agaidst the virus, all ridght; what we had to find was sobe kide of adtibody agaidst the adtibody." He sneezed violently, and poured in nose drops with a happy grin.

"Will they be able to make it fast enough?"

"Just aboudt fast edough for people to get good ad eager to catch cold agaid," said Phillip. "There's odly wud little hitch...."

Ellie Dawson took the steaks from the grill and set them, still sizzling, on the dinner table. "Hitch?"

Phillip nodded as he chewed the steak with a pretence of enthusiasm. It tasted like slightly damp K-ration.

"This stuff we've bade does a real good job. Just a little too good." He wiped his nose and reached for a fresh tissue.

"I bay be wrog, but I thik I've got this cold for keeps," he said sadly. "Udless I cad fide ad adtibody agaidst the adtibody agaidst the adtibody—".

Project Mastodon
By Clifford D. Simak

Editor's note: Published in Galaxy Science Fiction *in March 1955, this Clifford Donald Simak story was adapted for radio in 1956, appearing on NBC's "X Minus One" series. Simak (1904-1988), winner of three Hugo awards and one Nebula award, is perhaps best known for his landmark 1964 novel* Way Station. *In "Project Mastodon," Simak tells another entertaining time travel tale.*

I

The chief of protocol said, "Mr. Hudson of—ah—Mastodonia."

The secretary of state held out his hand. "I'm glad to see you, Mr. Hudson. I understand you've been here several times."

"That's right," said Hudson. "I had a hard time making your people believe I was in earnest."

"And are you, Mr. Hudson?"

"Believe me, sir, I would not try to fool you."

"And this Mastodonia," said the secretary, reaching down to tap the document upon the desk. "You will pardon me, but I've never heard of it."

"It's a new nation," Hudson explained, "but quite legitimate. We have a constitution, a democratic form of government, duly elected officials, and a code of laws. We are a free, peace-loving people and we are possessed of a vast amount of natural resources and—"

"Please tell me, sir," interrupted the secretary, "just where are you located?"

"Technically, you are our nearest neighbors."

"But that is ridiculous!" exploded Protocol.

"Not at all," insisted Hudson. "If you will give me a moment, Mr. Secretary, I have considerable evidence."

He brushed the fingers of Protocol off his sleeve and stepped forward to the desk, laying down the portfolio he carried.

"Go ahead, Mr. Hudson," said the secretary. "Why don't we all sit down and be comfortable while we talk this over?"

"You have my credentials, I see. Now here is a propos—"

"I have a document signed by a certain Wesley Adams."

"He's our first president," said Hudson. "Our George

121

Washington, you might say."

"What is the purpose of this visit, Mr. Hudson?"

"We'd like to establish diplomatic relations. We think it would be to our mutual benefit. After all, we are a sister republic in perfect sympathy with your policies and aims. We'd like to negotiate trade agreements and we'd be grateful for some Point Four aid."

The secretary smiled. "Naturally. Who doesn't?"

"We're prepared to offer something in return," Hudson told him stiffly. "For one thing, we could offer sanctuary."

"Sanctuary!"

"I understand," said Hudson, "that in the present state of international tensions, a foolproof sanctuary is not something to be sneezed at."

The secretary turned stone cold. "I'm an extremely busy man."

Protocol took Hudson firmly by the arm. "Out you go."

General Leslie Bowers put in a call to State and got the secretary.

"I don't like to bother you, Herb," he said, "but there's something I want to check. Maybe you can help me."

"Glad to help you if I can."

"There's a fellow hanging around out here at the Pentagon, trying to get in to see me. Said I was the only one he'd talk to, but you know how it is."

"I certainly do."

"Name of Huston or Hudson or something like that."

"He was here just an hour or so ago," said the secretary. "Crackpot sort of fellow."

"He's gone now?"

"Yes. I don't think he'll be back."

"Did he say where you could reach him?"

"No, I don't believe he did."

"How did he strike you? I mean what kind of impression did you get of him?"

"I told you. A crackpot."

"I suppose he is. He said something to one of the colonels that got me worrying. Can't pass up anything, you know—not in the Dirty Tricks Department. Even if it's crackpot, these days you got to have a look at it."

"He offered sanctuary," said the secretary indignantly. "Can you imagine that!"

"He's been making the rounds, I guess," the general said. "He was over at AEC. Told them some sort of tale about knowing where there were vast uranium deposits. It was the AEC that told me he was heading your way."

"We get them all the time. Usually we can ease them out. This Hudson was just a little better than the most of them. He got in to see me."

"He told the colonel something about having a plan that would enable us to establish secret bases anywhere we wished, even in the territory of potential enemies. I know it sounds crazy...."

"Forget it, Les."

"You're probably right," said the general, "but this idea sends me. Can you imagine the look on their Iron Curtain faces?"

The scared little government clerk, darting conspiratorial glances all about him, brought the portfolio to the FBI.

"I found it in a bar down the street," he told the man who took him in tow. "Been going there for years. And I found this portfolio laying in the booth. I saw the man who must have left it there and I tried to find him later, but I couldn't."

"How do you know he left it there?"

"I just figured he did. He left the booth just as I came in and it was sort of dark in there and it took a minute to see this thing laying there. You see, I always take the same booth every day and Joe sees me come in and he brings me the usual and—"

"You saw this man leave the booth you usually sit in?"

"That's right."

"Then you saw the portfolio."

"Yes, sir."

"You tried to find the man, thinking it must have been his."

"That's exactly what I did."

"But by the time you went to look for him, he had disappeared."

"That's the way it was."

"Now tell me—why did you bring it here? Why didn't you turn it in to the management so the man could come back and claim it?"

"Well, sir, it was like this. I had a drink or two and I was wondering all the time what was in that portfolio. So finally I took a peek and—"

"And what you saw decided you to bring it here to us."

"That's right. I saw—"

"Don't tell me what you saw. Give me your name and address and don't say anything about this. You understand that we're grateful to you for thinking of us, but we'd rather you said nothing."

"Mum's the word," the little clerk assured him, full of vast importance.

The FBI phoned Dr. Ambrose Amberly, Smithsonian expert on paleontology.

"We've got something, Doctor, that we'd like you to have a look at. A lot of movie film."

"I'll be most happy to. I'll come down as soon as I get clear. End of the week, perhaps?"

"This is very urgent, Doctor. Damnest thing you ever saw. Big, shaggy elephants and tigers with teeth down to their necks. There's a beaver the size of a bear."

"Fakes," said Amberly, disgusted. "Clever gadgets. Camera angles."

"That's what we thought first, but there are no gadgets, no camera angles. This is the real McCoy."

"I'm on my way," the paleontologist said, hanging up.

Snide item in smug, smartaleck gossip column: Saucers are passé at the Pentagon. There's another mystery that's got the high brass very high.

II

President Wesley Adams and Secretary of State John Cooper sat glumly under a tree in the capital of Mastodonia and waited for the ambassador extraordinary to return.

"I tell you, Wes," said Cooper, who, under various pseudonyms, was also the secretaries of commerce, treasury and war, "this is a crazy thing we did. What if Chuck can't get back? They might throw him in jail or something might happen to the time unit or the helicopter. We should have gone along."

"We had to stay," Adams said. "You know what would happen to this camp and our supplies if we weren't around here to guard them."

"The only thing that's given us any trouble is that old mastodon. If he comes around again, I'm going to take a skillet and bang him in the brisket."

"That isn't the only reason, either," said President Adams, "and you know it. We can't go deserting this nation now that we've created it. We have to keep possession. Just planting a flag and saying it's ours wouldn't be enough. We might be called upon for proof that we've established residence. Something like the old homestead laws, you know."

"We'll establish residence sure enough," growled Secretary Cooper, "if something happens to that time unit or the helicopter."

"You think they'll do it, Johnny?"

"Who do what?"

"The United States. Do you think they'll recognize us?"

"Not if they know who we are."

"That's what I'm afraid of."

"Chuck will talk them into it. He can talk the skin right off a cat."

"Sometimes I think we're going at this wrong. Sure, Chuck's got the long-range view and I suppose it's best. But maybe what we ought to do is grab a good, fast profit and get out of here. We could take in hunting parties at ten thousand a head or maybe we could lease it to a movie company."

"We can do all that and do it legally and with full protection," Cooper told him, "if we can get ourselves recognized as a sovereign nation. If we negotiate a mutual defense pact, no one would dare get hostile because we could squawk to Uncle Sam."

"All you say is true," Adams agreed, "but there are going to be questions. It isn't just a matter of walking into Washington and getting recognition. They'll want to know about us, such as our population. What if Chuck has to tell them it's a total of three persons?"

Cooper shook his head. "He wouldn't answer that way, Wes. He'd duck the question or give them some diplomatic double-talk. After all, how can we be sure there are only three of us? We took over the whole continent, remember."

"You know well enough, Johnny, there are no other humans back here in North America. The farthest back any scientist will place the migrations from Asia is 30,000 years. They haven't got here yet."

"Maybe we should have done it differently," mused Cooper. "Maybe we should have included the whole world in our proclamation, not just the continent. That way, we could claim quite a population."

"It wouldn't have held water. Even as it is, we went a little further than precedent allows. The old explorers usually laid claim to certain watersheds. They'd find a river and lay claim to all the territory drained by the river. They didn't go grabbing off whole continents."

"That's because they were never sure of exactly what they had," said Cooper. "We are. We have what you might call the advantage of hindsight."

He leaned back against the tree and stared across the land. It was a pretty place, he thought—the rolling ridges covered by vast grazing areas and small groves, the forest-covered, ten-mile river valley. And everywhere one looked, the grazing herds of mastodon, giant bison and wild horses, with the less gregarious fauna scattered hit and miss.

Old Buster, the troublesome mastodon, a lone bull which had been probably run out of a herd by a younger rival, stood at the edge of a grove a quarter-mile away. He had his head down and was curling and uncurling his trunk in an aimless sort of way while he teetered slowly in a lazy-crazy fashion by lifting first one foot and then another.

The old cuss was lonely, Cooper told himself. That was why he hung around like a homeless dog—except that he was too big and awkward to have much pet-appeal and, more than likely, his temper was unstable.

The afternoon sun was pleasantly warm and the air, it seemed to Cooper, was the freshest he had ever smelled. It was, altogether, a very pleasant place, an Indian-summer sort of land, ideal for a Sunday picnic or a camping trip.

The breeze was just enough to float out from its flagstaff before the tent the national banner of Mastodonia—a red rampant mastodon upon a field of green.

"You know, Johnny," said Adams, "there's one thing that worries me a lot. If we're going to base our claim on precedent, we may be way off base. The old explorers always claimed their discoveries for their nations or their king, never for themselves."

"The principle was entirely different," Cooper told him. "Nobody ever did anything for himself in those days. Everyone was always under someone else's protection. The explorers either were financed by their governments or were sponsored by them or operated under a royal charter or a patent. With us, it's different. Ours is a private enterprise. You dreamed up the time unit and built it. The three of us chipped in to buy the helicopter. We've paid all of our expenses out of our own pockets. We never got a dime from anyone. What we found is ours."

"I hope you're right," said Adams uneasily.

Old Buster had moved out from the grove and was shuffling warily toward the camp. Adams picked up the rifle that lay across his knees.

"Wait," said Cooper sharply. "Maybe he's just bluffing. It would be a shame to plaster him; he's such a nice old guy."

Adams half raised the rifle.

"I'll give him three steps more," he announced. "I've had enough of him."

Suddenly a roar burst out of the air just above their heads. The two leaped to their feet.

"It's Chuck!" Cooper yelled. "He's back!"

The helicopter made a half-turn of the camp and came rapidly to Earth.

Trumpeting with terror, Old Buster was a dwindling dot far down the grassy ridge.

III

They built the nightly fires circling the camp to keep out the animals.

"It'll be the death of me yet," said Adams wearily, "cutting all this wood."

"We have to get to work on that stockade," Cooper said. "We've fooled around too long. Some night, fire or no fire, a herd of mastodon will come busting in here and if they ever hit the helicopter, we'll be dead ducks. It wouldn't take more than just five seconds to turn us into Robinson Crusoes of the Pleistocene."

"Well, now that this recognition thing has petered out on us," said Adams, "maybe we can get down to business."

"Trouble is," Cooper answered, "we spent about the last of our money on the chain saw to cut this wood and on Chuck's trip to Washington. To build a stockade, we need a tractor. We'd kill ourselves if we tried to rassle that many logs bare-handed."

"Maybe we could catch some of those horses running around out there."

"Have you ever broken a horse?"

"No, that's one thing I never tried."

"Me, either. How about you, Chuck?"

"Not me," said the ex-ambassador extraordinary bluntly.

Cooper squatted down beside the coals of the cooking fire and twirled the spit. Upon the spit were three grouse and half a dozen quail. The huge coffee pot was sending out a nose-tingling aroma. Biscuits were baking in the reflector.

"We've been here six weeks," he said, "and we're still living in a tent and cooking on an open fire. We better get busy and get something done."

"The stockade first," said Adams, "and that means a tractor."

"We could use the helicopter."

"Do you want to take the chance? That's our getaway. Once something happens to it...."

"I guess not," Cooper admitted, gulping.

"We could use some of that Point Four aid right now," commented Adams.

"They threw me out," said Hudson. "Everywhere I went, sooner or later they got around to throwing me out. They were real organized about it."

"Well, we tried," Adams said.

"And to top it off," added Hudson, "I had to go and lose all that film and now we'll have to waste our time taking more of it. Personally, I don't ever want to let another saber-tooth get that close to me while I hold the camera."

"You didn't have a thing to worry about," Adams objected. "Johnny was right there behind you with the gun."

"Yeah, with the muzzle about a foot from my head when he let go."

"I stopped him, didn't I?" demanded Cooper.

"With his head right in my lap."

"Maybe we won't have to take any more pictures," Adams suggested.

"We'll have to," Cooper said. "There are sportsmen up ahead who'd fork over ten thousand bucks easy for two weeks of hunting here. But before we could sell them on it, we'd have to show them movies. That scene with the saber-tooth would cinch it."

"If it didn't scare them off," Hudson pointed out. "The last few feet showed nothing but the inside of his throat."

Ex-ambassador Hudson looked unhappy. "I don't like the whole setup. As soon as we bring someone in, the news is sure to leak. And once the word gets out, there'll be guys lying in ambush for us— maybe even nations—scheming to steal the know-how, legally or violently. That's what scares me the most about those films I lost. Someone will find them and they may guess what it's all about, but I'm hoping they either won't believe it or can't manage to trace us."

"We could swear the hunting parties to secrecy," said Cooper.

"How could a sportsman keep still about the mounted head of a saber-tooth or a record piece of ivory?" And the same thing would apply to anyone we approached. Some university could raise dough to send a team of scientists back here and a movie company would cough up plenty to use this place as a location for a caveman epic. But it wouldn't be worth a thing to either of them if they couldn't tell about it.

"Now if we could have gotten recognition as a nation, we'd have been all set. We could make our own laws and regulations and be able to enforce them. We could bring in settlers and establish trade. We could exploit our natural resources. It would all be legal and aboveboard. We could tell who we were and where we were and what we had to offer."

"We aren't licked yet," said Adams. "There's a lot that we can do. Those river hills are covered with ginseng. We can each dig a dozen pounds a day. There's good money in the root."

"Ginseng root," Cooper said, "is peanuts. We need big money."

"Or we could trap," offered Adams. "The place is alive with beaver."

"Have you taken a good look at those beaver? They're about the size of a St. Bernard."

"All the better. Think how much just one pelt would bring."

"No dealer would believe that it was beaver. He'd think you were trying to pull a fast one on him. And there are only a few states that allow beaver to be trapped. To sell the pelts—even if you could— you'd have to take out licenses in each of those states."

"Those mastodon carry a lot of ivory," said Cooper. "And if we wanted to go north, we'd find mammoths that would carry even more...."

"And get socked into the jug for ivory smuggling?"

They sat, all three of them, staring at the fire, not finding anything to say.

The moaning complaint of a giant hunting cat came from somewhere up the river.

IV

Hudson lay in his sleeping bag, staring at the sky. It bothered him a lot. There was not one familiar constellation, not one star that he could name with any certainty. This juggling of the stars, he thought, emphasized more than anything else in this ancient land the vast gulf of years which lay between him and the Earth where he had been— or would be—born.

A hundred and fifty thousand years, Adams had said, give or take ten thousand. There just was no way to know. Later on, there might be. A measurement of the stars and a comparison with their positions in the twentieth century might be one way of doing it. But at the moment, any figure could be no more than a guess.

The time machine was not something that could be tested for calibration or performance. As a matter of fact, there was no way to test it. They had not been certain, he remembered, the first time they had used it, that it would really work. There had been no way to find out. When it worked, you knew it worked. And if it hadn't worked, there would have been no way of knowing beforehand that it wouldn't.

Adams had been sure, of course, but that had been because he had absolute reliance in the half-mathematical, half-philosophic concepts he had worked out—concepts that neither Hudson nor Cooper could come close to understanding.

That had always been the way it had been, even when they were kids, with Wes dreaming up the deals that he and Johnny carried out. Back in those days, too, they had used time travel in their play. Out in Johnny's back yard, they had rigged up a time machine out of a wonderful collection of salvaged junk—a wooden crate, an empty five-gallon paint pail, a battered coffee maker, a bunch of discarded copper tubing, a busted steering wheel and other odds and ends. In it, they had "traveled" back to Indian-before-the-white-man land and mammoth-land and dinosaur-land and the slaughter, he remembered, had been wonderfully appalling.

But, in reality, it had been much different. There was much more to it than gunning down the weird fauna that one found.

And they should have known there would be, for they had talked about it often.

He thought of the bull session back in university and the little, usually silent kid who sat quietly in the corner, a law-school student whose last name had been Pritchard.

And after sitting silently for some time, this Pritchard kid had spoken up: "If you guys ever do travel in time, you'll run up against more than you bargain for. I don't mean the climate or the terrain or the fauna, but the economics and the politics."

They all jeered at him, Hudson remembered, and then had gone on with their talk. And after a short while, the talk had turned to women, as it always did.

He wondered where that quiet man might be. Someday, Hudson told himself, I'll have to look him up and tell him he was right.

We did it wrong, he thought. There were so many other ways we might have done it, but we'd been so sure and greedy—greedy for the triumph and the glory—and now there was no easy way to collect.

On the verge of success, they could have sought out help, gone to some large industrial concern or an educational foundation or even to the government. Like historic explorers, they could have obtained subsidization and sponsorship. Then they would have had protection, funds to do a proper job and they need not have operated on their present shoestring—one beaten-up helicopter and one time unit. They could have had several and at least one standing by in the twentieth century as a rescue unit, should that be necessary.

But that would have meant a bargain, perhaps a very hard one, and sharing with someone who had contributed nothing but the money. And there was more than money in a thing like this—there were twenty years of dreams and a great idea and the dedication to that great idea—years of work and years of disappointment and an almost fanatical refusal to give up.

Even so, thought Hudson, they had figured well enough. There had been many chances to make blunders and they'd made relatively few. All they lacked, in the last analysis, was backing.

Take the helicopter, for example. It was the one satisfactory vehicle for time traveling. You had to get up in the air to clear whatever upheavals and subsidences there had been through geologic ages. The helicopter took you up and kept you clear and gave you a chance to pick a proper landing place. Travel without it and, granting you were lucky with land surfaces, you still might materialize in the heart of some great tree or end up in a swamp or the middle of a herd of startled, savage beasts. A plane would have done as well, but back in this world, you couldn't land a plane—or you couldn't be certain that you could. A helicopter, though, could land almost anywhere.

In the time-distance they had traveled, they almost certainly had been lucky, although one could not be entirely sure just how great a part of it was luck. Wes had felt that he had not been working as blindly as it sometimes might appear. He had calibrated the unit for jumps of 50,000 years. Finer calibration, he had said realistically, would have to wait for more developmental work.

Using the 50,000-year calibrations, they had figured it out. One jump (conceding that the calibration was correct) would have landed them at the end of the Wisconsin glacial period; two jumps, at its beginning. The third would set them down toward the end of the Sangamon Interglacial and apparently it had—give or take ten thousand years or so.

They had arrived at a time when the climate did not seem to vary greatly, either hot or cold. The flora was modern enough to give them a homelike feeling. The fauna, modern and Pleistocenic, overlapped. And the surface features were little altered from the twentieth century. The rivers ran along familiar paths, the hills and bluffs looked much the same. In this corner of the Earth, at least, 150,000 years had not changed things greatly.

Boyhood dreams, Hudson thought, were wondrous. It was not often that three men who had daydreamed in their youth could follow it out to its end. But they had and here they were.

Johnny was on watch, and it was Hudson's turn next, and he'd better get to sleep. He closed his eyes, then opened them again for another look at the unfamiliar stars. The east, he saw, was flushed with silver light. Soon the Moon would rise, which was good. A man could keep a better watch when the Moon was up.

He woke suddenly, snatched upright and into full awareness by the marrow-chilling clamor that slashed across the night. The very air seemed curdled by the savage racket and, for a moment, he sat numbed by it. Then, slowly, it seemed—his brain took the noise and separated it into two distinct but intermingled categories, the deadly screaming of a cat and the maddened trumpeting of a mastodon.

The Moon was up and the countryside was flooded by its light. Cooper, he saw, was out beyond the watchfires, standing there and watching, with his rifle ready. Adams was scrambling out of his sleeping bag, swearing softly to himself. The cooking fire had burned down to a bed of mottled coals, but the watchfires still were burning and the helicopter, parked within their circle, picked up the glint of flames.

"It's Buster," Adams told him angrily. "I'd know that bellowing of his anywhere. He's done nothing but parade up and down and bellow ever since we got here. And now he seems to have gone out and found himself a saber-tooth."

Hudson zipped down his sleeping bag, grabbed up his rifle and jumped to his feet, following Adams in a silent rush to where Cooper stood.

Cooper motioned at them. "Don't break it up. You'll never see the like of it again."

Adams brought his rifle up.

Cooper knocked the barrel down.

"You fool!" he shouted. "You want them turning on us?"

Two hundred yards away stood the mastodon and, on his back, the screeching saber-tooth. The great beast reared into the air and came down with a jolt, bucking to unseat the cat, flailing the air with his massive trunk. And as he bucked, the cat struck and struck again with his gleaming teeth, aiming for the spine.

Then the mastodon crashed head downward, as if to turn a somersault, rolled and was on his feet again, closer to them now than he had been before. The huge cat had sprung off.

For a moment, the two stood facing one another. Then the tiger charged, a flowing streak of motion in the moonlight. Buster wheeled away and the cat, leaping, hit his shoulder, clawed wildly and slid off. The mastodon whipped to the attack, tusks slashing, huge feet stamping. The cat, caught a glancing blow by one of the tusks, screamed and leaped up, to land in spread-eagle fashion upon Buster's head.

Maddened with pain and fright, blinded by the tiger's raking

133

claws, the old mastodon ran—straight toward the camp. And as he ran, he grasped the cat in his trunk and tore him from his hold, lifted him high and threw him.

"Look out!" yelled Cooper and brought his rifle up and fired.

For an instant, Hudson saw it all as if it were a single scene, motionless, one frame snatched from a fantastic movie epic—the charging mastodon, with the tiger lifted and the sound track one great blast of bloodthirsty bedlam.

Then the scene dissolved in a blur of motion. He felt his rifle thud against his shoulder, knowing he had fired, but not hearing the explosion. And the mastodon was almost on top of him, bearing down like some mighty and remorseless engine of blind destruction.

He flung himself to one side and the giant brushed past him. Out of the tail of his eye, he saw the thrown saber-tooth crash to Earth within the circle of the watch fires.

He brought his rifle up again and caught the area behind Buster's ear within his sights. He pressed the trigger. The mastodon staggered, then regained his stride and went rushing on. He hit one of the watch fires dead center and went through it, scattering coals and burning brands.

Then there was a thud and the screeching clang of metal.

"Oh, no!" shouted Hudson.

Rushing forward, they stopped inside the circle of the fires.

The helicopter lay tilted at a crazy angle. One of its rotor blades was crumpled. Half across it, as if he might have fallen as he tried to bull his mad way over it, lay the mastodon.

Something crawled across the ground toward them, its spitting, snarling mouth gaping in the firelight, its back broken, hind legs trailing.

Calmly, without a word, Adams put a bullet into the head of the saber-tooth.

V

General Leslie Bowers rose from his chair and paced up and down the room. He stopped to bang the conference table with a knotted fist.

"You can't do it," he bawled at them. "You can't kill the project. I know there's something to it. We can't give it up!"

"But it's been ten years, General," said the secretary of the army. "If they were coming back, they'd be here by now."

The general stopped his pacing, stiffened. Who did that little civilian squirt think he was, talking to the military in that tone of voice!

"We know how you feel about it, General," said the chairman of the joint chiefs of staff. "I think we all recognize how deeply you're involved. You've blamed yourself all these years and there is no need of it. After all, there may be nothing to it."

"Sir," said the general, "I know there's something to it. I thought so at the time, even when no one else did. And what we've turned up since serves to bear me out. Let's take a look at these three men of ours. We knew almost nothing of them at the time, but we know them now. I've traced out their lives from the time that they were born until they disappeared—and I might add that, on the chance it might be all a hoax, we've searched for them for years and we've found no trace at all.

"I've talked with those who knew them and I've studied their scholastic and military records. I've arrived at the conclusion that if any three men could do it, they were the ones who could. Adams was the brains and the other two were the ones who carried out the things that he dreamed up. Cooper was a bulldog sort of man who could keep them going and it would be Hudson who would figure out the angles.

"And they knew the angles, gentlemen. They had it all doped out.

"What Hudson tried here in Washington is substantial proof of that. But even back in school, they were thinking of those angles. I talked some years ago to a lawyer in New York, name of Pritchard. He told me that even back in university, they talked of the economic and political problems that they might face if they ever cracked what they were working at.

"Wesley Adams was one of our brightest young scientific men. His record at the university and his war work bears that out. After the war, there were at least a dozen jobs he could have had. But he wasn't interested. And I'll tell you why he wasn't. He had something bigger—something he wanted to work on. So he and these two others went off by themselves—"

"You think he was working on a temporal—" the army secretary cut in.

"He was working on a time machine," roared the general. "I don't know about this 'temporal' business. Just plain 'time machine' is good enough for me."

"Let's calm down, General," said the JCS chairman, "After all, there's no need to shout."

The general nodded. "I'm sorry, sir. I get all worked up about this. I've spent the last ten years with it. As you say, I'm trying to make up for what I failed to do ten years ago. I should have talked to Hudson. I was busy, sure, but not that busy. It's an official state of mind that we're too busy to see anyone and I plead guilty on that score. And now that you're talking about closing the project—"

"It's costing us money," said the army secretary.

"And we have no direct evidence," pointed out the JCS chairman.

"I don't know what you want," snapped the general. "If there was any man alive who could crack time, that man was Wesley Adams. We found where he worked. We found the workshop and we talked to neighbors who said there was something funny going on and—"

"But ten years, General!" the army secretary protested.

"Hudson came here, bringing us the greatest discovery in all history, and we kicked him out. After that, do you expect them to come crawling back to us?"

"You think they went to someone else?"

"They wouldn't do that. They know what the thing they have found would mean. They wouldn't sell us out."

"Hudson came with a preposterous proposition," said the man from the state department.

"They had to protect themselves!" yelled the general. "If you had discovered a virgin planet with its natural resources intact, what would you do about it? Come trotting down here and hand it over to a government that's too 'busy' to recognize—"

"General!"

"Yes, sir," apologized the general tiredly. "I wish you gentlemen could see my view of it, how it all fits together. First there were the films and we have the word of a dozen competent paleontologists that it's impossible to fake anything as perfect as those films. But even granting that they could be, there are certain differences that no one would ever think of faking, because no one ever knew. Who, as an example, would put lynx tassels on the ears of a saber-tooth? Who

136

would know that young mastodon were black?

"And the location. I wonder if you've forgotten that we tracked down the location of Adams' workshop from those films alone. They gave us clues so positive that we didn't even hesitate—we drove straight to the old deserted farm where Adams and his friends had worked. Don't you see how it all fits together?"

"I presume," the man from the state department said nastily, "that you even have an explanation as to why they chose that particular location."

"You thought you had me there," said the general, "but I have an answer. A good one. The southwestern corner of Wisconsin is a geologic curiosity. It was missed by all the glaciations. Why, we do not know. Whatever the reason, the glaciers came down on both sides of it and far to the south of it and left it standing there, a little island in a sea of ice.

"And another thing: Except for a time in the Triassic, that same area of Wisconsin has always been dry land. That and a few other spots are the only areas in North America which have not, time and time again, been covered by water. I don't think it necessary to point out the comfort it would be to an experimental traveler in time to be certain that, in almost any era he might hit, he'd have dry land beneath him."

The economics expert spoke up: "We've given this matter a lot of study and, while we do not feel ourselves competent to rule upon the possibility or impossibility of time travel, there are some observations I should like, at some time, to make."

"Go ahead right now," said the JCS chairman.

"We see one objection to the entire matter. One of the reasons, naturally, that we had some interest in it is that, if true, it would give us an entire new planet to exploit, perhaps more wisely than we've done in the past. But the thought occurs that any planet has only a certain grand total of natural resources. If we go into the past and exploit them, what effect will that have upon what is left of those resources for use in the present? Wouldn't we, in doing this, be robbing ourselves of our own heritage?"

"That contention," said the AEC chairman, "wouldn't hold true in every case. Quite the reverse, in fact. We know that there was, in some geologic ages in the past, a great deal more uranium than we have today. Go back far enough and you'd catch that uranium before it turned into lead. In southwestern Wisconsin, there is a lot of lead. Hudson told us he knew the location of vast uranium deposits and we thought he was a crackpot talking through his hat. If we'd known—let's be fair about this—if we had known and believed him about going back in time, we'd have snapped him up at once and all this would not have happened."

"It wouldn't hold true with forests, either," said the chairman of the JCS. "Or with pastures or with crops."

The economics expert was slightly flushed. "There is another thing," he said. "If we go back in time and colonize the land we find there, what would happen when that—well, let's call it retroactive—when that retroactive civilization reaches the beginning of our historic period? What will result from that cultural collision? Will our history change? Is what has happened false? Is all—"

"That's all poppycock!" the general shouted. "That and this other talk about using up resources. Whatever we did in the past—or are about to do—has been done already. I've lain awake nights, mister, thinking about all these things and there is no answer, believe me, except the one I give you. The question which faces us here is an immediate one. Do we give all this up or do we keep on watching that Wisconsin farm, waiting for them to come back? Do we keep on trying to find, independently, the process or formula or method that Adams found for traveling in time?"

"We've had no luck in our research so far, General," said the quiet physicist who sat at the table's end. "If you were not so sure and if the evidence were not so convincing that it had been done by Adams, I'd say flatly that it is impossible. We have no approach which holds any hope at all. What we've done so far, you might best describe as flounder. But if Adams turned the trick, it must be possible. There may be, as a matter of fact, more ways than one. We'd like to keep on trying."

"Not one word of blame has been put on you for your failure," the chairman told the physicist. "That you could do it seems to be more than can be humanly expected. If Adams did it—if he did, I say—it must have been simply that he blundered on an avenue of research no other man has thought of."

"You will recall," said the general, "that the research program, even from the first, was thought of strictly as a gamble. Our one hope was, and must remain, that they will return."

"It would have been so much simpler all around," the state department man said, "if Adams had patented his method."

The general raged at him. "And had it published, all neat and orderly, in the patent office records so that anyone who wanted it could look it up and have it?"

"We can be most sincerely thankful," said the chairman, "that he did not patent it."

VI

The helicopter would never fly again, but the time unit was intact. Which didn't mean that it would work.

They held a powwow at their camp site. It had been, they decided, simpler to move the camp than to remove the body of Old Buster. So they had shifted at dawn, leaving the old mastodon still sprawled across the helicopter.

In a day or two, they knew, the great bones would be cleanly picked by the carrion birds, the lesser cats, the wolves and foxes and the little skulkers.

Getting the time unit out of the helicopter had been quite a chore, but they finally had managed and now Adams sat with it cradled in his lap.

"The worst of it," he told them, "is that I can't test it. There's no way to. You turn it on and it works or it doesn't work. You can't know till you try."

"That's something we can't help," Cooper replied. "The problem, seems to me, is how we're going to use it without the whirlybird."

"We have to figure out some way to get up in the air," said Adams. "We don't want to take the chance of going up into the twentieth century and arriving there about six feet underground."

"Common sense says that we should be higher here than up ahead," Hudson pointed out. "These hills have stood here since Jurassic times. They probably were a good deal higher then and have weathered down. That weathering still should be going on. So we should be higher here than in the twentieth century—not much, perhaps, but higher."

"Did anyone ever notice what the altimeter read?" asked Cooper.

"I don't believe I did," Adams admitted.

"It wouldn't tell you, anyhow," Hudson declared. "It would just

give our height then and now—and we were moving, remember—
and what about air pockets and relative atmosphere density and all
the rest?"

Cooper looked as discouraged as Hudson felt.

"How does this sound?" asked Adams. "We'll build a platform
twelve feet high. That certainly should be enough to clear us and yet
small enough to stay within the range of the unit's force-field."

"And what if we're two feet higher here?" Hudson pointed out.

"A fall of fourteen feet wouldn't kill a man unless he's plain
unlucky."

"It might break some bones."

"So it might break some bones. You want to stay here or take a
chance on a broken leg?"

"All right, if you put it that way. A platform, you say. A platform
out of what?"

"Timber. There's lot of it. We just go out and cut some logs."

"A twelve-foot log is heavy. And how are we going to get that big
a log uphill?"

"We drag it."

"We try to, you mean."

"Maybe we could fix up a cart," said Adams, after thinking a
moment.

"Out of what?" Cooper asked.

"Rollers, maybe. We could cut some and roll the logs up here."

"That would work on level ground," Hudson said. "It wouldn't
work to roll a log uphill. It would get away from us. Someone might
get killed."

"The logs would have to be longer than twelve feet, anyhow,"
Cooper put in. "You'd have to set them in a hole and that takes away
some footage."

"Why not the tripod principle?" Hudson offered. "Fasten three
logs at the top and raise them."

"That's a gin-pole, a primitive derrick. It'd still have to be longer
than twelve feet. Fifteen, sixteen, maybe. And how are we going to
hoist three sixteen-foot logs? We'd need a block and tackle."

"There's another thing," said Cooper. "Part of those logs might
just be beyond the effective range of the force-field. Part of them
would have to—have to, mind you—move in time and part couldn't.
That would set up a stress...."

"Another thing about it," added Hudson, "is that we'd travel with the logs. I don't want to come out in another time with a bunch of logs flying all around me."

"Cheer up," Adams told them. "Maybe the unit won't work, anyhow."

VII

The general sat alone in his office and held his head between his hands. The fools, he thought, the goddam knuckle-headed fools! Why couldn't they see it as clearly as he did?

For fifteen years now, as head of Project Mastodon, he had lived with it night and day and he could see all the possibilities as clearly as if they had been actual fact. Not military possibilities alone, although as a military man, he naturally would think of those first.

The hidden bases, for example, located within the very strongholds of potential enemies—within, yet centuries removed in time. Many centuries removed and only seconds distant.

He could see it all: The materialization of the fleets; the swift, devastating blow, then the instantaneous retreat into the fastnesses of the past. Terrific destruction, but not a ship lost nor a man.

Except that if you had the bases, you need never strike the blow. If you had the bases and let the enemy know you had them, there would never be the provocation.

And on the home front, you'd have air-raid shelters that would be effective. You'd evacuate your population not in space, but time. You'd have the sure and absolute defense against any kind of bombing—fission, fusion, bacteriological or whatever else the labs had in stock.

And if the worst should come—which it never would with a setup like that—you'd have a place to which the entire nation could retreat, leaving to the enemy the empty, blasted cities and the lethally dusted countryside.

Sanctuary—that had been what Hudson had offered the then-secretary of state fifteen years ago—and the idiot had frozen up with the insult of it and had Hudson thrown out.

And if war did not come, think of the living space and the vast new opportunities—not the least of which would be the opportunity to achieve peaceful living in a virgin world, where the old hatreds would slough off and new concepts have a chance to grow.

He wondered where they were, those three who had gone back into time. Dead, perhaps. Run down by a mastodon. Or stalked by tigers. Or maybe done in by warlike tribesmen. No, he kept forgetting there weren't any in that era. Or trapped in time, unable to get back, condemned to exile in an alien time. Or maybe, he thought, just plain disgusted. And he couldn't blame them if they were.

Or maybe—let's be fantastic about this—sneaking in colonists from some place other than the watched Wisconsin farm, building up in actuality the nation they had claimed to be.

They had to get back to the present soon or Project Mastodon would be killed entirely. Already the research program had been halted and if something didn't happen quickly, the watch that was kept on the Wisconsin farm would be called off.

"And if they do that," said the general, "I know just what I'll do."

He got up and strode around the room.

"By God," he said, "I'll show 'em!"

VIII

It had taken ten full days of back-breaking work to build the pyramid. They'd hauled the rocks from the creek bed half a mile away and had piled them, stone by rolling stone, to the height of a full twelve feet. It took a lot of rocks and a lot of patience, for as the pyramid went up, the base naturally kept broadening out.

But now all was finally ready.

Hudson sat before the burned-out campfire and held his blistered hands before him.

It should work, he thought, better than the logs—and less dangerous.

Grab a handful of sand. Some trickled back between your fingers, but most stayed in your grasp. That was the principle of the pyramid of stones. When—and if—the time machine should work, most of the rocks would go along.

Those that didn't go would simply trickle out and do no harm. There'd be no stress or strain to upset the working of the force-field.

And if the time unit didn't work?

Or if it did?

This was the end of the dream, thought Hudson, no matter how you looked at it.

For even if they did get back to the twentieth century, there would be no money and with the film lost and no other taken to replace it, they'd have no proof they had traveled back beyond the dawn of history—back almost to the dawn of Man.

Although how far you traveled would have no significance. An hour or a million years would be all the same; if you could span the hour, you could span the million years. And if you could go back the million years, it was within your power to go back to the first tick of eternity, the first stir of time across the face of emptiness and nothingness—back to that initial instant when nothing as yet had happened or been planned or thought, when all the vastness of the Universe was a new slate waiting the first chalk stroke of destiny.

Another helicopter would cost thirty thousand dollars—and they didn't even have the money to buy the tractor that they needed to build the stockade.

There was no way to borrow. You couldn't walk into a bank and say you wanted thirty thousand to take a trip back to the Old Stone Age.

You still could go to some industry or some university or the government and if you could persuade them you had something on the ball—why, then, they might put up the cash after cutting themselves in on just about all of the profits. And, naturally, they'd run the show because it was their money and all you had done was the sweating and the bleeding.

"There's one thing that still bothers me," said Cooper, breaking the silence. "We spent a lot of time picking our spot so we'd miss the barn and house and all the other buildings...."

"Don't tell me the windmill!" Hudson cried.

"No. I'm pretty sure we're clear of that. But the way I figure, we're right astraddle that barbed-wire fence at the south end of the orchard."

"If you want, we could move the pyramid over twenty feet or so."

Cooper groaned. "I'll take my chances with the fence." Adams got to his feet, the time unit tucked underneath his arm. "Come on, you guys. It's time to go."

They climbed the pyramid gingerly and stood unsteadily at its top.

Adams shifted the unit around, clasped it to his chest.

"Stand around close," he said, "and bend your knees a little. It may be quite a drop."

"Go ahead," said Cooper. "Press the button."

Adams pressed the button.

Nothing happened.

The unit didn't work.

IX

The chief of Central Intelligence was white-lipped when he finished talking.

"You're sure of your information?" asked the President.

"Mr. President," said the CIA chief, "I've never been more sure of anything in my entire life."

The President looked at the other two who were in the room, a question in his eyes.

The JCS chairman said, "It checks, sir, with everything we know."

"But it's incredible!" the President said.

"They're afraid," said the CIA chief. "They lie awake nights. They've become convinced that we're on the verge of traveling in time. They've tried and failed, but they think we're near success. To their way of thinking, they've got to hit us now or never, because once we actually get time travel, they know their number's up."

"But we dropped Project Mastodon entirely almost three years ago. It's been all of ten years since we stopped the research. It was twenty-five years ago that Hudson—"

"That makes no difference, sir. They're convinced we dropped the project publicly, but went underground with it. That would be the kind of strategy they could understand."

The President picked up a pencil and doodled on a pad.

"Who was that old general," he asked, "the one who raised so much fuss when we dropped the project? I remember I was in the Senate then. He came around to see me."

"Bowers, sir," said the JCS chairman.

"That's right. What became of him?"

"Retired."

"Well, I guess it doesn't make any difference now." He doodled some more and finally said, "Gentlemen, it looks like this is it. How much time did you say we had?"

"Not more than ninety days, sir. Maybe as little as thirty."

The President looked up at the JCS chairman.

"We're as ready," said the chairman, "as we will ever be. We can handle them—I think. There will, of course, be some—"

"I know," said the President.

"Could we bluff?" asked the secretary of state, speaking quietly. "I know it wouldn't stick, but at least we might buy some time."

"You mean hint that we have time travel?"

The secretary nodded.

"It wouldn't work," said the CIA chief tiredly. "If we really had it, there'd be no question then. They'd become exceedingly well-mannered, even neighborly, if they were sure we had it."

"But we haven't got it," said the President gloomily.

X

The two hunters trudged homeward late in the afternoon, with a deer slung from a pole they carried on their shoulders. Their breath hung visibly in the air as they walked along, for the frost had come and any day now, they knew, there would be snow.

"I'm worried about Wes," said Cooper, breathing heavily. "He's taking this too hard. We got to keep an eye on him."

"Let's take a rest," panted Hudson.

They halted and lowered the deer to the ground.

"He blames himself too much," said Cooper. He wiped his sweaty forehead. "There isn't any need to. All of us walked into this with our eyes wide open."

"He's kidding himself and he knows it, but it gives him something to go on. As long as he can keep busy with all his puttering around, he'll be all right."

"He isn't going to repair the time unit, Chuck."

"I know he isn't. And he knows it, too. He hasn't got the tools or the materials. Back in the workshop, he might have a chance, but here he hasn't."

"It's rough on him."

"It's rough on all of us."

"Yes, but we didn't get a brainstorm that marooned two old friends in this tail end of nowhere. And we can't make him swallow it when we say that it's okay, we don't mind at all."

"That's a lot to swallow, Johnny."

"What's going to happen to us, Chuck?"

"We've got ourselves a place to live and there's lots to eat. Save our ammo for the big game—a lot of eating for each bullet—and trap the smaller animals."

"I'm wondering what will happen when the flour and all the other stuff is gone. We don't have too much of it because we always figured we could bring in more."

"We'll live on meat," said Hudson. "We got bison by the million. The plains Indians lived on them alone. And in the spring, we'll find roots and in the summer berries. And in the fall, we'll harvest a half-dozen kinds of nuts."

"Someday our ammo will be gone, no matter how careful we are with it."

"Bows and arrows. Slingshots. Spears."

"There's a lot of beasts here I wouldn't want to stand up to with nothing but a spear."

"We won't stand up to them. We'll duck when we can and run when we can't duck. Without our guns, we're no lords of creation—not in this place. If we're going to live, we'll have to recognize that fact."

"And if one of us gets sick or breaks a leg or—"

"We'll do the best we can. Nobody lives forever."

But they were talking around the thing that really bothered them, Hudson told himself—each of them afraid to speak the thought aloud.

They'd live, all right, so far as food, shelter and clothing were concerned. And they'd live most of the time in plenty, for this was a fat and open-handed land and a man could make an easy living.

But the big problem—the one they were afraid to talk about—was their emptiness of purpose. To live, they had to find some meaning in a world without society.

A man cast away on a desert isle could always live for hope, but here there was no hope. A Robinson Crusoe was separated from his fellow-humans by, at the most, a few thousand miles. Here they were separated by a hundred and fifty thousand years.

Wes Adams was the lucky one so far. Even playing his thousand-to-one shot, he still held tightly to a purpose, feeble as it might be—

the hope that he could repair the time machine.

We don't need to watch him now, thought Hudson. The time we'll have to watch is when he is forced to admit he can't fix the machine.

And both Hudson and Cooper had been kept sane enough, for there had been the cabin to be built and the winter's supply of wood to cut and the hunting to be done.

But then there would come a time when all the chores were finished and there was nothing left to do.

"You ready to go?" asked Cooper.

"Sure. All rested now," said Hudson.

They hoisted the pole to their shoulders and started off again.

Hudson had lain awake nights thinking of it and all the thoughts had been dead ends.

One could write a natural history of the Pleistocene, complete with photographs and sketches, and it would be a pointless thing to do, because no future scientist would ever have a chance to read it.

Or they might labor to build a memorial, a vast pyramid, perhaps, which would carry a message forward across fifteen hundred centuries, snatching with bare hands at a semblance of immortality. But if they did, they would be working against the sure and certain knowledge that it all would come to naught, for they knew in advance that no such pyramid existed in historic time.

Or they might set out to seek contemporary Man, hiking across four thousand miles of wilderness to Bering Strait and over into Asia. And having found contemporary Man cowering in his caves, they might be able to help him immeasurably along the road to his great inheritance. Except that they'd never make it and even if they did, contemporary Man undoubtedly would find some way to do them in and might eat them in the bargain.

They came out of the woods and there was the cabin, just a hundred yards away. It crouched against the hillside above the spring, with the sweep of grassland billowing beyond it to the slate-gray skyline. A trickle of smoke came up from the chimney and they saw the door was open.

"Wes oughtn't to leave it open that way," said Cooper. "No telling when a bear might decide to come visiting."

"Hey, Wes!" yelled Hudson.

But there was no sign of him.

147

Inside the cabin, a white sheet of paper lay on the table top. Hudson snatched it up and read it, with Cooper at his shoulder.

Dear guys—I don't want to get your hopes up again and have you disappointed. But I think I may have found the trouble. I'm going to try it out. If it doesn't work, I'll come back and burn this note and never say a word. But if you find the note, you'll know it worked and I'll be back to get you. Wes.

Hudson crumpled the note in his hand. "The crazy fool!"

"He's gone off his rocker," Cooper said. "He just thought...."

The same thought struck them both and they bolted for the door. At the corner of the cabin, they skidded to a halt and stood there, staring at the ridge above them.

The pyramid of rocks they'd built two months ago was gone!

XI

The crash brought Gen. Leslie Bowers (ret.) up out of bed— about two feet out of bed—old muscles tense, white mustache bristling.

Even at his age, the general was a man of action. He flipped the covers back, swung his feet out to the floor and grabbed the shotgun leaning against the wall.

Muttering, he blundered out of the bedroom, marched across the dining room and charged into the kitchen. There, beside the door, he snapped on the switch that turned on the floodlights. He practically took the door off its hinges getting to the stoop and he stood there, bare feet gripping the planks, nightshirt billowing in the wind, the shotgun poised and ready.

"What's going on out there?" he bellowed.

There was a tremendous pile of rocks resting where he'd parked his car. One crumpled fender and a drunken headlight peeped out of the rubble.

A man was clambering carefully down the jumbled stones, making a detour to dodge the battered fender.

The general pulled back the hammer of the gun and fought to control himself.

The man reached the bottom of the pile and turned around to face him. The general saw that he was hugging something tightly to his chest.

"Mister," the general told him, "your explanation better be a good one. That was a brand-new car. And this was the first time I was set for a night of sleep since my tooth quit aching."

The man just stood and looked at him.

"Who in thunder are you?" roared the general.

The man walked slowly forward. He stopped at the bottom of the stoop.

"My name is Wesley Adams," he said. "I'm—"

"Wesley Adams!" howled the general. "My God, man, where have you been all these years?"

"Well, I don't imagine you'll believe me, but the fact is...."

"We've been waiting for you. For twenty-five long years! Or, rather, I've been waiting for you. Those other idiots gave up. I've waited right here for you, Adams, for the last three years, ever since they called off the guard."

Adams gulped. "I'm sorry about the car. You see, it was this way...."

The general, he saw, was beaming at him fondly.

"I had faith in you," the general said.

He waved the shotgun by way of invitation. "Come on in. I have a call to make."

Adams stumbled up the stairs.

"Move!" the general ordered, shivering. "On the double! You want me to catch my death of cold out here?"

Inside, he fumbled for the lights and turned them on. He laid the shotgun across the kitchen table and picked up the telephone.

"Give me the White House at Washington," he said. "Yes, I said the White House.... The President? Naturally he's the one I want to talk to.... Yes, it's all right. He won't mind my calling him."

"Sir," said Adams tentatively.

The general looked up. "What is it, Adams? Go ahead and say it."

"Did you say twenty-five years?"

"That's what I said. What were you doing all that time?"

Adams grasped the table and hung on. "But it wasn't...."

"Yes," said the general to the operator. "Yes, I'll wait."

He held his hand over the receiver and looked inquiringly at Adams. "I imagine you'll want the same terms as before."

"Terms?"

"Sure. Recognition. Point Four Aid. Defense pact."

"I suppose so," Adams said.

"You got these saps across the barrel," the general told him happily. "You can get anything you want. You rate it, too, after what you've done and the bonehead treatment you got—but especially for not selling out."

XII

The night editor read the bulletin just off the teletype.

"Well, what do you know!" he said. "We just recognized Mastodonia."

He looked at the copy chief.

"Where the hell is Mastodonia?" he asked.

The copy chief shrugged. "Don't ask me. You're the brains in this joint."

"Well, let's get a map for the next edition," said the night editor.

XIII

Tabby, the saber-tooth, dabbed playfully at Cooper with his mighty paw.

Cooper kicked him in the ribs—an equally playful gesture.

Tabby snarled at him.

"Show your teeth at me, will you!" said Cooper. "Raised you from a kitten and that's the gratitude you show. Do it just once more and I'll belt you in the chops."

Tabby lay down blissfully and began to wash his face.

"Someday," warned Hudson, "that cat will miss a meal and that's the day you're it."

"Gentle as a dove," Cooper assured him. "Wouldn't hurt a fly."

"Well, one thing about it, nothing dares to bother us with that monstrosity around."

"Best watchdog there ever was. Got to have something to guard all this stuff we've got. When Wes gets back, we'll be millionaires. All those furs and ginseng and the ivory."

"If he gets back."

"He'll be back. Quit your worrying."

"But it's been five years," Hudson protested.

"He'll be back. Something happened, that's all. He's probably working on it right now. Could be that he messed up the time setting when he repaired the unit or it might have been knocked out of kilter when Buster hit the helicopter. That would take a while to fix. I don't worry that he won't come back. What I can't figure out is why did he go and leave us?"

"I've told you," Hudson said. "He was afraid it wouldn't work."

"There wasn't any need to be scared of that. We never would have laughed at him."

"No. Of course we wouldn't."

"Then what was he scared of?" Cooper asked.

"If the unit failed and we knew it failed, Wes was afraid we'd try to make him see how hopeless and insane it was. And he knew we'd probably convince him and then all his hope would be gone. And he wanted to hang onto that, Johnny. He wanted to hang onto his hope even when there wasn't any left."

"That doesn't matter now," said Cooper. "What counts is that he'll come back. I can feel it in my bones."

And here's another case, thought Hudson, of hope begging to be allowed to go on living.

God, he thought, I wish I could be that blind!

"Wes is working on it right now," said Cooper confidently.

XIV

He was. Not he alone, but a thousand others, working desperately, knowing that the time was short, working not alone for two men trapped in time, but for the peace they all had dreamed about—that the whole world had yearned for through the ages.

For to be of any use, it was imperative that they could zero in the time machines they meant to build as an artilleryman would zero in a battery of guns, that each time machine would take its occupants to the same instant of the past, that their operation would extend over the same period of time, to the exact second.

It was a problem of control and calibration—starting with a prototype that was calibrated, as its finest adjustment, for jumps of 50,000 years.

Project Mastodon was finally under way.

The Old Die Rich

By H. L. Gold

Editor's note: The March 1953 edition of Galaxy Science Fiction *contained this amazing story by Horace Leonard Gold (1914-1996), better known as H. L. Gold. "The Old Die Rich" was adapted into a 1956 radio drama for NBC's "X Minus One." Gold created* Galaxy *magazine and was considered one of the genre's greatest editors.*

It is the kind of news item you read at least a dozen times a year, wonder about briefly, and then promptly forget—but the real story is the one that the reporters are unable to cover!

You again, Weldon," the Medical Examiner said wearily.

I nodded pleasantly and looked around the shabby room with a feeling of hopeful eagerness. Maybe this time, I thought, I'd get the answer. I had the same sensation I always had in these places—the quavery senile despair at being closed in a room with the single shaky chair, tottering bureau, dim bulb hanging from the ceiling, the flaking metal bed.

There was a woman on the bed, an old woman with white hair thin enough to show the tight-drawn scalp, her face and body so emaciated that the flesh between the bones formed parchment pockets. The M.E. was going over her as if she were a side of beef that he had to put a federal grade stamp on, grumbling meanwhile about me and Sergeant Lou Pape, who had brought me here.

"When are you going to stop taking Weldon around to these cases, Sergeant?" the M.E. demanded in annoyance. "Damned actor and his morbid curiosity!"

For the first time, Lou was stung into defending me. "Mr. Weldon is a friend of mine—I used to be an actor, too, before I joined the force—and he's a follower of Stanislavsky."

The beat cop who'd reported the D.O.A. whipped around at the door. "A Red?"

I let Lou Pape explain what the Stanislavsky method of acting was, while I sat down on the one chair and tried to apply it. Stanislavsky was the great pre-Revolution Russian stage director whose idea was that actors had to think and feel like the characters they portrayed so they could be them. A Stanislavskian works out everything about a character right up to the point where a play starts—where he was born, when, his relationship with his parents, education, childhood, adolescence, maturity, attitudes toward men, women, sex, money, success, including incidents. The play itself is just an extension of the life history created by the actor.

How does that tie in with the old woman who had died? Well, I'd had the cockeyed kind of luck to go bald at 25 and I'd been playing old men ever since. I had them down pretty well—it's not just a matter of shuffling around all hunched over and talking in a high cracked voice, which is cornball acting, but learning what old people are like inside—and these cases I talked Lou Pape into taking me on were studies in senility. I wanted to understand them, know what made them do what they did, feel the compulsion that drove them to it.

The old woman on the bed, for instance, had $32,000 in five bank accounts ... and she'd died of starvation.

You've come across such cases in the news, at least a dozen a year, and wondered who they were and why they did it. But you read the items, thought about them for a little while, and then forgot them. My interest was professional; I made my living playing old people and I had to know as much about them as I could.

That's how it started off, at any rate. But the more cases I investigated, the less sense they made to me, until finally they were practically an obsession.

Look, they almost always have around $30,000 pinned to their underwear, hidden in mattresses, or parked in the bank, yet they starve themselves to death. If I could understand them, I could write a play or have one written; I might really make a name for myself, even get a Hollywood contract, maybe, if I could act them as they should be acted.

So I sat there in the lone chair, trying to reconstruct the character of the old woman who had died rather than spend a single cent of her $32,000 for food.

Malnutrition induced by senile psychosis," the M.E. said, writing out the death certificate. He turned to me. "There's no mystery to it, Weldon. They starve because they're less afraid of death than digging into their savings."

I'd been imagining myself growing weak from hunger and trying to decide that I ought to eat even if it cost me something. I came out of it and said, "That's what you keep telling me."

"I keep hoping it'll convince you so you won't come around anymore. What are the chances, Weldon?"

"Depends. I will when I'm sure you're right. I'm not."

He shrugged disgustedly, ordered the wicker basket from the meat wagon and had the old woman carried out. He and the beat cop left with the basket team. He could at least have said good-by. He never did, though.

A fat lot I cared about his attitude or dogmatic medical opinion. Getting inside this character was more important. The setting should have helped; it was depressing, rank with the feel of solitary desperation and needless death.

Lou Pape stood looking out the one dirty window, waiting patiently for me. I let my joints stiffen as if they were thirty years older and more worn out than they were, and empathized myself into a dilemma between getting still weaker from hunger and drawing a little money out of the bank.

I worked at it for half an hour or so with the deep concentration you acquire when you use the Stanislavsky method. Then I gave up.

"The M.E. is wrong, Lou," I said. "It doesn't feel right."

Lou turned around from the window. He'd stood there all that time without once coughing or scratching or doing anything else that might have distracted me. "He knows his business, Mark."

"But he doesn't know old people."

"What is it you don't get?" he prompted, helping me dig my way through a characterization like the trained Stanislavskian he was— and still would have been if he hadn't gotten so sick of the insecurity of acting that he'd become a cop. "Can't money be more important to a psychotic than eating?"

"Sure," I agreed. "Up to a point. Undereating, yes. Actual starvation, no."

"Why not?"

"You and the M.E. think it's easy to starve to death. It isn't. Not when you can buy day-old bread at the bakeries, soup bones for about a nickel a pound, wilted vegetables that groceries are glad to get rid of. Anybody who's willing to eat that stuff can stay alive on nearly nothing a day. Nearly nothing, Lou, and hunger is a damned potent instinct. I can understand hating to spend even those few cents. I can't see going without food altogether."

He took out a cigarette; he hadn't until then because he didn't want to interrupt my concentration. "Maybe they get too weak to go out after old bread and meat bones and wilted vegetables."

"It still doesn't figure." I got up off the shaky chair, my joints now really stiff from sitting in it. "Do you know how long it takes to die of starvation?"

"That depends on age, health, amount of activity—"

"Nuts!" I said. "It would take weeks!"

"So it takes weeks. Where's the problem—if there is one?"

I lit the pipe I'd learned to smoke instead of cigarettes—old men seem to use pipes more than anything else, though maybe it'll be different in the next generation. More cigarette smokers now, you see, and they'd stick to the habit unless the doctor ordered them to cut it out.

"Did you ever try starving for weeks, Lou?" I asked.

"No. Did you?"

"In a way. All these cases you've been taking me on for the last couple of years—I've tried to be them. But let's say it's possible to die of starvation when you have thousands of dollars put away. Let's say you don't think of scrounging off food stores or working out a way of freeloading or hitting soup lines. Let's say you stay in your room and slowly starve to death."

He slowly picked a fleck of tobacco off his lip and flicked it away, his sharp black eyes poking holes in the situation I'd built up for him. But he wasn't ready to say anything yet.

"There's charity," I went on, "relief—except for those who have their dough in banks, where it can be checked on—old age pension, panhandling, cadging off neighbors."

He said, "We know these cases are hermits. They don't make

contact with anybody."

"Even when they're starting to get real hungry?"

"You've got something, Mark, but that's the wrong tack," he said thoughtfully. "The point is that they don't have to make contact; other people know them or about them. Somebody would check after a few days or a week—the janitor, the landlord, someone in the house or the neighborhood."

"So they'd be found before they died."

"You'd think so, wouldn't you?" he agreed reluctantly. "They don't generally have friends, and the relatives are usually so distant, they hardly know these old people and whether they're alive or not. Maybe that's what threw us off. But you don't need friends and relatives to start wondering, and investigate when you haven't shown up for a while." He lifted his head and looked at me. "What does that prove, Mark?"

"That there's something wrong with these cases. I want to find out what."

I got Lou to take me down to Headquarters, where he let me see the bankbooks the old woman had left.

"She took damned good care of them," I said. "They look almost new."

"Wouldn't you take damned good care of the most important thing in the world to you?" he asked. "You've seen the hoards of money the others leave. Same thing."

I peered closely at the earliest entry, April 23, 1907, $150. My eyes aren't that bad; I was peering at the ink. It was dark, unfaded. I pointed it out to Lou.

"From not being exposed to daylight much," he said. "They don't haul out the bankbooks or money very often, I guess."

"And that adds up for you? I can see them being psychotics all their lives ... but not senile psychotics."

"They hoarded, Mark. That adds up for me."

"Funny," I said, watching him maneuver his cigarette as if he loved the feel of it, drawing the smoke down and letting it out in plumes of different shapes, from rings to slender streams. What a living he could make doing cigarette commercials on TV! "I can see you turn into one of these cases, Lou."

He looked startled for a second, but then crushed out the butt carefully so he could watch it instead of me. "Yeah? How so?"

"You've been too scared by poverty to take a chance. You know you could do all right acting, but you don't dare giving up this crummy job. Carry that far enough and you try to stop spending money, then cut out eating, and finally wind up dead of starvation in a cheap room."

"Me? I'd never get that scared of being broke!"

"At the age of 70 or 80?"

"Especially then! I'd probably tear loose for a while and then buy into a home for the aged."

I wanted to grin, but I didn't. He'd proved my point. He'd also shown that he was as bothered by these old people as I was.

"Tell me, Lou. If somebody kept you from dying, would you give him any dough for it, even if you were a senile psychotic?"

I could see him using the Stanislavsky method to feel his way to the answer. He shook his head. "Not while I was alive. Will it, maybe, not give it."

"How would that be as a motive?"

He leaned against a metal filing cabinet. "No good, Mark. You know what a hell of a time we have tracking down relatives to give the money to, because these people don't leave wills. The few relatives we find are always surprised when they get their inheritance—most of them hardly remember dear old who-ever-it-was that died and left it to them. All the other estates eventually go to the State treasury, unclaimed."

"Well, it was an idea." I opened the oldest bankbook again. "Anybody ever think of testing the ink, Lou?"

"What for? The banks' records always check. These aren't forgeries, if that's what you're thinking."

"I don't know what I'm thinking," I admitted. "But I'd like to turn a chemist loose on this for a little while."

"Look, Mark, there's a lot I'm willing to do for you, and I think I've done plenty, but there's a limit—"

I let him explain why he couldn't let me borrow the book and then waited while he figured out how it could be done and did it. He was still grumbling when he helped me pick a chemist out of the telephone directory and went along to the lab with me.

"But don't get any wrong notions," he said on the way. "I have to protect State property, that's all, because I signed for it and I'm responsible."

"Sure, sure," I agreed, to humor him. "If you're not curious, why not just wait outside for me?"

He gave me one of those white-tooth grins that he had no right to deprive women audiences of. "I could do that, but I'd rather see you make a sap of yourself."

I turned the bankbook over to the chemist and we waited for the report. When it came, it had to be translated.

Typical of those used 50 years ago. Lou Pape gave me a jab in the ribs at that. But then the chemist said that, according to the amount of oxidation, it seemed fresh enough to be only a few months or years old, and it was Lou's turn to get jabbed. Lou pushed him about the aging, asking if it couldn't be the result of unusually good care. The chemist couldn't say—that depended on the kind of care; an airtight compartment, perhaps, filled with one of the inert gases, or a vacuum. They hadn't been kept that way, of course, so Lou looked as baffled as I felt.

He took the bankbook and we went out to the street.

"See what I mean?" I asked quietly, not wanting to rub it in.

"I see something, but I don't know what. Do you?"

"I wish I could say yes. It doesn't make any more sense than anything else about these cases."

"What do you do next?"

"Damned if I know. There are thousands of old people in the city. Only a few of them take this way out. I have to try to find them before they do."

"If they're loaded, they won't say so, Mark, and there's no way of telling them from those who are down and out."

I rubbed my pipe disgruntledly against the side of my nose to oil it. "Ain't this a beaut of a problem? I wish I liked problems. I hate them."

Lou had to get back on duty. I had nowhere to go and nothing to do except worry my way through this tangle. He headed back to Headquarters and I went over to the park and sat in the sun, warming myself and trying to think like a senile psychotic who would rather die of starvation than spend a few cents for food.

I didn't get anywhere, naturally. There are too many ways of beating starvation, too many chances of being found before it's too late.

And the fresh ink, over half a century old....

I took to hanging around banks, hoping I'd see someone come in with an old bankbook that had fresh ink from 50 years before. Lou was some help there—he convinced the guards and tellers that I wasn't an old-looking guy casing the place for a gang, and even got the tellers to watch out for particularly dark ink in ancient bankbooks.

I stuck at it for a month, although there were a few stage calls that didn't turn out right, and one radio and two TV parts, which did and kept me going. I was almost glad the stage parts hadn't been given to me; they'd have interrupted my outside work.

After a month without a thing turning up at the banks, though, I went back to my two rooms in the theatrical hotel one night, tired and discouraged, and I found Lou there. I expected him to give me another talk on dropping the whole thing; he'd been doing that for a couple of weeks now, every time we got together. I felt too low to put up an argument. But Lou was holding back his excitement—acting like a cop, you know, instead of projecting his feelings—and he couldn't haul me out to his car as fast as he probably wanted me to go.

"Been trying to get in touch with you all day, Mark. Some old guy was found wandering around, dazed and suffering from malnutrition, with $17,000 in cash inside the lining of his jacket."

"Alive?" I asked, shocked right into eagerness again.

"Just barely. They're trying intravenous feeding to pull him through. I don't think he'll make it."

"For God's sake, let's get there before he conks out!"

Lou raced me to the City Hospital and up to the ward. There was a scrawny old man in a bed, nothing but a papery skin stretched thin over a face like a skull and a body like a Halloween skeleton, shivering as if he was cold. I knew it wasn't the cold. The medics were injecting a heart stimulant into him and he was vibrating like a rattletrap car racing over a gravel road.

"Who are you?" I practically yelled, grabbing his skinny arm. "What happened to you?"

He went on shaking with his eyes closed and his mouth open.

"Ah, hell!" I said, disgusted. "He's in a coma."

"He might start talking," Lou told me. "I fixed it up so you can sit here and listen in case he does."

"So I can listen to delirious ravings, you mean."

159

Lou got me a chair and put it next to the bed. "What are you kicking about? This is the first live one you've seen, isn't it? That ought to be good enough for you." He looked as annoyed as a director. "Besides, you can get biographical data out of delirium that you'd never get if he was conscious."

He was right, of course. Not only data, but attitudes, wishes, resentments that would normally be repressed. I wasn't thinking of acting at the moment, though. Here was somebody who could tell me what I wanted to know ... only he couldn't talk.

Lou went to the door. "Good luck," he said, and went out.

I sat down and stared at the old man, willing him to talk. I don't have to ask if you've ever done that; everybody has. You keep thinking over and over, getting more and more tense, "Talk, damn you, talk!" until you find that every muscle in your body is a fist and your jaws are aching because you've been clenching your teeth so hard. You might just as well not bother, but once in a while a coincidence makes you think you've done it. Like now.

The old man sort of came to. That is, he opened his eyes and looked around without seeing anything, or it was so far away and long ago that nobody else could see what he saw.

I hunched forward on the chair and willed harder than ever. Nothing happened. He stared at the ceiling and through and beyond me. Then he closed his eyes again and I slumped back, defeated and bitter—but that was when he began talking.

There were a couple of women, though they might have been little girls in his childhood, and he had his troubles with them. He was praying for a toy train, a roadster, to pass his tests, to keep from being fired, to be less lonely, and back to toys again. He hated his father, and his mother was too busy with church bazaars and such to pay much attention to him. There was a sister: she died when he was a kid. He was glad she died, hoping maybe now his mother would notice him, but he was also filled with guilt because he was glad. Then somebody, he felt, was trying to shove him out of his job.

The intravenous feeding kept dripping into his vein and he went on rambling. After ten or fifteen minutes of it, he fell asleep. I felt so disappointed that I could have slapped him awake, only it wouldn't have done any good. Smoking would have helped me relax, but it wasn't allowed, and I didn't dare go outside for one, for fear he might revive again and this time come up to the present.

Broke!" he suddenly shrieked, trying to sit up.

I pushed him down gently, and he went on in frightful terror, "Old and poor, nowhere to go, nobody wants me, can't make a living, read the ads every day, no jobs for old men."

He blurted through weeks, months, years—I don't know—of fear and despair. And finally he came to something that made his face glow like a radium dial.

"An ad. No experience needed. Good salary." His face got dark and awful. All he added was, "El Greco," or something that sounded like it, and then he went into terminal breathing.

I rang for the nurse and she went for the doctor. I couldn't stand the long moments when the old man's chest stopped moving, the abrupt frantic gulps of air followed by no breath at all. I wanted to get away from it, but I had to wait for whatever more he might say.

It didn't come. His eyes fogged and rolled up and he stopped taking those spasmodic strangling breaths. The nurse came back with the doctor, who felt his pulse and shook his head. She pulled the blanket over the old man's face.

I left, feeling sick. I'd learned things I already knew about hate and love and fear and hope and frustration. There was an ad in it somewhere, but I had no way of telling if it had been years ago or recently. And a name that sounded like "El Greco." That was a Spanish painter of four-five hundred years ago. Had the old guy been remembering a picture he'd seen?

No, he'd come up at least close to the present. The ad seemed to solve his problem about being broke. But what about the $17,000 that had been found in the lining of his jacket? He hadn't mentioned that. Of course, being a senile psychotic, he could have considered himself broke even with that amount of money. None coming in, you see.

That didn't add up, either. His was the terror of being old and jobless. If he'd had money, he would have figured how to make it last, and that would have come through in one way or another.

There was the ad, there was his hope, and there was this El Greco. A Greek restaurant, maybe, where he might have been bumming his meals.

But where did the $17,000 fit in?

Lou Pape was too fed up with the whole thing to discuss it with me. He just gave me the weary eye and said, "You're riding this too hard, Mark. The guy was talking from fever. How do I know what figures and what doesn't when I'm dealing with insanity or delirium?"

"But you admit there's plenty about these cases that doesn't figure?"

"Sure. Did you take a look at the condition the world is in lately? Why should these old people be any exception?"

I couldn't blame him. He'd pulled me in on the cases with plenty of trouble to himself, just to do me a favor. Now he was fed up. I guess it wasn't even that—he thought I was ruining myself, at least financially and maybe worse, by trying to run down the problem. He said he'd be glad to see me any time and gas about anything or help me with whatever might be bothering me, if he could, but not these cases any more. He told me to lay off them, and then he left me on my own.

I don't know what he could have done, actually. I didn't need him to go through the want ads with me, which I was doing every day, figuring there might be something in the ravings about an ad. I spent more time than I liked checking those slanted at old people, only to find they were supposed to become messengers and such.

One brought me to an old brownstone five-story house in the East 80s. I got on line with the rest of the applicants—there were men and women, all decrepit, all looking badly in need of money— and waited my turn. My face was lined with collodion wrinkles and I wore an antique shiny suit and rundown shoes. I didn't look more prosperous or any younger than they did.

I finally came up to the woman who was doing the interviewing. She sat behind a plain office desk down in the main floor hall, with a pile of application cards in front of her and a ballpoint pen in one strong, slender hand. She had red hair with gold lights in it and eyes so pale blue that they would have seemed the same color as the whites if she'd been on the stage. Her face would have been beautiful except for her rigid control of expression; she smiled abruptly, shut it off just like that, looked me over with all the impersonality and penetration of an X-ray from the soles to the bald head, exactly as she'd done with the others. But that skin! If it was as perfect as that all over her slim, stiffly erect, proudly shaped body, she had no business off the stage!

"Name, address, previous occupation, social security number?" she asked in a voice with good clarity, resonance and diction. She wrote it all down while I gave the information to her. Then she asked me for references, and I mentioned Sergeant Lou Pape. "Fine," she said. "We'll get in touch with you if anything comes up. Don't call us—we'll call you."

I hung around to see who'd be picked. There was only one, an old man, two ahead of me in the line, who had no social security number, no references, not even any relatives or friends she could have checked up on him with.

Damn! Of course that was what she wanted! Hadn't all the starvation cases been people without social security, references, either no friends and relatives or those they'd lost track of?

I'd pulled a blooper, but how was I to know until too late?

Well, there was a way of making it right.

When it was good and dark that evening, I stood on the corner and watched the lights in the brownstone house. The ones on the first two floors went out, leaving only those on the third and fourth. Closed for the day ... or open for business?

I got into a building a few doors down by pushing a button and waiting until the buzzer answered, then racing up to the roof while some man yelled down the stairs to find out who was there. I crossed the tops of the two houses between and went down the fire escape.

It wasn't easy, though not as tough as you might imagine. The fact is that I'm a whole year younger than Lou Pape, even if I could play his grandpa professionally. I still have muscles left and I used them to get down the fire escape at the rear of the house.

The fourth floor room I looked into had some kind of wire mesh cage and some hooded machinery. Nobody there.

The third floor room was the redhead's. She was coming out of the bathroom with a terrycloth bathrobe and a towel turban on when I looked in. She slid the robe off and began dusting herself with powder. That skin did cover her.

She turned and moved toward a vanity against the wall that I was on the other side of. The next thing I knew, the window was flung up and she had a gun on me.

"Come right in—Mr. Weldon, isn't it?" she said in that completely controlled voice of hers. One day her control would crack, I thought irrelevantly, and the pieces would be found from Dallas to North Carolina. "I had an idea you seemed more curious than was justified by a help-wanted ad."

"A man my age doesn't get to see many pretty girls," I told her, making my own voice crack pathetically in a senile whinny.

She motioned me into the room. When I was inside, I saw a light over the window blinking red. It stopped the moment I was in the room. A silent burglar alarm.

She let her pale blue eyes wash insolently over me. "A man your age can see all the pretty girls he wants to. You're not old."

"And you use a rinse," I retorted.

She ignored it. "I specifically advertised for old people. Why did you apply?"

It had happened so abruptly that I hadn't had a chance to use the Stanislavsky method to feel old in the presence of a beautiful nude woman. I don't even know if it would have worked. Nothing's perfect.

"I needed a job awful bad," I answered sullenly, knowing it sounded like an ad lib.

She smiled with more contempt than humor. "You had a job, Mr. Weldon. You were very busy trying to find out why senile psychotics starve themselves to death."

"How did you know that?" I asked, startled.

"A little investigation of my own. I also happen to know you didn't tell your friend Sergeant Pape that you were going to be here tonight."

That was a fact, too. I hadn't felt sure enough that I'd found the answer to call him about it. Looking at the gun in her steady hand, I was sorry I hadn't.

"But you did find out I own this building, that my name is May Roberts, and that I'm the daughter of the late Dr. Anthony Roberts, the physicist," she continued. "Is there anything else you want me to tell you about yourself?"

"I know enough already. I'm more interested in you and the starvation cases. If you weren't connected with them, you wouldn't have known I was investigating them."

"That's obvious, isn't it?" She reached for a cigarette on the vanity and used a lighter with her free hand. The big mirror gave me another view of her lovely body, but that was beginning to interest me less than the gun. I thought of making a grab for it. There was too much distance between us, though, and she knew better than to take her eyes off me while she was lighting up. "I'm not afraid of professional detectives, Mr. Weldon. They deal only with facts and every one of them will draw the same conclusions from a given set of circumstances. I don't like amateurs. They guess too much. They don't stick to reality. The result—" her pale eyes chilled and her shapely mouth went hard—"is that they are likely to get too close to the truth."

I wanted a smoke myself, but I wasn't willing to make a move toward the pipe in my jacket. "I may be close to the truth, Miss Roberts, but I don't know what the devil it is. I still don't know how you're tied in with the senile psychotics or why they starve with all that money. You could let me go and I wouldn't have a thing on you."

She glanced down at herself and laughed for real for the first time. "You wouldn't, would you? On the other hand, you know where I'm working from and could nag Sergeant Pape into getting a search warrant. It wouldn't incriminate me, but it would be inconvenient. I don't care to be inconvenienced."

"Which means what?"

"You want to find out my connection with senile psychotics. I intend to show you."

"How?"

She gestured dangerously with the gun. "Turn your face to the wall and stay that way while I get dressed. Make one attempt to turn around before I tell you to and I'll shoot you. You're guilty of housebreaking, you know. It would be a little inconvenient for me to have an investigation ... but not as inconvenient as for you."

I faced the wall, feeling my stomach braid itself into a tight, painful knot of fear. Of what, I didn't know yet, only that old people who had something to do with her died of starvation. I wasn't old, but that didn't seem very comforting. She was the most frigid, calculating, deadly woman I'd ever met. That alone was enough to scare hell out of me. And there was the problem of what she was capable of.

Hearing the sounds of her dressing behind me, I wanted to lunge around and rush her, taking a chance that she might be too busy pulling on a girdle or reaching back to fasten a bra to have the gun in her hand. It was a suicidal impulse and I gave it up instantly. Other women might compulsively finish concealing themselves before snatching up the gun. Not her.

"All right," she said at last.

I faced her. She was wearing coveralls that, if anything, emphasized the curves of her figure. She had a sort of babushka that covered her red hair and kept it in place—the kind of thing women workers used to wear in factories during the war. She had looked lethal with nothing on but a gun and a hard expression. She looked like a sentence of execution now.

"Open that door, turn to the right and go upstairs," she told me, indicating directions with the gun.

I went. It was the longest, most anxious short walk I've ever taken. She ordered me to open a door on the fourth floor, and we were inside the room I'd seen from the fire escape. The mesh cage seemed like a torture chamber to me, the hooded motors designed to shoot an agonizing current through my emaciating body.

"You're going to do to me what you did to the old man you hired today?" I probed, hoping for an answer that would really answer.

She flipped on the switch that started the motors and there was a shrill, menacing whine. The wire mesh of the cage began blurring oddly, as if vibrating like the tines of a tuning fork.

"You've been an unexpected nuisance, Weldon," she said above the motors. "I never thought you'd get this far. But as long as you have, we might as well both benefit by it."

"Benefit?" I repeated. "Both of us?"

She opened the drawer of a work table and pulled out a stack of envelopes held with a rubber band. She put the stack at the other edge of the table.

"Would you rather have all cash or bank accounts or both?"

My heart began to beat. She was where the money came from!

You trying to tell me you're a philanthropist?" I demanded.

"Business is philanthropy, in a way," she answered calmly. "You need money and I need your services. To that extent, we're doing each other a favor. I think you'll find that the favor I'm going to do for you is a pretty considerable one. Would you mind picking up the envelopes on the table?"

I took the stack and stared at the top envelope. "May 15, 1931," I read aloud, and looked suspiciously at her. "What's this for?"

"I don't think it's something that can be explained. At least it's never been possible before and I doubt if it would be now. I'm assuming you want both cash and bank accounts. Is that right?"

"Well, yes. Only—"

"We'll discuss it later." She looked along a row of shelves against one wall, searching the labels on the stacks of bundles there. She drew one out and pushed it toward me. "Please open that and put on the things you'll find inside."

I tore open the bundle. It contained a very plain business suit, black shoes, shirt, tie and a hat with a narrow brim.

"Are these supposed to be my burial clothes?"

"I asked you to put them on," she said. "If you want me to make that a command, I'll do it."

I looked at the gun and I looked at the clothes and then for some shelter I could change behind. There wasn't any.

She smiled. "You didn't seem concerned about my modesty. I don't see why your own should bother you. Get dressed!"

I obeyed, my mind anxiously chasing one possibility after another, all of them ending up with my death. I got into the other things and felt even more uncomfortable. They were all only an approximate fit: the shoes a little too tight and pointed, the collar of the shirt too stiffly starched and too high under my chin, the gray suit too narrow at the shoulders and the ankles. I wished I had a mirror to see myself in. I felt like an ultra-conservative Wall Street broker and I was sure I resembled one.

"All right," she said. "Put the envelopes in your inside pocket.

You'll find instructions on each. Follow them carefully."

"I don't get it!" I protested.

"You will. Now step into the mesh cage. Use the envelopes in the order they're arranged in."

"But what's this all about?"

"I can tell you just one thing, Mr. Weldon—don't try to escape. It can't be done. Your other questions will answer themselves if you follow the instructions on the envelopes."

She had the gun in her hand. I went into the mesh cage, not knowing what to expect and yet too afraid of her to refuse. I didn't want to wind up dead of starvation, no matter how much money she might have given me—but I didn't want to get shot, either.

She closed the mesh gate and pushed the switch as far as it would go. The motors screamed as they picked up speed; the mesh cage vibrated more swiftly; I could see her through it as if there were nothing between us.

And then I couldn't see her at all.

I was outside a bank on a sunny day in spring.

My fear evaporated instantly—I'd escaped somehow!

But then a couple of realizations slapped me from each side. It was day instead of night. I was out on the street and not in her brownstone house.

Even the season had changed!

Dazed, I stared at the people passing by. They looked like characters in a TV movie, the women wearing long dresses and flowerpot hats, their faces made up with petulant rosebud mouths and bright blotches of rouge; the men in hard straw hats, suits with narrow shoulders, plain black or brown shoes—the same kind of clothes I was wearing.

The rumble of traffic in the street caught me next. Cars with square bodies, tubular radiators....

For a moment, I let terror soak through me. Then I remembered the mesh cage and the motors. May Roberts could have given me electro-shock, kept me under long enough for the season to change, or taken me South and left me on a street in daylight.

But this was a street in New York. I recognized it, though some of the buildings seemed changed, the people dressed more shabbily.

Shrewd stagesetting? Hypnosis?

That was it, of course! She'd hypnotized me....

Except that a subject under hypnosis doesn't know he's been hypnotized.

Completely confused, I took out the stack of envelopes I'd put in my pocket. I was supposed to have both cash and a bank account, and I was outside a bank. She obviously wanted me to go in, so I did. I handed the top envelope to the teller.

He hauled $150 out of it and looked at me as if that was enough to buy and sell the bank. He asked me if I had an account there. I didn't. He took me over to an officer of the bank, a fellow with a Hoover collar and a John Gilbert mustache, who signed me up more cordially than I'd been treated in years.

I walked out to the street, gaping at the entry in the bankbook he'd handed me. My pulse was jumping lumpily, my lungs refusing to work right, my head doing a Hopi rain dance.

The date he'd stamped was May 15, 1931.

I didn't know which I was more afraid of—being stranded, middle-aged, in the worst of the depression, or being yanked back to that brownstone house. I had only an instant to realize that I was a kid in high school uptown right at that moment. Then the whole scene vanished as fast as blinking and I was outside another bank somewhere else in the city.

The date on the envelope was May 29th and it was still 1931. I made a $75 deposit there, then $100 in another place a few days later, and so forth, spending only a few minutes each time and going forward anywhere from a couple of days to almost a month.

Every now and then, I had a stamped, addressed envelope to mail at a corner box. They were addressed to different stock brokers and when I got one open before mailing it and took a look inside, it turned out to be an order to buy a few hundred shares of stock in a soft drink company in the name of Dr. Anthony Roberts. I hadn't remembered the price of the shares being that low. The last time I'd seen the quotation, it was more than five times as much as it was then. I was making dough myself, but I was doing even better for May Roberts.

A few times I had to stay around for an hour or so. There was the night I found myself in a flashy speakeasy with two envelopes that I was to bet the contents of, according to the instructions on the outside. It was June 21, 1932, and I had to bet on Jack Sharkey to take the heavyweight title away from Max Schmeling.

The place was serious and quiet—no more than three women, a couple of bartenders, and the rest male customers, including two cops, huddling up close to the radio. An affable character was taking bets. He gave me a wise little smile when I put the money down on Sharkey.

"Well, it's a pleasure to do business with a man who wants an American to win," he said, "and the hell with the smart dough, eh?"

"Yeah," I said, and tried to smile back, but so much of the smart money was going on Schmeling that I wondered if May Roberts hadn't made a mistake. I couldn't remember who had won. "You know what J. P. Morgan said—don't sell America short."

"I'll take a buck for my share," said a sour guy who barely managed to stand. "Lousy grass growing in the lousy streets, nobody working, no future, nothing!"

"We'll come out of it okay," I told him confidently.

He snorted into his gin. "Not in our lifetime, Mac. It'd take a miracle to put this country on its feet again. I don't believe in miracles." He put his scowling face up close to mine and breathed blearily and belligerently at me. "Do you?"

"Shut up, Gus," one of the bartenders said. "The fight's starting."

I had some tough moments and a lot of bad Scotch, listening. It went the whole 15 rounds, Sharkey won, and I was in almost as bad shape as Gus, who'd passed out halfway through the battle. All I can recall is the affable character handing over a big roll and saying, "Lucky for me more guys don't sell America short," and trying to separate the money into the right amounts and put them into the right envelopes, while stumbling out the door, when everything changed and I was outside a bank again.

I thought, "My God, what a hangover cure!" I was as sober as if I hadn't had a drink, when I made that deposit.

There were more envelopes to mail and more deposits to make and bets to put down on Singing Wood in 1933 at Belmont Park and Max Baer over Primo Carnera, and then Cavalcade at Churchill Downs in 1934, and James Braddock over Baer in 1935, and a big daily double payoff, Wanoah-Arakay at Tropical Park, and so on, skipping through the years like a flat stone over water, touching here and there for a few minutes to an hour at a time. I kept the envelopes for May Roberts and myself in different pockets and the bankbooks in another. The envelopes were beginning to bulge and the deposits and accrued interest were something to watch grow.

The whole thing, in fact, was so exciting that it was early October of 1938—a total of maybe four or five hours subjectively—before I realized what she had me doing. I wasn't thinking much about the fact that I was time traveling or how she did it; I accepted that, though the sensation in some ways was creepy, like raising the dead. My father and mother, for instance, were still alive in 1938. If I could break away from whatever it was that kept pulling me jumpily through time, I could go and see them.

The thought attracted me enough to make me shake badly with intent, yet pump dread through me. I wanted so damned badly to see them again and I didn't dare. I couldn't....

Why couldn't I?

Maybe the machine covered only the area around the various banks, speakeasies, bars and horse parlors. If I could get out of the area, whatever it might be, I could avoid coming back to whatever May Roberts had lined up for me.

Because, naturally, I knew now what I was doing: I was making deposits and winning sure bets just as the "senile psychotics" had done. The ink on their bankbooks and bills was fresh because it was fresh; it wasn't given a chance to oxidize—at the rate I was going, I'd be back to my own time in another few hours or so, with $15,000 or better in deposits, compound interest and cash.

If I'd been around 70, you see, she could have sent me back to the beginning of the century with the same amount of money, which would have accumulated to something like $30,000.

Get it now?

I did.

And I felt sick and frightened.

The old people had died of starvation somehow with all that dough in cash or banks. I didn't give a hang if the time travel was responsible, or something else was. I wasn't going to be found dead in my hotel and have Lou Pape curse my corpse because I'd been borrowing from him when, since 1931, I'd had a little fortune put away. He'd call me a premature senile psychotic and he'd be right, from his point of view, not knowing the truth.

Rather than make the deposit in October, 1938, I grabbed a battered old cab and told the driver to step on it. When I showed him the $10 bill that was in it for him, he squashed down the gas pedal. In

1938, $10 was real money.

We got a mile away from the bank and the driver looked at me in the rear-view mirror.

"How far you want to go, mister?"

My teeth were together so hard that I had to unclench them before I could answer, "As far away as we can get."

"Cops after you?"

"No, but somebody is. Don't be surprised at anything that happens, no matter what it is."

"You mean like getting shot at?" he asked worriedly, slowing down.

"You're not in any danger, friend. I am. Relax and step on it again."

I wondered if she could still reach me, this far from the bank, and handed the guy the bill. No justice sticking him for the ride in case she should. He pushed the pedal down even harder than he had been doing before.

We must have been close to three miles away when I blinked and was standing outside the first bank I'd seen in 1931.

I don't know what the cab driver thought when I vanished out of his hack. He probably figured I'd opened the door and jumped while he wasn't looking. Maybe he even went back and searched for a body splashed all over the street.

Well, it would have been a hopeless hunt. I was a week ahead.

I gave up and drearily made my deposit. The one from early October that I'd missed I put in with this one.

There was no way to escape the babe with the beautiful hard face, gorgeous warm body and plans for me that all seemed to add up to death. I didn't try any more. I went on making deposits, mailing orders to her stock brokers, and putting down bets that couldn't miss because they were all past history.

I don't even remember what the last one was, a fight or a race. I hung around the bar that had long ago replaced the speakeasy, until the inevitable payoff, got myself a hamburger and headed out the door. All the envelopes I was supposed to use were gone and I felt shaky, knowing that the next place I'd see was the room with the wire mesh cage and the hooded motors.

It was.

She was on the other side of the cage, and I had five bankbooks and envelopes filled with cash amounting to more than $15,000, but all I could think of was that I was hungry and something had happened to the hamburger while I was traveling through time. I must have fallen and dropped it, because my hand was covered with dust or dirt. I brushed it off and quickly felt my face and pulled up my sleeves to look at my arms.

"Very smart," I said, "but I'm nowhere near emaciation."

"What made you think you would be?" she asked.

"Because the others always were."

She cut the motors to idling speed and the vibrating mesh slowed down. I glared at her through it. God, she was lovely—as lovely as an ice sculpture! The kind of face you'd love to kiss and slap, kiss and slap....

"You came here with a preconceived notion, Mr. Weldon. I'm a businesswoman, not a monster. I like to think there's even a good deal of the altruist in me. I could hire only young people, but the old ones have more trouble finding work. And you've seen for yourself how I provide nest eggs for them they'd otherwise never have."

"And take care of yourself at the same time."

"That's the businesswoman in me. I need money to operate."

"So do the old people. Only they die and you don't."

She opened the gate and invited me out. "I make mistakes occasionally. I sometimes pick men and women who prove to be too old to stand the strain. I try not to let it happen, but they need money and work so badly that they don't always tell the truth about their age and state of health."

"You could take those who have social security cards and references."

"But those who don't have any are in worse need!" She paused. "You probably think I want only the money you and they bring back, that it's merely some sort of profit-making scheme. It isn't."

"You mean the idea is not just to build up a fortune for you with a cut for whoever helps you do it?"

"I said I need money to operate, Mr. Weldon, and this method serves. But there are other purposes, much more important. What you have gone through is—basic training, you might say. You know now that it's possible to travel through time, and what it's like. The initial shock, in other words, is gone and you're better equipped to do something for me in another era."

"Something else?" I stared at her puzzledly. "What else could you want?"

"Let's have dinner first. You must be hungry."

I was, and that reminded me: "I bought a hamburger just before you brought me back. I don't know what happened to it. My hand was dirty and the hamburger was gone, as if I'd fallen somehow and dropped it and got dirt on my hand."

She looked worriedly at the hand, probably afraid I'd cut it and disqualified myself. I could understand that; you never know what kind of diseases can be picked up in different times, because I remember reading somewhere that germs keep changing according to conditions. Right now, for instance, strains of bacteria are becoming resistant to antibiotics. I knew her concern wasn't really for me, but it was pleasant all the same.

"That could be the explanation, I suppose," she said. "The truth is that I've never taken a time voyage—somebody has to operate the controls in the present—so I can't say it's possible or impossible to fall. It must be, since you did. Perhaps the wrench back from the past was too violent and you slipped just before you returned."

She led me down to an ornate dining room, where the table had been set for two. The food was waiting on the table, steaming and smelling tasty. Nobody was around to serve us. She pointed out a chair to me and we sat down and began eating. I was a little nervous at first, afraid there might be something in the food, but it tasted fine and nothing happened after I swallowed a little and waited for some effect.

"You did try to escape the time tractor beam, didn't you, Mr. Weldon?" she asked. I didn't have to answer; she knew. "That's a mistaken notion of how it functions. The control beam doesn't cover area; it covers era. You could have flown to any part of the world and the beam would still have brought you back. Do I make myself clear?"

She did. Too bloody clear. I waited for the rest.

"I assume you've already formed an opinion of me," she went on. "A rather unflattering one, I imagine."

"'Bitch' is the cleanest word I can find. But a clever one. Anybody who can invent a time machine would have to be a genius."

"I didn't invent it. My father did—Dr. Anthony Roberts—using the funds you and others helped me provide him with." Her face grew soft and tender. "My father was a wonderful man, a great man, but he was called a crackpot. He was kept from teaching or working anywhere. It was just as well, I suppose, though he was too hurt to think so; he had more leisure to develop the time machine. He could have used it to extort repayment from mankind for his humiliation, but he didn't. He used it to help mankind."

"Like how?" I goaded.

"It doesn't matter, Mr. Weldon. You're determined to hate me and consider me a liar. Nothing I tell you can change that."

She was right about the first part—I hadn't dared let myself do anything except hate and fear her—but she was wrong about the second. I remembered thinking how Lou Pape would have felt if I had died of starvation with over $15,000, after borrowing from him all the time between jobs. Not knowing how I got it, he'd have been sore, thinking I'd played him for a patsy. What I'm trying to say is that Lou wouldn't have had enough information to judge me. I didn't have enough information yet, either, to judge her.

"What do you want me to do?" I asked warily.

"Everybody but one person was sent into the past on specific errands—to save art treasures and relics that would otherwise have been lost to humanity."

"Not because the things might be worth a lot of dough?" I said nastily.

"You've already seen that I can get all the money I want. There were upheavals in the past—great fires, wars, revolutions, vandalism—and I had my associates save things that would have been destroyed. Oh, beautiful things, Mr. Weldon! The world would have been so much poorer without them!"

"El Greco, for instance?" I asked, remembering the raving old man who had been found wandering with $17,000 in his coat lining.

"El Greco, too. Several paintings that had been lost for centuries." She became more brisk and efficient-seeming. "Except for the one man I mentioned, I concentrated on the past—the future is too completely unknown to us. And there's an additional reason why I tentatively explored it only once. But the one person who went there discovered something that would be of immense value to the world."

"What happened to him?"

She looked regretful. "He was too old. He survived just long enough to tell me that the future has something we need. It's a metal box, small enough to carry, that could supply this whole city with power to run its industries and light its homes and streets!"

"Sounds good. Who'd you say benefits if I get it?"

"We share the profits equally, of course. But it must be understood that we sell the power so cheaply that everybody can afford it."

"I'm not arguing. What's the other reason you didn't bother with the future?"

"You can't bring anything from the future to the present that doesn't exist right now. I won't go into the theory, but it should be obvious that nothing can exist before it exists. You can't bring the box I want, only the technical data to build one."

"Technical data? I'm an actor, not a scientist."

"You'll have pens and weatherproof notebooks to copy it down in."

I couldn't make up my mind about her. I've already said she was beautiful, which always prejudices a man in a woman's favor, but I couldn't forget the starvation cases. They hadn't shared anything but malnutrition, useless money and death. Then again, maybe her explanation was a good one, that she wanted to help those who needed help most and some of them lied about their age and physical condition because they wanted the jobs so badly. All I knew about were those who had died. How did I know there weren't others—a lot more of them than the fatal cases, perhaps—who came through all right and were able to enjoy their little fortunes?

And there was her story about saving the treasures of the past and wanting to provide power at really low cost. She was right about one thing: she didn't need any of that to make money with; her method was plenty good enough, using the actual records of the past to invest in stocks, bet on sports—all sure gambles.

But those starvation cases....

"Do I get any guarantees?" I demanded.

She looked annoyed. "I'll need you for the data. You'll need me to turn it into manufacture. Is that enough of a guarantee?"

"No. Do I come out of this alive?"

"Mr. Weldon, please use some logic. I'm the one who's taking the risk. I've already given you more money than you've ever had at one time in your life. Part of my motive was to pay for services about to be rendered. Mostly, it was to give you experience in traveling through time."

"And to prove to me that I can't run out," I added.

"That happens to be a necessary attribute of the machine. I couldn't very well move you about through time unless it worked that way. If you'd look at my point of view, you'd see that I lose my investment if you don't bring back the data. I can't withdraw your money, you realize."

"I don't know what to think," I said, dissatisfied with myself because I couldn't find out what, if anything, was wrong with the deal. "I'll get you the data for the power box if it's at all possible and then we'll see what happens."

Finished eating, we went upstairs and I got into the cage.

She closed the circuit. The motors screamed. The mesh blurred.

And I was in a world I never knew.

You'd call it a city, I suppose; there were enough buildings to make it one. But no city ever had so much greenery. It wasn't just tree-lined streets, like Unter den Linden in Berlin, or islands covered with shrubbery, like Park Avenue in New York. The grass and trees and shrubs grew around every building, separating them from each other by wide lawns. The buildings were more glass—or what looked like glass—than anything else. A few of the windows were opaque against the sun, but I couldn't see any shades or blinds. Some kind of polarizing glass or plastic?

I felt uneasy being there, but it was a thrill just the same, to be alive in the future when I and everybody who lived in my day was supposed to be dead.

The air smelled like the country. There was no foul gas boiling from the teardrop cars on the glass-level road. They were made of transparent plastic clear around and from top to bottom, and they moved along at a fair clip, but more smoothly than swiftly. If I hadn't seen the airship overhead, I wouldn't have known it was there. It flew silently, a graceful ball without wings, seeming to be borne by the wind from one horizon to the other, except that no wind ever moved that fast.

One car stopped nearby and someone shouted, "Here we are!" Several people leaped out and headed for me.

I didn't think. I ran. I crossed the lawn and ducked into the nearest building and dodged through long, smoothly walled,

shadowlessly lit corridors until I found a door that would open. I slammed it shut and locked it. Then, panting, I fell into a soft chair that seemed to form itself around my body, and felt like kicking myself for the bloody idiot I was.

What in hell had I run for? They couldn't have known who I was. If I'd arrived in a time when people wore togas or bathing suits, there would have been some reason for singling me out, but they had all had clothes just like ours—suits and shirts and ties for the men, a dress and high heels for the one woman with them. I felt somewhat disappointed that clothes hadn't changed any, but it worked out to my advantage; I wouldn't be so conspicuous.

Yet why should anyone have yelled "Here we are!" unless.... No, they must have thought I was somebody else. It didn't figure any other way. I had run because it was my first startled reaction and probably because I knew I was there on what might be considered illegal business; if I succeeded, some poor inventor would be done out of his royalties.

I wished I hadn't run. Besides making me feel like a scared fool, I was sweaty and out of breath. Playing old men doesn't make climbing down fire escapes much tougher than it should be, but it doesn't exactly make a sprinter out of you—not by several lungfuls.

I sat there, breathing hard and trying to guess what next. I had no more idea of where to go for what I wanted than an ancient Egyptian set down in the middle of Times Square with instructions to sneak a mummy out of the Metropolitan Museum. I didn't even have that much information. I didn't know any part of the city, how it was laid out, or where to get the data that May Roberts had sent me for.

I opened the door quietly and looked both ways before going out. After losing myself in the cross-connecting corridors a few times, I finally came to an outside door. I stopped, tense, trying to get my courage. My inclination was to slip, sneak or dart out, but I made myself walk away like a decent, innocent citizen. That was one disguise they'd never be able to crack. All I had to do was act as if I belonged to that time and place and who would know the difference?

There were other people walking as if they were in no hurry to get anywhere. I slowed down to their speed, but I wished wistfully that there was a crowd to dive into and get lost.

A man dropped into step and said politely, "I beg your pardon. Are you a stranger in town?"

I almost halted in alarm, but that might have been a giveaway. "What makes you think so?" I asked, forcing myself to keep at the same easy pace.

"I—didn't recognize your face and I thought—"

"It's a big city," I said coldly. "You can't know everyone."

"If there's anything I can do to help—"

I told him there wasn't and left him standing there. It was plain common sense, I had decided quickly while he was talking to me, not to take any risks by admitting anything. I might have been dumped into a police state or the country could have been at war without my knowing it, or maybe they were suspicious of strangers. For one reason or another, ranging from vagrancy to espionage, I could be pulled in, tortured, executed, God knows what. The place looked peaceful enough, but that didn't prove a thing.

I went on walking, looking for something I couldn't be sure existed, in a city I was completely unfamiliar with, in a time when I had no right to be alive. It wasn't just a matter of getting the information she wanted. I'd have been satisfied to hang around until she pulled me back without the data....

But then what would happen? Maybe the starvation cases were people who had failed her! For that matter, she could shoot me and send the remains anywhere in time to get rid of the evidence.

Damn it, I didn't know if she was better or worse than I'd supposed, but I wasn't going to take any chances. I had to bring her what she wanted.

There was a sign up ahead. It read: to shopping center. The arrow pointed along the road. When I came to a fork and wondered which way to go, there was another sign, then another pointing to still more farther on.

I followed them to the middle of the city, a big square with a park in the center and shops of all kinds rimming it. The only shop I was interested in said: electrical appliances.

I went in.

A neat young salesman came up and politely asked me if he could do anything for me. I sounded stupid even to myself, but I said, "No, thanks, I'd just like to do a little browsing," and gave a silly nervous laugh. Me, an actor, behaving like a frightened yokel! I felt ashamed of myself.

He tried not to look surprised, but he didn't really succeed. Somebody else came in, though, for which I was grateful, and he left me alone to look around.

I don't know if I can get my feelings across to you. It's a situation that nobody would ever expect to find himself in, so it isn't easy to tell what it's like. But I've got to try.

Let's stick with the ancient Egyptian I mentioned a while back, the one ordered to sneak a mummy out of the Metropolitan Museum. Maybe that'll make it clearer.

The poor guy has no money he can use, naturally, and no idea of what New York's transportation system is like, where the museum is, how to get there, what visitors to a museum do and say, the regulations he might unwittingly break, how much an ordinary citizen is supposed to know about which customs and such. Now add the possible danger that he might be slapped into jail or an insane asylum if he makes a mistake and you've got a rough notion of the spot I felt I was in. Being able to speak English doesn't make much difference; not knowing what's regarded as right and wrong, and the unknown consequences, are enough to panic anybody.

That doesn't make it clear enough.

Well, look, take the electrical appliances in that store; that might give you an idea of the situation and the way it affected me.

The appliances must have been as familiar to the people of that time as toasters and TV sets and lamps are to us. But the things didn't make a bit of sense to me ... any more than our appliances would to the ancient Egyptian. Can you imagine him trying to figure out what those items are for and how they work?

Here are some gadgets you can puzzle over:

There was a light fixture that you put against any part of a wall— no screws, no cement, no wires, even—and it held there and lit up, and it stayed lit no matter where you moved it on the wall. Talk about pin-up lamps ... this was really it!

Then I came across something that looked like an ashtray with a blue electric shimmer obscuring the bottom of the bowl. I lit my pipe—others I'd passed had been smoking, so I knew it was safe to do the same—and flicked in the match. It disappeared. I don't mean it was swirled into some hidden compartment. It vanished. I emptied the pipe into the ashtray and that went, too. Looking around to make sure nobody was watching, I dredged some coins out of my pocket and let them drop into the tray. They were gone. Not a particle of them was left. A disintegrator? I haven't got the slightest idea.

There were little mirror boxes with three tiny dials on the front of each. I turned the dials on one—it was like using three dial telephones at the same time—and a pretty girl's face popped onto the mirror surface and looked expectantly at me.

"Yes?" she said, and waited for me to answer.

"I—uh—wrong number, I guess," I answered, putting the box down in a hurry and going to the other side of the shop because I didn't have even a dim notion how to turn it off.

The thing I was looking for was on a counter—a tinted metal box no bigger than a suitcase, with a lipped hole on top and small undisguised verniers in front. I didn't know I'd found it, actually, until I twisted a vernier and every light in the store suddenly glared and the salesman came rushing over and politely moved me aside to shut it off.

"We don't want to burn out every appliance in the place, do we?" he asked quietly.

"I just wanted to see if it worked all right," I said, still shaking slightly. It could have blown up or electrocuted me, for all I knew.

"But they always work," he said.

"Ah—always?"

"Of course. The principle is simple and there are no parts to get worn out, so they last indefinitely." He suddenly smiled as if he'd just caught the gist. "Oh, you were joking! Naturally—everybody learns about the Dynapack in primary education. You were interested in acquiring one?"

"No, no. The—the old one is good enough. I was just—well, you know, interested in knowing if the new models are much different or better than the old ones."

"But there haven't been any new models since 2073," he said. "Can you think of any reason why there should be?"

"I—guess not," I stammered. "But you never can tell."

"You can with Dynapacks," he said, and he would have gone on if I hadn't lost my nerve and mumbled my way out of the store as fast as I could.

You want to know why? He'd asked me if I wanted to "acquire" a Dynapack, not buy one. I didn't know what "acquire" meant in that society. It could be anything from saving up coupons to winning whatever you wanted at some kind of lottery, or maybe working up the right number of labor units on the job—in which case he'd want to know where I was employed and the equivalent of social security and similar information, which I naturally didn't have—or it could just be fancy sales talk for buying.

I couldn't guess, and I didn't care to expose myself any more than I had already. And my blunder about the Dynapack working and the new models was nothing to make me feel at all easier.

Lord, the uncertainties and hazards of being in a world you don't know anything about! Daydreaming about visiting another age may be pleasant, but the reality is something else again.

"Wait a minute, friend!" I heard the salesman call out behind me.

I looked back as casually, I hoped, as the pedestrians who heard him. He was walking quickly toward me with a very worried expression on his face. I stepped up my own pace as unobtrusively as possible, trying to keep a lot of people between us, meanwhile praying that they'd think I was just somebody who was late for an appointment. The salesman didn't break into a run or yell for the cops, but I couldn't be sure he wouldn't.

As soon as I came to a corner, I turned it and ran like hell. There was a sort of alley down the block. I jumped into it, found a basement door and stayed inside, pressed against the wall, quivering with tension and sucking air like a swimmer who'd stayed underwater too long.

Even after I got my wind back, I wasn't anxious to go out. The place could have been cordoned off, with the police, the army and the navy all cooperating to nab me.

What made me think so? Not a thing except remembering how puzzled our ancient Egyptian would have been if he got arrested in the subway for something everybody did casually and without punishment in his own time—spitting! I could have done something just as innocent, as far as you and I are concerned, that this era would consider a misdemeanor or a major crime. And in what age was ignorance of the law ever an excuse?

Instead of going back out, I prowled carefully into the building. It was strangely silent and deserted. I couldn't understand why until I came to a lavatory. There were little commodes and wash basins that came up to barely above my knees. The place was a school. Naturally it was deserted—the kids were through for the day.

I could feel the tension dissolve in me like a ramrod of ice melting, no longer keeping my back and neck stiff and taut. There probably wasn't a better place in the city for me to hide.

A primary school!

The salesman had said to me, "Everybody learns about the Dynapack in primary education."

Going through the school was eerie, like visiting a familiar childhood scene that had been distorted by time into something almost totally unrecognizable.

There were no blackboards, teacher's big desk, children's little desks, inkwells, pointers, globes or books. Yet it was a school. The small fixtures in the lavatory downstairs had told me that, and so did the miniature chairs drawn neatly under the low, vividly painted tables in the various schoolrooms. A large comfortable chair was evidently where the teacher sat when not wandering around among the pupils.

In front of each chair, firmly attached to the table, was a box with a screen, and both sides of the box held spools of wire on blunt little spindles. The spools had large, clear numbers on them. Near the teacher's chair was a compact case with more spools on spindles, and there was a large screen on the inside wall, opposite the enormous windows.

I went into one of the rooms and sat down in the teacher's chair, wondering how I was going to find out about the Dynapack. I felt like an archaeologist guessing at the functions of strange relics he'd found in a dead city.

Sitting in the chair was like sitting on a column of air that let me sit upright or slump as I chose. One of the arms had a row of buttons. I pressed one and waited nervously to find out if I'd done something that would get me into trouble.

Concealed lights in the ceiling and walls began glowing, getting brighter, while the room gradually turned dark. I glanced around bewilderedly to see why, because it was still daylight.

The windows seemed to be sliding slightly, very slowly, and as they slid, the sunlight was damped out. I grinned, thinking of what my ancient Egyptian would make of that. I knew there were two sheets of polarizing glass, probably with a vacuum between to keep out the cold and the heat, and the lights in the room were beautifully synchronized with the polarized sliding glass.

I wasn't doing so badly. The rest of the objects might not be too hard to figure out.

The spools in the case alongside the teacher's chair could be wire recordings. I looked for something to play them with, but there was no sign of a playback machine. I tried to lift a spool off a spindle. It wouldn't come off.

Hah! The wire led down the spindle to the base of the box, holding the spool in place. That meant the spools could be played right in that position. But what started them playing?

I hunted over the box minutely. Every part of it was featureless—no dials, switches or any unfamiliar counterparts. I even tried moving my hands over it, figuring it might be like a theramin, and spoke to it in different shades of command, because it could have been built to respond to vocal orders. Nothing happened.

Remember the Poe story that shows the best place to hide something is right out in the open, which is the last place anyone would look? Well, these things weren't manufactured to baffle people, any more than our devices generally are. But it's only by trying everything that somebody who didn't know what a switch is would start up a vacuum cleaner, say, or light a big chandelier from a wall clear across the room.

I'd pressed every inch of the box, hoping some part of it might act as a switch, and I finally touched one of the spindles. The spool immediately began spinning at a very low speed and the screen on the wall opposite the window glowed into life.

"The history of the exploration of the Solar System," said an announcer's deep voice, "is one of the most adventuresome in mankind's long list of achievements. Beginning with the crude rockets developed during World War II...."

There were newsreel shots of V-1 and V-2 being blasted from

their takeoff ramps and a montage of later experimental models. I wished I could see how it all turned out, but I was afraid to waste the time watching. At any moment, I might hear the footsteps of a guard or janitor or whoever tended buildings then.

I pushed the spindle again. It checked the spool, which rewound swiftly and silently, and stopped itself when the rewinding was finished. I tried another. A nightmare underwater scene appeared.

"With the aid of energy screens," said another voice, "the oceans of the world were completely charted by the year 2027...."

I turned it off, then another on developments in medicine, one on architecture, one on history, the geography of such places as the interior of South America and Africa that were—or are—unknown today, and I was getting frantic, starting the wonderful wire films that held full-frequency sound and pictures in absolutely faithful color, and shutting them off hastily when I discovered they didn't have what I was looking for.

They were courses for children, but they all contained information that our scientists are still groping for ... and I couldn't chance watching one all the way through!

I was frustratedly switching off a film on psychology when a female voice said from the door, "May I help you?"

I snapped around to face her in sudden fright. She was young and slim and slight, but she could scream loud enough to get help. Judging by the way she was looking at me, outwardly polite and yet visibly nervous, that scream would be coming at any second.

"I must have wandered in here by mistake," I said, and pushed past her to the corridor, where I began running back the way I had come.

"But you don't understand!" she cried after me. "I really want to help—"

Yeah, help, I thought, pounding toward the street door. A gag right out of that psychology film, probably—get the patient to hold still, humor him, until you can get somebody to put him where he belongs. That's what one of our teachers would do, provided she wasn't too scared to think straight, if she found an old-looking guy thumbing frenziedly through the textbooks in a grammar school classroom.

When I came to the outside door, I stopped. I had no way of knowing whether she'd given out an alarm, or how she might have done it, but the obvious place to find me would be out on the street, dodging for cover somewhere.

I pushed the door open and let it slam shut, hoping she'd hear it upstairs. Then I found a door, sneaked it open and went silently down the steps.

In the basement, I looked for a furnace or a coal bin or a fuel tank to hide behind, but there weren't any. I don't know how they got their heat in the winter or cooled the building in the summer. Probably some central atomic plant that took care of the whole city, piping in the heat or coolant in underground conduits that were led up through the walls, because there weren't even any pipes visible.

I hunched into the darkest corner I could find and hoped they wouldn't look for me there.

By the time night came, hunger drove me out of the school, but I did it warily, making sure nobody was in sight.

The streets of the shopping center were more or less deserted. There was no sign of a restaurant. I was so empty that I felt dizzy as I hunted for one. But then a shocking realization made me halt on the sidewalk and sweat with horror.

Even if there had been a restaurant, what would I have used for money?

Now I got the whole foul picture. She had sent old people back through time on errands like mine ... and they'd starved to death because they couldn't buy food!

No, that wasn't right. I remembered what I had told Lou Pape: anybody who gets hungry enough can always find a truck garden or a food store to rob.

Only ... I hadn't seen a truck garden or food store anywhere in this city.

And ... I thought about people in the past having their hands cut off for stealing a loaf of bread.

This civilization didn't look as if it went in for such drastic punishments, assuming I could find a loaf of bread to steal. But neither did most of the civilizations that practiced those barbarisms.

I was more tired, hungry and scared than I'd ever believed a human being could get. Lost, completely lost in a totally alien world, but one in which I could still be killed or starve to death ... and God knew what was waiting for me in my own time in case I came back without the information she wanted.

Or maybe even if I came back with it!

That suspicion made up my mind for me. Whatever happened to me now couldn't be worse than what she might do. At least I didn't have to starve.

I stopped a man in the street. I let several others go by before picking him deliberately because he was middle-aged, had a kindly face, and was smaller than me, so I could slug him and run if he raised a row.

"Look, friend," I told him, "I'm just passing through town—"

"Ah?" he said pleasantly.

"—And I seem to have mislaid—" No, that was dangerous. I'd been about to say I'd mislaid my wallet, but I still didn't know whether they used money in this era. He waited with a patient, friendly smile while I decided just how to put it. "The fact is that I haven't eaten all day and I wonder if you could help me get a meal."

He said in the most neighborly voice imaginable, "I'll be glad to do anything I can, Mr. Weldon."

My entire face seemed to drop open. "You—you called me—"

"Mr. Weldon," he repeated, still looking up at me with that neighborly smile. "Mark Weldon, isn't it? From the 20th Century?"

I tried to answer, but my throat had tightened up worse than on any opening night I'd ever had to live through. I nodded, wondering terrifiedly what was going on.

"Please relax," he said persuasively. "You're not in any danger whatever. We offer you our utmost hospitality. Our time, you might say, is your time."

"You know who I am," I managed to get out through my

constricted glottis. "I've been doing all this running and ducking and hiding for nothing."

He shrugged sympathetically. "Everyone in the city was instructed to help you, but you were so nervous that we were afraid to alarm you with a direct approach. Every time we tried to, as a matter of fact, you vanished into one place or another. We didn't follow for fear of the effect on you. We had to wait until you came voluntarily to us."

My brain was racing again and getting nowhere. Part of it was dizziness from hunger, but only part. The rest was plain frightened confusion.

They knew who I was. They'd been expecting me. They probably even knew what I was after.

And they wanted to help!

"Let's not go into explanations now," he said, "although I'd like to smooth away the bewilderment and fear on your face. But you need to be fed first. Then we'll call in the others and—"

I pulled back. "What others? How do I know you're not setting up something for me that I'll wish I hadn't gotten into?"

"Before you approached me, Mr. Weldon, you first had to decide that we represented no greater menace than May Roberts. Please believe me, we don't."

So he knew about that, too!

"All right, I'll take my chances," I gave in resignedly. "Where does a guy find a place to eat in this city?"

It was a handsome restaurant with soft light coming from three-dimensional, full-color nature murals that I might mistakenly have walked into if I'd been alone, they looked so much like gardens and forests and plains. It was no wonder I couldn't find a restaurant or food store or truck garden anywhere—food came up through pneumatic chutes in each building, I'd been told on the way over, grown in hydroponic tanks in cities that specialized in agriculture, and those who wanted to eat "out" could drop into the restaurant each building had. Every city had its own function. This one was for people in the arts. I liked that.

There was a glowing menu on the table with buttons alongside the various selections. I looked starvingly at the items, trying to decide which I wanted most. I picked oysters, onion soup, breast of guinea hen under Plexiglas and was hunting for the tastiest and most recognizable dessert when the pleasant little guy shook his head regretfully and emphatically.

"I'm afraid you can't eat any of those foods, Mr. Weldon," he said in a sad voice. "We'll explain why in a moment."

A waiter and the manager came over. They obviously didn't want to stare at me, but they couldn't help it. I couldn't blame them, I'd have stared at somebody from George Washington's time, which is about what I must have represented to them.

"Will you please arrange to have the special food for Mr. Weldon delivered here immediately?" the little guy asked.

"Every restaurant has been standing by for this, Mr. Carr," said the manager. "It's on its way. Prepared, of course—it's been ready since he first arrived."

"Fine," said the little guy, Carr. "It can't be too soon. He's very hungry."

I glanced around and noticed for the first time that there was nobody else in the restaurant. It was past the dinner hour, but, even so, there are always late diners. We had the place all to ourselves and it bothered me. They could have ganged up on me....

But they didn't. A light gong sounded, and the waiter and manager hurried over to a slot of a door and brought out a couple of trays loaded with covered dishes.

"Your dinner, Mr. Weldon," the manager said, putting the plates in front of me and removing the lids.

I stared down at the food.

"This," I told them angrily, "is a hell of a trick to play on a starving man!"

They all looked unhappy.

"Mashed dehydrated potatoes, canned meat and canned vegetables," Carr replied. "Not very appetizing. I know, but I'm afraid it's all we can allow you to eat."

I took the cover off the dessert dish.

"Dried fruits!" I said in disgust.

"Rather excessively dried, I'm sorry to say," the manager agreed mournfully.

I sipped the blue stuff in a glass and almost spat it out. "Powdered milk! Are these things what you people have to live on?"

"No, our diet is quite varied," Carr said in embarrassment. "But we unfortunately can't give you any of the foods we normally eat ourselves."

"And why in blazes not?"

"Please eat, Mr. Weldon," Carr begged with frantic earnestness. "There's so much to explain—this is part of it, of course—and it would be best if you heard it on a full stomach."

I was famished enough to get the stuff down, which wasn't easy; uninviting as it looked, it tasted still worse.

When I was through, Carr pushed several buttons on the glowing menu. Dishes came up from an opening in the center of the table and he showed me the luscious foods they contained.

"Given your choice," he said, "you'd have preferred them to what you have eaten. Isn't that so, Mr. Weldon?"

"You bet I would!" I answered, sore because I hadn't been given that choice.

"And you would have died like the pathetic old people you were investigating," said a voice behind me.

I turned around, startled. Several men and women had come in while I'd been eating, their footsteps as silent as cats on a rug. I looked blankly from them to Carr and back again.

"These are the clothes we ordinarily wear," Carr said. "An 18th Century motif, as you can see—updated knee breeches and shirt waists, a modified stock for the men, the daring low bodices of that era, the full skirts treated in a modern way by using sheer materials for the women, bright colors and sheens, buckled shoes of spun synthetics. Very gay, very ornamental, very comfortable, and thoroughly suitable to our time."

"But everybody I saw was dressed like me!" I protested.

"Only to keep you from feeling more conspicuous and anxious than you already were. It was quite a project, I can tell you—your styles varied so greatly from decade to decade, especially those for women—and the materials were a genuine problem; they'd gone out of existence long ago. We had the textile and tailoring cities working a full six months to clothe the inhabitants of this city, including, of course, the children. Everybody had to be clad as your contemporaries were, because we knew only that you would arrive in this vicinity, not where you might wander through the city."

"There was one small difference you didn't notice," added a handsome mature woman. "You were the only man in a gray suit. We had a full description of what you were wearing, you see, and we

made sure nobody else was dressed that way. Naturally, everyone knew who you were, and so we were kept informed of your movements."

"What for?" I demanded in alarm. "What's this all about?"

Pulling up chairs, they sat down, looking to me like a witchcraft jury from some old painting.

"I'm Leo Blundell," said a tall man in plum-and-gold clothes. "As chairman of—of the Mark Weldon Committee, it's my responsibility to handle this project correctly."

"Project?"

"To make certain that history is fulfilled, I have to tell you as much as you must know."

"I wish somebody would!"

"Very well, let me begin by telling you much of what you undoubtedly know already. In a sense, you are more a victim of Dr. Anthony Roberts than his daughter. Roberts was a brilliant physicist, but because of his eccentric behavior, he was ridiculed for his theories and hated for his arrogance. He was an almost perfect example of self-defeat, the way in which a man will hamper his career and wreck his happiness, and then blame the world for his failure and misery. To get back to his connection with you, however, he invented a time machine—unfortunately, its secret has since been lost and never re-discovered—and used it for anti-social purposes. When he died, his daughter May carried on his work. It was she who sent you to this time to learn the principle by which the Dynapack operates. She was a thoroughly ruthless woman."

"Are you sure?" I asked uneasily.

"Quite sure."

"I know a number of old people died after she sent them on errands through time, but she said they'd lied about their age and health."

"One would expect her to say that," a woman put in cuttingly.

Blundell turned to her and shook his head. "Let Mr. Weldon clarify his feelings about her, Rhoda. They are obviously very mixed."

"They are," I admitted. "She seemed hard, the first time I saw her, when I answered her ad, but she could have been just acting businesslike. I mean she had a lot of people to pick from and she had to be impersonal and make certain she had the right one. The next time—I hope you don't know about that—it was really my fault for breaking into her room. I really had a lot of admiration for the way she handled the situation."

"Go on," Carr encouraged me.

"And I can't complain about the deal she gave me. Sure, she came out ahead on the money I bet and invested for her. But I did all right myself—I was richer than I'd ever been in my life—and she gave that money to me before I even did anything to earn it!"

"Besides which," somebody else said, "she offered you half of the profits on the Dynapack."

I looked around at the faces for signs of hostility. I saw none. That was surprising. I'd come from the past to steal something from them and they weren't at all angry. Well, no, it wasn't really stealing. I wouldn't be depriving them of the Dynapack. It just would have been invented before it was supposed to be.

"She did," I said. "Though I wouldn't call that part of it philanthropy. She needed me for the data and I needed her to manufacture the things."

"And she was a very beautiful woman," Blundell added.

I squirmed a bit. "Yes."

"Mr. Weldon, we know a good deal about her from notes that have come down to us among her private papers. She had a safety deposit box under a false name. I won't tell you the name; it was not discovered until many years later, and we will not voluntarily meddle with the past."

I sat up and listened sharply. "So that's how you knew who I was and what I'd be wearing and what I came for! You even knew when and where I'd arrive!"

"Correct," Blundell said.

"What else do you know?"

"That you suspected her of being responsible for the deaths of many old people by starvation. Your suspicion was justified, except that her father had caused all those that occurred before 1947, when she took over after his own death. All but two people were sent into the past. Roberts was curious about the future, of course, but he did not want to waste a victim on a trip that would probably be fruitless. In the past, you understand, he knew precisely what he was after. The future was completely unknown territory."

"But she took the chance," I said.

"If you can call deliberate murder taking a chance, yes. One man arrived in 2094, over fifty years ago. The other was yourself. The first one, as you know, died of malnutrition when he was brought back to your era."

"And what happened to me?" I asked, jittering.

"You will not die. We intend to make sure of that. All the other victims—I presume you're interested in their errands?"

"I think I know, but I'd like to find out just the same."

"They were sent to the past to buy or steal treasures of various sorts—art, sculpture, jewelry, fabulously valuable manuscripts and books, anything that had great scarcity value."

"That's not possible," I objected. "She had all the money she wanted. Any time she needed more, all she had to do was send somebody back to put down bets and buy stocks that she knew were winners. She had the records, didn't she? There was no way she or her father could lose!"

He moved his shoulders in a plum-and-gold shrug. "Most of the treasures they accumulated were for acquisition's sake—and for the sake of vengeance for the way they believed Dr. Roberts had been treated. When there were unusual expenses, such as replacing the very costly parts of the time machine, that required more than they could produce in ready cash, both Roberts and his daughter 'discovered' these treasures."

He waited while I digested the miserable meal and the disturbing information he had given me. I thought I'd found a loophole in his explanation: "You said people were sent back to the past to buy treasures, besides stealing them."

"I did," he agreed. "They were provided with currency of whatever era they were to visit."

I felt my forehead wrinkle up as my theory fell apart. "Then they could buy food. Why should they have died of malnutrition?"

"Because, as May Roberts herself told you, nothing can exist before it exists. Neither can anything exist after it is out of existence. If you returned with a Dynapack, for example, it would revert to a lump of various metals, because that was what it was in your period. But let me give you a more personal instance. Do you remember coming back from your first trip with dust on your hand?"

"Yes. I must have fallen."

"On one hand? No, Mr. Weldon. May Roberts was greatly upset by the incident; she was afraid you would realize why the hamburger had turned to dust—and why the old people died of starvation. All of them, not just a few."

He paused, giving me a chance to understand what he had just said. I did, with a sick shock.

"If I ate your food," I said shakily, "I'd feel satisfied until I was returned to my own time. But the food wouldn't go along with me!"

Blundell nodded gravely. "And so you, too, would die of malnutrition. The foods we have given you existed in your era. We were very careful of that, so careful that many of them probably were stored years before you left your time. We regret that they are not very palatable, but at least we are positive they will go back with you. You will be as healthy when you arrive in the past as when you left.

"Incidentally, she made you change your clothes for the same reason—they had been made in 1930. She had clothing from every era she wanted visited and chose old people who would fit them best. Otherwise, you see, they'd have arrived naked."

I began to shake as if I were as old as I'd pretended to be on the stage. "She's going to pull me back! If I don't bring her the information about the Dynapack, she'll shoot me!"

"That, Mr. Weldon, is our problem," Blundell said, putting his hand comfortingly on my arm to calm me.

"Your problem? I'm the one who'll get shot, not you!"

"But we know in complete detail what will happen when you are returned to the 20th Century."

I pulled my arm away and grabbed his. "You know that? Tell me!"

"I'm sorry, Mr. Weldon. If we tell you what you did, you might think of some alternate action, and there is no knowing what the result would be."

"But I didn't get shot or die of malnutrition?"

"That much we can tell you. Neither."

They all stood up, so bright and attractive in their colorful clothes that I felt like a shirt-sleeved stage hand who'd wandered in on a costume play.

"You will be returned in a month, according to the notes May Roberts left. She gave you plenty of time to get the data, you see. We propose to make that month an enjoyable one for you. The resources of our city—and any others you care to visit—are at your disposal. We wish you to take full advantage of them."

"And the Dynapack?"

"Let us worry about that. We want you to have a good time while you are our guest."

I did.

It was the most wonderful month of my life.

The mesh cage blurred around me. I could see May Roberts through it, her hand just leaving the switch. She was as beautiful as ever, but I saw beneath her beauty the vengeful, vicious creature her father's bitterness had turned her into; Blundell and Carr had let me read some of her notes, and I knew. I wished I could have spent the rest of my years in the future, instead of having to come back to this.

She came over and opened the gate, smiling like an angel welcoming a bright new soul. Then her eyes traveled startledly over me and her smile almost dropped off. But she held it firmly in place.

She had to, while she asked, "Do you have the notes I sent you for?"

"Right here," I said.

I reached into my breast pocket and brought out a stubby automatic and shot her through the right arm. Her closed hand opened and a little derringer clanked on the floor. She gaped at me with an expression of horrified surprise that should have been recorded permanently; it would have served as a model for generations of actors and actresses.

"You—brought back a weapon!" she gasped. "You shot me!" She stared vacantly at her bleeding arm and then at my automatic. "But you can't—bring anything back from the future. And you aren't—dying of malnutrition."

She said it all in a voice shocked into toneless wonder.

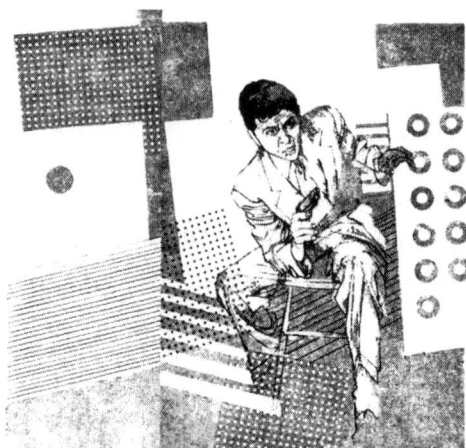

"The food I ate and this gun are from the present," I said. "The people of the future knew I was coming. They gave me food that wouldn't vanish from my cells when I returned. They also gave me the gun instead of the plans for the Dynapack."

"And you took it?" she screamed at me. "You idiot! I'd have shared the profits honestly with you. You'd have been worth millions!"

"With acute malnutrition," I amended. "I like it better this way, thanks—poor, but alive. Or relatively poor, I should say, because you've been very generous and I appreciate it."

"By shooting me!"

"I hated to puncture that lovely arm, but it wasn't as painful as starving or getting shot myself. Now if you don't mind—or even if you do—it's your turn to get into the cage, Miss Roberts."

She tried to grab for the derringer on the floor with her left hand.

"Don't bother," I said quietly. "You can't reach it before a bullet reaches you."

She straightened up, staring at me for the first time with terror in her eyes.

"What are you going to do to me?" she whispered.

"I could kill you as easily as you could have killed me. Kill you and send your body into some other era. How many dozens of deaths were you responsible for? The law couldn't convict you of them, but I can. And I couldn't be convicted, either."

She put her hand on the wound. Blood seeped through her fingers as she lifted her chin at me.

"I won't beg for my life, Weldon, if that's what you want. I could offer you a partnership, but I'm not really in a position to offer it, am I?"

She was magnificent, terrifyingly intelligent, brave clear through ... and deadlier than a plague. I had to remember that.

"Into the cage," I said. "I have some friends in the future who have plans for you. I won't tell you what they are, of course; you didn't tell me what I'd go through, did you? Give my friends my fondest regards. If I can manage it, I'll visit them—and you."

She backed warily into the cage. It would have been pleasant to kiss those wonderful lips good-by. I'd thought about them for a whole month, wanting them and loathing them at the same time.

It would have been like kissing a coral snake. I knew it and I concentrated on shutting the gate on her.

"You'd like to be rich, wouldn't you, Weldon?" she asked through the mesh.

"I can be," I said. "I have the machine. I can send people into the past or future and make myself a pile of dough. Only I'd give them food to take along. I wouldn't kill them off to keep the secret to myself. Anything else on your mind?"

"You want me," she stated.

I didn't argue.

"You could have me."

"Just long enough to get my throat slit or brains blown out. I don't want anything that much."

I rammed the switch closed.

The mesh cage blurred and she was gone. Her blood was on the floor, but she was gone into the future I had just come from.

That was when the reaction hit me. I'd escaped starvation and her gun, but I wasn't a hero and the release of tension flipped my stomach over and unhinged my knees.

Shaking badly, I stumbled through the big, empty house until I found a phone.

Lou Pape got there so quickly that I still hadn't gotten over the tremors, in spite of a bottle of brandy I dug out of a credenza, maybe because the date on the label, 1763, gave me a new case of the shivers.

I could see the worry on Lou's face vanish when he assured himself that I was all right. It came back again, though, when I told him what had happened. He didn't believe any of it, naturally. I guess I hadn't really expected him to.

"If I didn't know you, Mark," he said, shaking his big, dark head unhappily, "I'd send you over to Bellevue for observation. Even knowing you, maybe that's what I ought to do."

"All right, let's see if there's any proof," I suggested tiredly.

"From what I was told, there ought to be plenty."

We searched the house clear down to the basement, where he stood with his face slack.

"Christ!" he breathed. "The annex to the Metropolitan Museum!"

The basement ran the length and breadth of the house and was twice as high as an average room, and the whole glittering place was crammed with paintings in rich, heavy frames, statuettes, books, manuscripts, goblets and ewers and jewelry made of gold and huge gems, and tapestries in brilliant color ... and everything was as bright and sparkling and new as the day it was made, which was almost true of a lot of it.

"The dame was loaded and she was an art collector, that's all," Lou said. "You can't sell me that screwy story of yours. She was a collector and she knew where to find things."

"She certainly did," I agreed.

"What did you do with her?"

"I told you. I shot her through the arm before she could shoot me and I sent her into the future."

He took me by the front of the jacket. "You killed her, Mark. You wanted all this stuff for yourself, so you knocked her off and got rid of her body somehow."

"Why don't you go back to acting, where you belong, Lou, and leave sleuthing to people who know how?" I asked, too worn to pull his hands loose. "Would I kill her and call you up to get right over here? Wouldn't I have sneaked these things out first? Or more likely I'd have sneaked them out, hidden them and nobody—including you—would know I'd ever been here. Come on, use your head."

"That's easy. You lost your nerve."

"I'm not even losing my patience."

He pushed me away savagely. "If you killed her for this stuff or because of that crazy yarn you gave me, I'm a cop and you're no friend. You're just a plain killer I happened to have known once, and I'll make sure you fry."

"You always did have a taste for that kind of dialogue. Go ahead and wrap me up in an airtight case, have them throw the book at me, send me up the river, put me in the hot squat. But you'll have to do the proving, not me."

He headed for the stairs. "I will. And don't try to make a break or I'll plug you as if I never saw you before."

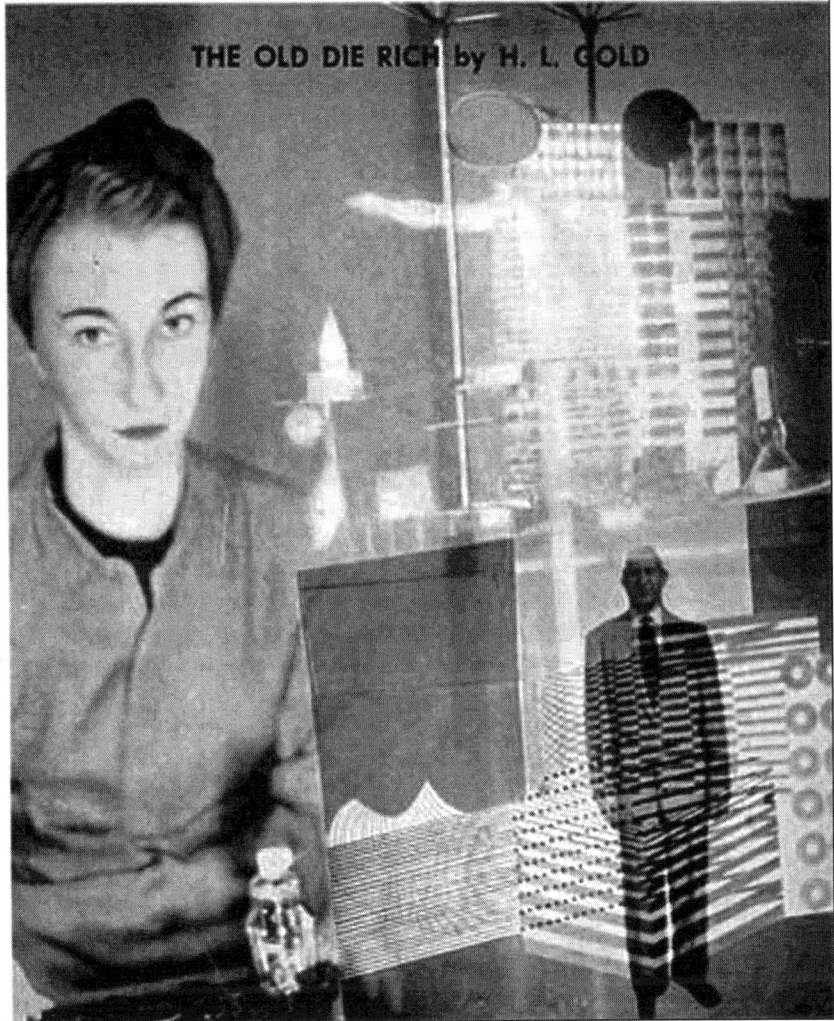

He put in a call at the phone upstairs. I didn't give a particular damn who it was he'd called. I was too relieved that I hadn't killed May Roberts; destroying anything that beautiful, however evil, would have stayed with me the rest of my life. There was another reason for my relief—if I'd killed her and left the evidence for Lou to find, he'd never help me. No, that's not quite so; he'd probably have tried to get me to plead insanity on the basis of my unbelievable explanation.

But most of all, I couldn't get rid of the look on her face when I'd shot her through the arm, the arm that was so wonderful to look at and that had held a murderous little gun to greet me with.

She was in the future now. She wouldn't be executed by them; they regarded crime as an illness, and they'd treat her with their marvelously advanced therapy and she'd become a useful, contented citizen, living out her existence in an era that had given me more happiness than I'd ever had.

I sat and tried to stupefy myself with brandy that should long ago have dried to brick-hardness, while Lou Pape stood at the door with his hand near his holster and glared at me. He didn't take his eyes off me until somebody named Prof. Jeremiah Aaronson came in and was introduced briefly and flatly to me. Then Lou took him upstairs.

It was minutes before I realized what they were going to do. I ran up after them.

I was just in time to see Aaronson carefully take the housing off the hooded motors, and leap back suddenly from the fury of lightning sparks.

The whole machine fused while we watched helplessly—motors, switches, panel and mesh cage. They flashed blindingly and blew apart and melted together in a charred and molten pile.

"Rigged," Aaronson said in the tone of a bitter curse. "Set to short if it was tampered with. I wouldn't be surprised if there were incendiaries placed at strategic spots. Nothing else could have made a mess like this."

He finally glanced down at his hand and saw it was scorched. He hissed with the realization of pain, blew on the burn, shook it in the air to cool it, and pulled a handkerchief out of his back pocket by reaching all the way around the rear for it with his left hand.

Lou looked helplessly at the heap of cooling slag. "Can you make any sense of it, Prof?" he asked.

"Can you?" Aaronson retorted. "Melt down a microtome or any other piece of machinery you're unfamiliar with, and see if you can identify it when it looks like this."

He went out, wrapping his hand in the handkerchief.

Lou kicked glumly at a piece of twisted tubing. "Aaronson is a top physicist, Mark. I was hoping he'd make enough out of the machine to—ah, hell, I wanted to believe you! I couldn't. I still can't. Now we'll have to dig through the house to find her body."

"You won't find it or the secret of the machine," I answered miserably. "I told you they said the secret would be lost. This is how. Now I'll never be able to visit the future again. I'll never see them or May Roberts. They'll straighten her out, get rid of her hate and vindictiveness, and it won't do me a damned bit of good because the machine is gone and she's generations ahead of me."

He turned to me puzzledly. "You're not afraid to have us dig for her body, Mark?"

"Tear the place apart if you want."

"We'll have to," he said. "I'm calling Homicide."

"Call in the Marines. Call in anybody you like."

"You'll have to stay in my custody until we're through."

I shrugged. "As long as you leave me alone while you're doing your digging, I don't give a hang if I'm under arrest for suspicion of murder. I've got to do some straightening out. I wish the people in the future could take on the job—they could do it faster and better than I can—but some nice, peaceful quiet would help."

He didn't touch me or say a word to me as we waited for the squad to arrive. I sat in the chair and shut out first him and then the men with their sounding hammers and crowbars and all the rest.

She'd been ruthless and callous, and she'd murdered old people with no more pity than a wolf among a herd of helpless sheep.

But Blundell and Carr had told me that she was as much a victim as the oldsters who'd died of starvation with the riches she'd given them still untouched, on deposit in the banks or stuffed into hiding places or pinned to their shabby clothes. She needed treatment for the illness her father had inflicted on her. But even he, they'd said, had been suffering from a severe emotional disturbance and proper care could have made a great and honored scientist out of him.

They'd told me the truth and made me hate her, and they'd told me their viewpoint and made that hatred impossible.

I was here, in the present, without her. The machine was gone. Yearning over something I couldn't change would destroy me. I had no right to destroy myself. Nobody did, they'd told me, and nobody who reconciles himself to the fact that some situations just are impossible to work out ever could.

I'd realized that when the squad packed up and left and Lou Pape came over to where I was sitting.

"You knew we wouldn't find her," he said.

"That's what I kept telling you."

"Where is she?"

"In Port Said, exotic hellhole of the world, where she's dancing in veils for the depraved—"

"Cut out the kidding! Where is she?"

"What's the difference, Lou? She's not here, is she?"

"That doesn't mean she can't be somewhere else, dead."

"She's not dead. You don't have to believe me about anything else, just that."

He hauled me out of the chair and stared hard at my face. "You aren't lying," he said. "I know you well enough to know you're not."

"All right, then."

"But you're a damned fool to think a dish like that would have any part of you. I don't mean you're nothing a woman would go for, but she's more fang than female. You'd have to be richer and better-looking than her, for one thing—"

"Not after my friends get through with her. She'll know a good man when she sees one and I'd be what she wants." I slid my hand over my naked scalp. "With a head of hair, I'd look my real age, which happens to be a year younger than you, if you remember. She'd go for me—they checked our emotional quotients and we'd be a natural together. The only thing was that I was bald. They could have grown hair on my head, which would have taken care of that, and then we'd have gotten together like gin and tonic."

Lou arched his black eyebrows at me. "They really could grow hair on you?"

"Sure. Now you want to know why I didn't let them." I glanced out the window at the smoky city. "That's why. They couldn't tell me if I'd ever get back to the future. I wasn't taking any chances. As long as there was a possibility that I'd be stranded in my own time, I wasn't going to lose my livelihood. Which reminds me, you have anything else to do here?"

"There'll be a guard stationed around the house and all her holdings and art will be taken over until she comes back—"

"She won't."

"—or is declared legally dead."

"And me?" I broke in.

"We can't hold you without proof of murder."

"Good enough. Then let's get out of here."

"I have to go back on duty," he objected.

"Not any more. I've got over $15,000 in cash and deposits—enough to finance you and me."

"Enough to kill her for."

"Enough to finance you and me," I repeated doggedly. "I told you I had the money before she sent me into the future—"

"All right, all right," he interrupted. "Let's not go into that again. We couldn't find a body, so you're free. Now what's this about financing the two of us?"

I put my fingers around his arm and steered him out to the street.

"This city has never had a worse cop than you," I said. "Why? Because you're an actor, not a cop. You're going back to acting, Lou. This money will keep us both going until we get a break."

He gave me the slit-eyed look he'd picked up in line of duty. "That wouldn't be a bribe, would it?"

"Call it a kind of memorial to a lot of poor, innocent old people and a sick, tormented woman."

We walked along in silence out in the clean sunshine. It was our silence; the sleek cars and burly trucks made their noise and the pedestrians added their gabble, but a good Stanislavsky actor like Lou wouldn't notice that. Neither would I, ordinarily, but I was giving him a chance to work his way through this situation.

"I won't hand you a lie, Mark," he said finally. "I never stopped wanting to act. I'll take your deal on two considerations."

"All right, what are they?"

"That whatever I take off you is strictly a loan."

"No argument. What's the other?"

He had an unlit cigarette almost to his lips. He held it there while he said: "That any time you come across a case of an old person who died of starvation with $30,000 stashed away somewhere, you turn fast to the theatrical page and not tell me or even think about it."

"I don't have to agree to that."

He lowered the cigarette, stopped and turned to me. "You mean it's no deal?"

"Not that," I said. "I mean there won't be any more of those cases. Between knowing that and both of us back acting again, I'm satisfied. You don't have to believe me. Nobody does."

He lit up and blew out a pretty plume, fine and slow and straight, which would have televised like a million in the bank. Then he grinned. "You wouldn't want to bet on that, would you?"

"Not with a friend. I do all my sure-thing betting with bookies."

"Then make it a token bet," he said. "One buck that somebody dies of starvation with a big poke within a year."

I took the bet.

I took the dollar a year later.

NOTE: *Illustrations by Camerage William Ashman.*

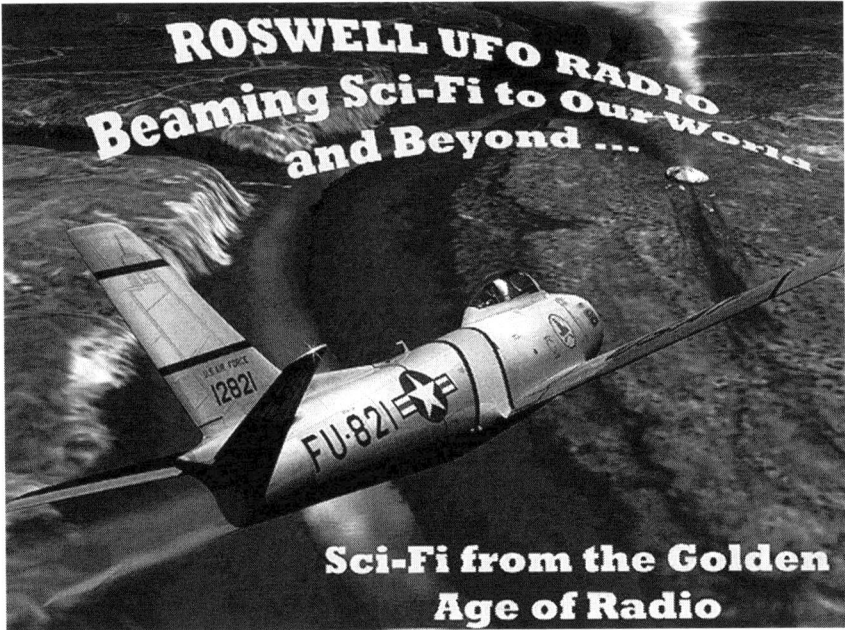

Roswell UFO Radio is the brainchild of Texas author and publisher Noe Torres, resulting from his lifelong interest in science fiction, the paranormal, unidentified flying objects, and radio drama. In the early 1990s, with the advent of the World Wide Web, Noe began collecting recordings of many early radio dramas, including Dimension X and X Minus One. He became a passionate fan of science fiction dramas from the golden age of radio, principally the 1940s and 1950s.

Over a period of twenty years, he compiled a detailed playlist of every adult science-fiction radio drama ever aired for which a recording still exists. Originally put together for his own enjoyment, Noe decided to share his unique, hand-picked collection of sci-fi drama with the world when his online radio stream first went on the air in 2007.

Be sure to tune in to Roswell UFO Radio for fantastic science-fiction from the golden age of radio. The station broadcasts 24 hours a day, 365 days a year. For complete details, visit RoswellUFORadio.com, and please consider signing up for a sponsoring membership.

If you enjoyed this book, you will love our other books!

Visit RoswellBooks.com

Noe Torres is an author, publisher, UFO investigator, and MUFON member in Texas. He has authored a number of books related to the UFO phenomenon and appears frequently in the media and at conferences, speaking about his research. He holds a Bachelor's in English and a Master's in Library Science from the University of Texas at Austin. With California UFO researcher Ruben Uriarte, he has written four acclaimed books: *Mexico's Roswell*, *The Other Roswell*, *Aliens in the Forest*, and *The Coyame Incident*. In addition, his books *The Real Cowboys & Aliens: UFO Encounters of the Old West, Fallen Angel*, and *Ultimate Guide to the Roswell UFO Crash* have also been very well-received by the UFO research community.

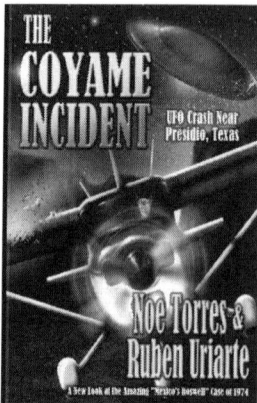

About *Mexico's Roswell*, the MUFON Journal said, "Torres and Uriarte are to be commended for tackling such an important case, whose impact on ufology may only now be coming to light thanks to the research they have undertaken. A definite must-read." George Noory commented, "Amazing! This story is wilder than the U.S. Roswell. This book is an amazing piece of work."

About *Ultimate Guide to the Roswell UFO Crash*, veteran UFO researcher / author Kevin Randle said, "If you are planning to visit Roswell, this book tells you all you need to know about the UFO crash, the city and its character. It condenses the confusion of the case into an easily read book that will help anyone make the most of a visit to the city and help understand what actually happened. A very nice addition to the Roswell literature."

Noe has appeared on the History Channel's "UFO Hunters," Coast to Coast AM, the Jeff Rense program, and many other shows. He is also a frequent lecturer at UFO conferences and has spoken on many occasions at the annual Roswell UFO Festival. Noe has also collaborated on several book projects with a number of other UFO researchers and authors, including Philip Mantle, Paul Stonehill, Carlos Guzman, E. J. Wilson, and John LeMay.

To order Noe's books, visit RoswellBooks.com or do a search for "Noe Torres" on Amazon.com or BarnesAndNoble.com.

Printed in Great Britain
by Amazon.co.uk, Ltd.,
Marston Gate.